Critical Acclaim for *Eatin*

"Helen Ellis's murderously comic nove
even as it bats around issues
self-mutilation."

". . . sometimes shocking, ofte

"If there is a prize awarded for Most Outrageous Opening Scene, surely Ellis is a prime contender. . . . This is a first novel with all the polish and style of a much-published author; it is mean-spirited, glorifies revenge, and is chillingly, killingly funny."

—Valerie Ryan, *The Seattle Times*

". . . dark, funny satire . . ."

—*Seventeen*

"The home of the Crimson Tide will never be the same. . . ."

—Randall Curb, *Oxford American*

". . . darkly comic farce . . ."

—Rhonda Johnson, *Entertainment Weekly*

". . . poignant . . ."

—Jennifer Becker, *Boston Herald*

"Southern Gothic never had it so funny as it does in Helen Ellis's hilarious if chilling debut novel."

—Susan Larson, *The Times-Picayune*

". . . a crackling, crazy Southern novel . . . Ellis's voice is funny, smart, and quick . . . while these might not be women we would choose to encounter, their stories, like good gossip—and good villains—are hard to resist."

—Sarah Dessen, *The News and Observer* (Raleigh)

"Ellis barbecues the odd habits of Crimson Tide fans and Tuscaloosa society, serves it up with a hefty dollop of sex and society catfights, and finishes with just desserts. Tasty!"

—*The Tampa Tribune*

". . . a down and dirty catfight of a novel . . . *Eating the Cheshire Cat* is a surprisingly engaging, darkly humorous debut that makes us cheer for the bad girls. Most of all, its shamelessly entertaining."

—Stephen M. Deusner, *The Commercial Appeal* (Memphis)

"... darkly funny ..."

—Maureen Duffin-Ward, *The Herald-Sun* (Durham)

"Ellis displays substantial insight into the nuances of Southern living. . . . But it is her deliciously catty humor and breathless storytelling that turn the Alabama of this Southern gothic satire into a chillingly funny Wonderland, complete with three desperate Alices."

—*Publishers Weekly*

"Oh, the things these girls do to each other in the name of beauty, ambition, friendship and sisterhood! *Eating the Cheshire Cat* is a wicked, funny, page-turner of a story. Helen Ellis is bursting on the scene with a pitch-perfect voice. She is an original."

—Dani Shapiro, author of *Slow Motion*

"In *Eating the Cheshire Cat*, Helen Ellis proves to our delight that you can take the girl out of the South, but you can't take the South out of the girl. Consuming this quirky, original first novel will be pure pleasure to readers, Southern and otherwise."

—Rosemary Daniell, author of *Fatal Flowers* and *The Woman Who Spilled Words All Over Herself*

"*Eating the Cheshire Cat* offers us a delightful new voice."

—Billie Letts, author of *Where the Heart Is*

"*Eating the Cheshire Cat* is rich and lively and enormously funny, with the most outrageous mother-daughter duo south of the Mason-Dixon. My congratulations to Helen Ellis. I know readers will love this novel."

—Michael Lee West, author of *American Pie*

"This is darkly Southern gothic humor, both witty and disturbing, that throws into sharp relief the madness lurking beneath obsessive social rituals."

—Georgia Metcalfe, *Daily Mail* (London)

"With great verve and wit, Helen Ellis tackles head-on this fluffy pink corner of the American cliché, behind which lie sharp nails (fake, of course), a thousand hair-rollers and echoes of the horror flick *Carrie*. . . . A fine debut, and an immensely enjoyable read."

—Anthea Lawson, *The Times* (London)

SCRIBNER PAPERBACK FICTION
Simon & Schuster, Inc.
Rockefeller Center
1230 Avenue of the Americas
New York, NY 10020

This book is a work of fiction. Names, characters, places, and incidents either are products of the author's imagination or are used fictitiously. Any resemblance to actual events or locales or persons, living or dead, is entirely coincidental.

First Scribner Paperback Fiction edition 2001

Designed by Brooke Zimmer
Manufactured in the United States of America

1 3 5 7 9 10 8 6 4 2

The Library of Congress had cataloged the Scribner edition as follows:

Ellis, Helen.
Eating the Cheshire cat : a novel / Helen Ellis.
p. cm.
I. Title.
PS3555.L5965E28 2000
813'.54—dc21 99-16217
CIP

ISBN 0-684-86440-1
0-684-86441-X (Pbk)

Eating the Cheshire Cat

A Novel by **Helen Ellis**

Scribner Paperback Fiction
Published by Simon & Schuster
New York London Toronto Sydney Singapore

This book is for my parents
Mike and Helen Holmes Ellis
who taught me the importance of
a really good story

Thanks to my Wednesday night workshop: Ann Napolitano and Hannah Tinti who read every word and taught me a few new ones—patience, trust, and fearlessness.

Thanks to my friends from Tuscaloosa: Victoria (Vicki Buckley) Curran who listened to every story read aloud since we were sixth graders and Dr. Elizabeth (Liz Ponder) McGraw who explained what would happen when I did bad things to bodies.

Thanks to the women in my family, Elizabeth and Boots, who read final drafts and screamed in all the right spots.

Thanks to those who will always be invited to the party: Patti Stockinger, Kristen Fincken Mahan, Amanda Eubanks Mussalli, Audrey Rosenthal, and Ellen Miller.

Thanks to Alain Wertheimer, Charles Heilbronn, and Koula Delianides, who gave me a "real" job which allowed me to fulfill my dream.

Thanks to my mentors at New York University, who gave me the courage to put down a bad novel and go back to this one, and to Alice McDermott and the Sewanee Writers' Conference, who gave me the strength to start over again.

Thanks to my agent, Chris Calhoun, and editor, Gillian Blake, who both read this book in one night and fought for it, bettered it, and brought it to life. And thanks to Joy Jacobs, who works just as hard and makes our team complete.

Thanks to the vacuum shift at the Writers' Room.

And especially thanks to Alexander Haris, my love, my guppy, who after so many years surprises me still.

"But I don't want to go among mad people,"
Alice remarked.
"Oh, you can't help that," said the Cat: "we're
all mad here. I'm mad. You're mad."
"How do you know I'm mad?" said Alice.
"You must be," said the Cat, "or you wouldn't
have come here."

—Lewis Carroll
Alice's Adventures in Wonderland, 1865

And if a man starts to weaken,
That's his shame,
For Bama's pluck and grit have
Writ her name in Crimson Flame.

—Ethelred Lundy (Epp) Sykes
"Yea Alabama" Fight Song, 1926

PART ONE

Wonderland

Sarina

On the eve of her sixteenth birthday, Sarina Summers got an overnight stay at Druid City Hospital. As her mother helped her through the emergency room doors, Sarina knew there was no turning back. This was it. She was serious about her future.

"What happened to this child?" the doctor exclaimed. "This child is drunk as a skunk and her fingers are broke!"

Sarina could not answer. She was totally shit-faced.

"Honey?" Mrs. Summers said.

"Miss?" said the doctor as he held Sarina's eyes open by the brows. He lit up her pupils with a tiny flashlight. "Let me know if you can hear me." He flicked the flashlight on and off. "Anybody home?"

"Honestly," said Mrs. Summers. "Does she need to be fully conscious for this? Could you just fix her fingers, please?"

Sarina nodded furiously and tried to sit up on the gurney. She offered her hands to the doctor. She said, "Hurts." The room was spinning faster now. Noises echoed. She fell back. The impact against the pillow pushed her long brown curls across her white-washed cheeks.

"I know it hurts," said Mrs. Summers and, with her hands, combed the hair away.

Sarina tried to focus her attention on how good her mother's nails felt against her scalp. How the square-shaped acrylics were softer than what her mother grew naturally. It was a dull, comforting sensation. Her mother's magic fingers. For a moment, she was calm. Sarina said, "Mmm."

"Yes," said Mrs. Summers. "That's my girl. Show the nice doctor that you're ready."

Sarina felt the back of her mother's hand against her jaw, her forehead.

The doctor said, "What she's ready to do is get her stomach pumped."

"Oh, no," Mrs. Summers said. "No, that's uncalled for. Fix her fingers. She'll sleep it off. She's drunk, not poisoned."

"I assure you," said the doctor, "she's as good as poisoned."

"Hurts," said Sarina. She rolled her head from side to side.

"Sarina," said the doctor. "Are you with us? Can you tell us what happened?"

Sarina kept her eyes shut. She choked back the sobs that crawled up her throat.

"Mrs. Summers," said the doctor, "I don't know what kind of drinker your daughter is."

"She's not one."

"Well, ma'am, she is one tonight."

Mrs. Summers crossed her arms and pressed down her breasts.

The doctor said, "From the smell of her and from her limited response, I'd say she's put down a bottle of Jack Daniel's."

Sarina heard her mother let out a long sigh.

The doctor said, "Believe me, I want what's best for your daughter. Her fingers can wait." The doctor motioned to a woman in green scrubs drinking something from a Styrofoam cup. He said, "Nurse, take this patient to room nine. Prep her and get the hose."

The nurse held the rim of the cup in her teeth and used her free hands to push Sarina down the hallway.

Sarina reached her hands, the bones of her two smallest fingers sticking out of the skin like straws, first in the air, then over her head toward her mother's voice as it fell away with the pace of the gurney.

Sarina heard her mother ask, "Can't I sit with her?"

She heard the doctor's voice. "Waiting room." She heard him say, "It's the right thing."

She lost them.

The nurse pushed Sarina's arms down. "Keep still. This will be over before you know it."

Sarina rocked in the darkness. The gurney like a hammock. The cool, clear corridor like her big backyard.

The party was great, thought Sarina as the nurse pried her teeth apart and the doctor pushed the hard warm hose to the back of her throat and then down and down.

"Don't fight it," said the doctor.

"You're doing so good," said the nurse.

Sarina tried not to gag. She tried to be still. *Mom,* she thought, *You said the worst part was over. You didn't tell me this part.* "Hurts," Sarina tried to say, but all that came out was a strained gurgling noise.

"Almost over," said the doctor.

"You're doing so good," said the nurse.

Sarina kept her eyes closed the way her mother had taught her (*In painful situations, you want to keep yourself from seeing what's happening*). Sarina reasoned with herself. *I'll just go to sleep.* Over the course of the evening, she slipped in and out of consciousness.

When she came to, the light through the blinds showed her it was morning. She felt as if she had slept for a week. She bet her eyes were bloodshot. Her neck ached from the position her arms were set. They were raised like Barbie's in the box. Outside the window of the closed metal door, Sarina could see the heads of her mother and the doctor.

"Mother," she said, surprised by the scratch in her voice. "Mom," she said a little bit louder. She watched her mother turn her head, bring her hand over her mouth, push open the door, and take three long strides to sit on the bed.

"Honey," Mrs. Summers gushed, "how are you feeling?"

"My throat hurts."

"I bet it does," Mrs. Summers said. She looked accusingly over her shoulder at the doctor.

The doctor said, "Sarina, can you tell us what happened?"

"Yes," said Mrs. Summers. "What on earth?"

Sarina said nothing.

"Did you fall?" said the doctor.

"Did you shut your hands in the car door?" Mrs. Summers suggested.

Sarina shook her head as the doctor and her mother continued to guess.

"Volleyball?"

"Did you stick your fingers in the fan?"

"Moving furniture?"

"Did that nasty camp trunk shut on you?"

Sarina shook her head at all of these. She said, "I can't remember."

"Well," said the doctor. "In any case, you're lucky your mother found you. That must have been some party."

"It didn't happen at the party."

"I would have seen it," said Mrs. Summers.

"*Ho*-kay," said the doctor. "I've given your mother a prescription to help the pain when you come off the morphine. Take one pill when you need to. They'll make you sleepy, which is okay, but they'll make you nauseous if you don't take them on a full stomach."

"My throat hurts," said Sarina.

Mrs. Summers again looked over her shoulder at the doctor.

"Well," said the doctor. "Try to force something down. It will hurt a lot more coming up than it will going down. The nurse will be in to help you with your checkout." He put his hands in his pockets and pulled the door open with his hands still in his lab coat.

Sarina and her mother were alone.

"How do your fingers feel?"

"I don't really feel them. I'm pretty woozy."

Mrs. Summers stood up and smiled down at her daughter. "You've had some birthday."

Sarina nodded.

Mrs. Summers ran her fingers across the soft pad that covered the metal splint of Sarina's left pinky. She frowned. She said, "They cut your nail."

Sarina twisted her mouth in disapproval.

Mrs. Summers peered over the bed to examine Sarina's other pinky. They were identical, like two pieces of chalk. Mrs. Summers lightened. She smiled as big as her face would hold. She said, "They're going to be beautiful!"

"I know," said Sarina.

The nurse came in.

As she was helped out of bed, helped into a wheelchair, helped into her mother's car, Sarina remembered her party the night before.

The invitations had read, "Please Join Me for a Sweet Sixteen Luau!"

Her mother had gone all out. She had cooked for days. She wrapped pineapple chunks in bacon and soaked them in honey. She went to Winn-Dixie and Piggly Wiggly and

Kroger's to gather enough from Alabama's low supply of coconuts to gut them and make punch with the insides, drinks with the outsides. She bought tiny umbrellas and hung tissue-paper lanterns. She had the florist make leis for all the teenagers.

When Sarina got home from the last day of tenth grade, she walked into the backyard, dropped her books, and spun until she could not stand it anymore. Hypnotized by the pastel colors and rented picnic tables, she dropped to her knees and fell back onto her hands. "Mom!" she said. "This is *so* great! I can't believe you did this!"

Mrs. Summers sat down on the cement step in front of the sliding glass doors to the den. She smoothed her bangs into her new bob haircut sprung loose by the humidity of the approaching summer. The haircut was meant to make her look thin. To make herself look thin, Mrs. Summers wore tunic tops, black pants, and two coats of Maybelline Great Lash. Mrs. Summers smiled at her daughter sprawled in the grass like a little girl. She said, "You're not a little girl anymore."

"Maw-hum!" Sarina opened her mouth and rolled her eyes. She got to her feet and rushed to her mother. She sat in her lap and hugged her neck. "Stop!" She put her head against her mother's. She said, "Gawd, it's not like I did anything special."

"But you will," Mrs. Summers said. "You'll do so many great things."

Sarina rolled her eyes again. She stuck her flat tongue between her teeth freed from braces a few weeks after Christmas. "Come on," Sarina said, tugging her mother off the step. "Help me get ready. It's an hour to five and you *know* one of the boys will show up right on time."

Mrs. Summers said, "Okay." She pulled open the sliding door and followed her daughter into the den. As she slid the door shut, Mrs. Summers stared out into the big backyard. She thought, *Once the sun goes down, those pines will almost look like palms.* She said, "Did you see the roses your father sent? They're in your room."

Sarina had reached her room by this point. She called to her mother, "Mom! Come on!"

Mrs. Summers turned from the party-in-waiting. With her back against the glass, she prayed for it not to rain, then walked through the house to sit in her daughter's room while Sarina put her hair in rollers, lined her lips, and asked for help with the zipper to the sundress they had chosen two months ago.

After the party, Sarina grinned and swayed like a punching bag in the center of the kitchen.

Mrs. Summers said, "Somebody's had too much punch."

Sarina said, "Somebody spiked it!"

Mrs. Summers looked at the ceiling. She put her index finger to her chin. She said, "I wonder who."

Sarina gawked. "You are too cool."

"I suppose I am," said Mrs. Summers. She pointed to the glazed ham. "Put some tinfoil on that, will you?"

Sarina did as she was told and helped her mother lift the ham and slide it onto the bottom shelf of the fridge.

"That's the last of it," Mrs. Summers said. "You ready?"

"Uh-huh!"

Mrs. Summers slapped her daughter's face so hard Sarina lost a clip-on earring. She studied her daughter, who stretched her eyes wide and bit her lip in an effort not to cry.

Mrs. Summers frowned. "No you're not." She offered her daughter a sheet of Bounty to dry her tears. "I bet that smarts. Goddamn weak punch."

She took her daughter by the wrist to the rumpus room

downstairs. She sat her in a chair by the edge of the Ping-Pong table. From her apron pocket, Mrs. Summers produced a shot glass and bottle of whisky. She said, "Pour yourself a drink and I'll get things ready."

As Sarina screwed the lid off the bottle, she took a good look at her crooked pinkies. The top joints bent toward the other fingers. Her father used to tease her. He said it was like those pinkies were trying to do a U-turn.

On a routine physical, Mrs. Summers had asked the pediatrician, "Can these be fixed?"

"Not in any way you'd want to," the pediatrician had told her. "There's no doctor who'll do it. What your daughter's got is a recessive trait. Like widow's peaks and attached earlobes."

Sarina filled the shot glass to the lip. She held it with both hands. She whispered, "Like braces."

She had four more shots.

Mrs. Summers stood behind her and ran her fingers through her daughter's hair. She twisted it. Let it loose. Started a braid. "How you doing?" she asked and put the back of her hand against Sarina's damp forehead. "Feeling no pain?"

"Don't slap me again."

Mrs. Summers said, "I won't."

Mrs. Summers walked around the Ping-Pong table. She poured a shot. She put it in her daughter's hands. "Drink, honey."

Sarina nursed the whisky. "I don't feel so good."

"That's a good sign," said her mother. "Keep working that drink. Shut your eyes. Don't pay any attention to me."

Sarina let the whisky drain into her mouth. She tried to decipher the weird sounds in the room. A giant thud on the Ping-Pong table. A lot of ripping. Then her mother took the shot glass away. She fiddled with Sarina's wrists and hands and fingers.

"Have another," Mrs. Summers said. "Be a good girl."

Sarina could feel the shot glass at her mouth. She felt her mother tilt her head back and guide the liquid down.

She took a peep.

In front of her, Sarina saw her arms outstretched, her wrists duct-taped to a cinder block. Except for her pinkies, her fingers were curled into fists and taped. Her pinkies laid out and taped. The cinder block taped to the table. Her mother standing before it all.

"Oh," cried Sarina. She was too drunk to speak.

"Be a good girl," Mrs. Summers said as she picked up the ax. She lifted it, blade backwards, over her shoulder. "Keep your eyes closed."

Sarina did as she was told.

On the ride home from the hospital, Sarina thought *It wasn't that bad.* The last thing she remembered was her mother bringing the ax down and the crack of the first of her two fingers breaking.

Bitty Jack

THE SUMMER Sarina turned thirteen years old, Bitty Jack Carlson met her, crooked fingers and all.

The afternoon Sarina arrived in Summons County, Camp Chickasaw was three days under way and no one in the cabin had taken the bunk beneath Bitty Jack. Although it had not happened since she was eight or nine, Bitty Jack Carlson was a known bed wetter. While the chances of her mattress springing a leak were slim, in the paranoid minds of just-turned-teenagers Bitty Jack's urine could rain down like tiny anvils.

"Not under the Pee Queen!" all thirty girls had cried to their counselors.

On the first day of camp, Bitty Jack was banished to the empty bunks in the corner of the cabin. While the other girls played Get-to-Know-You-Games, Bitty Jack sat on her top bed, her back to the others, and wrote a letter to her parents.

Mama and Daddy, it read, *please come get me.*

Bitty Jack snuck out of the back bathroom door. She walked up the biggest hill—past the tennis courts and archery range, the road to the pool, the path to Lovers' Leap—to her family's house, now dubbed "The Caretakers."

In exchange for a small salary and year-round residency, the Carlsons took care of Camp Chickasaw grounds during the off-season and, from June to August, ran maintenance and laundry. When schools let out, the camp owners arrived with big Hellos and How-Do-You-Dos. They raised their right hands and boomed, "HOW, HOW, HOW!" They turned up the volume of the Carlsons' quiet life. In the summer, the lake was drowned out by go-carts, by *Sound of Music* rehearsals, by fake-out color wars. Everyone was encouraged to scream their spirit to the sky. To Bitty Jack, even the birds chirped louder.

Although Summons County, Alabama, was poor, with a population less than a hundred, Chickasaw was an exclusive camp with a long wait list. Parents from six Southern states shipped their pride-and-joys with trunks-full of underwear labeled and pressed. The Carlsons' jobs took up twelve hours a day, so Bitty Jack was put in a cabin to live with the rich girls. The night before each season started, Mrs. Carlson helped her daughter roll her clothes into her daddy's army duffel bag.

Bitty Jack got her name from her father. Mrs. Carlson had wanted to name her Mary or Tiffany Ann, a special girl's name, but that did not happen. She came three months premature and stayed in the hospital for weeks. It seemed like she slept all the time, her lungs working hard, her veins moving blood so close to her skin. When the doctors told her mother that during labor something inside her quit working, this would be her only child, raise it right, Big Jack spoke up. He said, "I ain't gonna have no boys, but that's okay. This itty-bitty one'll be all right." When the threat of death left the infant ward, her mother filled out the birth certificate. During the first rain of the summer, Bitty Jack left the hospital in the cradle of her daddy's scrubbed, calloused hands.

Bitty Jack climbed the wooden stairs to her house. She clutched the letter as the handrail shook with each step. The screen door whined as she let herself in. Her mother was down the hill in the laundry and her father was cutting grass farther down by the lake. In her room, the bed was made, her stuffed animals lined by seniority like she'd left them. One crack of sunlight cut through the drawn curtains and sliced her bed in half, leaving the patchwork quilt hot. Bitty Jack lay the envelope on the pattern of six frogs jump-roping that her mother had sewn as the quilt's center patch.

She said, "Mama and Daddy, please come see."

With the hopes of one of her parents stopping by for a Coke, Bitty Jack paused at each light switch on her way out of the house. She sighed many sighs. She said, "Shoot."

When Sarina showed up, Bitty Jack's parents still had not mentioned the letter. She wondered if on the day she moved back to her house, she would find the envelope where she placed it. The seal unbroken, pink color tinted brown.

Sarina stood in the doorway to the cabin. She surveyed the room at rest period.

At this point, the girls had just finished lunch. While their counselors gossiped on the front porch, the girls fought off naps induced by ground beef casserole and too much bug juice. They lay on their beds and fondled teenybopper magazines. They freed from the staples foldout mini-posters of the latest prime-time high school hunks. They played Go Fish and Slap Jack. They painted their nails colors their mothers would never approve of. *Mmmm . . . yum . . .* contraband Blow Pops. They placed big-money twenty-five-cent bets on whom among them would be felt up first.

"I've done it," Sarina said as she made her way to the only empty bunk in the cabin.

"Done what?" said the four-foot-five boobie bookie taking the bets.

"What?" said her cohort counting out the cabin's quarters.

Bitty Jack knew what. Before Sarina reached the bunk below hers, Bitty Jack knew that Sarina had gone further than she had even allowed herself to imagine. Sarina walked like a young lady who had spent some time at second base. She stuck out her chest as if to show the cleat marks. Bitty Jack tugged at the weak elastic of her bra strap. She watched Sarina closely as she kept her back to the girls and further comments to herself. Bitty Jack heard Sarina's suitcase zipper yawn. She knew that this would be the last sound from the new girl until the room was quieted.

The boobie bookie said, "Done what?"

Captain Quarters said, "What?"

Unaware, the other girls buzzed.

The boobie bookie said, "Shhhhh!"

Captain Quarters said, "Hush, ya'll!"

Sarina unpacked as the rest of the room was silenced by a series of mean looks and hand gestures. Some of the girls climbed down from their bunks, got up off the floor, moved closer to Sarina.

The boobie bookie said, "Tell."

Bitty Jack felt the metal frame sway as Sarina sat down. She peered over the edge of her mattress and saw Sarina cross her legs like a woman. Sarina's white socks were a shade darker than her skin, but nobody dared make fun of how pale she was. So as not to miss a word, the girls leaned forward like deaf dogs.

Sarina said, "I've done skin on skin."

The girls said, "No way!" They followed with, "Agggh!"

Captain Quarters said, "When? With who?"

"Stewart Steptoe, and is last night near enough?"

Sarina was the only Tuscaloosa girl there. No one knew a Stewart Steptoe but his name was pronounced with such authority they had to believe. Bitty Jack hung her head upside down. She spoke for the first time during rest period. She said, "For real?"

Sarina jerked away from Bitty's blood-swollen face (bifocals loose, eyes upside down, cheeks sagging like a bat). "No," she said, "I'm lying, you four-eyed freak."

The girls squealed. They actually applauded.

Bitty Jack swung her body back and lay flat, her head sinking slowly into her fire-retardant foam pillow. She thought *Maybe if I don't move, it will be like nothing's happening*. Bitty Jack stayed still while the girls' laughter threatened to lift her body off the bed and toss it around like a bag of day-old cotton candy.

"Go on," said the boobie bookie. "Tell us *exactly* what happened. How did he do it? Was it your first time?"

Sarina said, "Hardly."

"Tell," said the girls. "Tell, tell!" they chanted.

Bitty Jack kept still as the girls forgot about her and zeroed in on the whisper slinking out of Sarina's mouth. As Bitty Jack listened to the story of the backyard woods, she hoped that Sarina's bubble gum–flavored gloss would glue her lips shut. But Sarina kept her story moving with ease. Phrases like "and then he undid" and "I made myself look" and "he didn't say anything when I" floated up and hovered over Bitty Jack like clouds.

Bitty Jack wondered what she would have to do to hold the girls' attention like Sarina. She wondered if she would ever outgrow what her mama called her awkward stage. Could she ever afford new glasses? Could she dress better? Wear makeup so it looked right? Would her acne ever clear? Would her hair lose the oil, gain body, gain bounce? Bitty Jack wondered what it felt like to lay on the leaves and let a boy see her from the waist up. Would he feel so good she could ignore the roots and rocks, the hiss of the dragonflies, the smell of his jeans?

To retell a half hour of ecstasy, Sarina took all forty-five minutes remaining of rest period. She stopped when a counselor stuck her head in and called, "Who wants volleyball, who wants crafts?"

The girls waited to see which Sarina would choose. When

Sarina said, "Macramé's cool," their souls were captured. They would follow her anywhere. They exited en masse.

Bitty Jack crawled down from her bunk. She faked cramps and, on the way to the infirmary, went to find her mama.

Her mama said, "Baby, girls like that don't grow up to be nothing special."

Bitty Jack said, "No?"

"No, baby girl. This is it for girls like her. Maybe she'll make it big in high school next year. But what do you care?"

"She shares my bunk."

"Well now, that's true. But every time she don't treat you right, you just remember that her life will be sad in a few years. In a few years, no one's going to think she's so cute. No one'll care what she has to say. She'll get married because she's supposed to and then she'll disappear."

Bitty Jack said, "Swear?"

Her mama said, "You know I cain't swear, but I'll promise you this. If you're patient and keep your eyes peeled, she'll get old and you can watch how unhappy that makes her."

Bitty Jack said, "When I get old, will I be unhappy?"

Her mama said, "Baby girl, not if you can help it."

Bitty Jack did not know what she could do to help anything. She wondered if she could ever change into a woman who could. Sarina was only thirteen and already content as the center of attention. Bitty Jack was a bystander thrust out of the loop.

As the summer continued, Bitty Jack tried to be brave. She spoke up when someone cut in front of her for shower rotation. Even when she was full, she forced down an extra helping so the girls would quit calling her Bird-Legs Anorexic. She ran the bases quickly. With each serve, she got the volleyball over the net. She read by herself. She kept away from the new girl.

Sometimes, after curfew or whenever the chance presented itself, Bitty Jack would carry on conversations with the bathroom mirror. Maybe it was a teacher she spoke to. A counselor. Her mama. Sometimes she made up an imaginary boyfriend. She'd close her eyes and kiss her own reflection, steam up the mirror, ignore the flavor of Formula 409.

Recently she spoke with only Sarina. She imagined a babbling, boring Sarina. One who wished she could be her friend. One that pleaded. One that begged. At first, Bitty Jack would be apologetic. "I'm so *sorry*." Then sarcastic. "I'm *so* sorry." Then mean. "I'm not sorry." Then cold. She'd widen her eyes as if to say, "Some nerve." She'd think about slapping her. Making the other girls scared.

During the off-season, her parents caught her at this all the time. While her mother watered the outside houseplants, she would spot her daughter through an open window.

"Big Jack," she'd say, "come get a look at this!"

As he ran, her father's key ring jangled on his hip. Before he saw her, Bitty Jack would scream and tromp off to her room. She would crawl under her bed where there was just enough room for her to keep her glasses on. She would ignore her mother's calls because she knew, at supper time, her daddy would come and get her.

Bitty would hear the stairs strain and the door open and his weight sink the springs. Her daddy would sit patiently at the foot of the bed and say, "Come on outta there, kid. You ain't got nothing to be ashamed of. You're okay. You're just practicing for life and your mother thinks it's cute."

Bitty would immediately slide out from under the bed, but remain just as flat as she was before.

Her father would say, "Who's Daddy's little rake?" Then he'd step on her toes and pull her rigid body upright.

When Sarina caught Bitty Jack talking to the bathroom mirror, she said, "Who the hell are you talking to?"

"Nobody." Bitty watched her reflection burn red from ears to nose.

Sarina stepped out of the bathroom. She shouted to everyone in the cabin, "Get a load of the freak show! Bitty Jack Carlson's talking to herself. She's got no friends so she's talking to herself!"

"No way!" called the boobie bookie.

"Freak!" called Captain Quarters.

"Freak show! Freak show!" The girls chanted and, to keep the rhythm, Sarina beat a broom handle against the bathroom wall.

Bitty Jack washed her hands until the bell for afternoon activity sounded. She twirled the pink Carress and wished for camp to hurry up and end. She wished for embarrassing moments the likes of which her parents gave her. From those, her daddy always helped her recover.

Her daddy was good at relieving Bitty Jack's blues. He let her help him with duties at Chickasaw assemblies. When Maria Von Trapp took the stage on Play Night, Bitty Jack steadied the spotlight and shook a cookie sheet to make thunder. She hosed down canoes at lake races. She gathered the bases after softball tournaments.

Bonfires were what Bitty Jack liked most.

Once a week everyone would gather down by the lake. They'd squeeze onto the bleachers and form rows on the grass. On the other side of the lake, Big Jack had stacked ten logs in teepee formation. He'd stuffed twigs and straw inside. It was the makings of a beautiful fire. Bitty Jack was small enough to fit inside that teepee. When she heard the campers' cheers echo across the water, she knew it was time to get down and do her thing.

"Fire, fire, we want fire! F-I-R," clap, clap, clap, "E!"

With a Chock Full O'Nuts can rimmed with sulfuric acid and a mayonnaise jar filled with sulfur and charcoal dust, Bitty Jack would get on her knees and elbows and fit her body halfway between two logs. She'd empty the powder mix in the center of the twigs. She'd sit the Chock Full O'Nuts can behind the powder pile and tie a string around its middle. As the cheers got louder, she'd scoot out and run to meet her father fifteen yards away. On his count of three, she'd yank the string and the acid on the chemical combo would cause a small explosion and start the fire. As the heat burned her cheeks and the cheers continued, Bitty Jack would bask in the glow of a job well done, the flames so high, and her daddy's clear pride.

Near the end of the season, Sarina promised to show the girls how to give head on the field-trip bus. She said, "If I have to, I'll use my Sweetarts roll." She cut out of breakfast early to be the first in the showers. The other girls could hardly protest.

Usually the girls showered before dinner and socials, but that morning, they were going to the Alabama State Fair. It was stationed in Summons County the last weeks of summer. There would be tenth-grade boys on the Chickasaw bus. High school boys were worth extra prep time. All the girls agreed.

With travel rollers, curling irons, crimpers, Water Piks, and hair dryers, they blew fuses every other day. Bitty let her shoulder-length brown hair dry naturally. While the girls rescued roller clips from the drain, Bitty Jack would sit on the porch and paint her short nails pink. At times like this, she did not mind the other girls. When a fuse blew, the girls would screech and a half made-up counselor would trudge to the main house to make a report. The owners would call Bitty Jack's house and, with his overall chest pocket full of fuses, Big Jack would make a trip to the dysfunctional cabin. He was reliable.

Except on August 25. That was the Carlsons' wedding anniversary. Throughout camp season, it was the only day the two of them left the campgrounds. They checked into the Moonwink Inn. They registered under Big Jack's mother's maiden name. They were gone. Unavailable. Under-cover-lovers. Do not disturb. The twenty-fifth was for making whoopee, fireworks, home-churned love.

The field trip was on August 26.

During the campers' breakfast, laundry and maintenance were already at work. Big Jack showed up at Bitty's cabin to fix the fuse. Later, he told Bitty and her mother that the cabin seemed empty. The front lights were out and he went inside. He headed toward the bathroom and opened the fuse box. As he unscrewed the blown fuse, he heard a noise in one of the wooden stalls. He didn't see any feet. He thought it was a raccoon or a mouse. Maybe a snake. He pulled his flashlight from his tool belt. He raised it above his head and took two silent steps and peered over and into the stall.

There was Sarina.

She sat cross-legged on the toilet. Her wet hair curtained her face and clung to the shoulders of her terry-cloth robe. Big Jack could see the disarranged part down the center of her scalp. Her bangs stood up straight from where she must have wiped her forehead. She was moving her head methodically. Up and down. Slowly then quickly. Big Jack thought she must be one of those bulimics he had seen on TV. He did not know what to do. Should he stop her mid-heave? And then she started making those sounds. Not throw-up sounds like his wife had made when she was pregnant with Bitty. Sounds like that girl was choking on something.

Big Jack said, "You okay?"

Sarina lifted her head and caught sight of Big Jack. Her lips lodged at the fat cheeks of the blow dryer, she quickly withdrew the nozzle from her mouth. Unlike his daughter's hues of embarrassment, Sarina looked like she just might kill him. This was not a look he'd ever gotten from Bitty Jack. But then, he had never caught his daughter trying to lick the life into a Vidal Sassoon Model 2000.

Sarina cried, "Go away!"

Big Jack said, "Sorry." He stepped back from the stall. He slipped the flashlight through a loop on his tool belt. He returned to the fuse box.

Sarina pushed open the door. It slammed against another stall and the lock stuck from her force. In front of the toilet, Sarina stood, knees slightly bent, robe tied tight, hair heavy, hair dryer in her fist, by her side like a gun. "Go!"

Big Jack fished for a fuse in his pocket. He said, "Look, I got to fix this for you. Hold your horses. Hold on a minute."

Sarina said, "Get out of here, now!"

Big Jack produced a new fuse. He held it up for her to see. He said, "All I have to do is screw this in. Hold on. Give me one minute."

Sarina stomped her feet. Her shame lit to anger. She screamed, "Get out! Get out! Get out!"

Big Jack sighed. He would not humor her hissy fit. He turned his back to her and screwed in the fuse.

Sarina ran out of the bathroom, through the rows of bunk beds, onto the porch. All the way, screaming, "Get him out of here! Get him out!"

On the path back to the cabin, Bitty heard Sarina go nuts. When she saw Sarina, mouth agape, hair limp, fists pounding the paint off the porch banister, Bitty slowed her pace to lag even further behind the other girls.

"What happened?" asked the red-headed counselor as she helped Sarina back into the cabin.

"What?" asked the girls as they walked Sarina to her bed.

The red-headed counselor sat beside Sarina. The girls huddled around. Her route to the top bunk blocked, Bitty stood in Sarina's firing range.

"Her father's a perv!"

Big Jack stepped out of the bathroom.

Bitty said, "Daddy?"

Sarina said, "Get him out of here! He's a perv!"

Bitty looked at her father. Again, she asked, "Daddy?"

The counselor said, "What happened, Jack?"

"I came to fix the fuse. I accidentally walked in on her. She was fully clothed. I didn't see a thing."

"I was on the toilet," Sarina bawled.

"You weren't *on* the toilet."

"Was too and you saw everything!"

Big Jack put his hands on his hips. He hung his head. He shook it. He said to the counselor, "She's overreacting." He walked past the girls, stopping to rest a hand on Bitty Jack's shoulder.

"Daddy," Bitty said.

"Pervert!" Sarina yelled.

"Pervert!" the girls chimed in. "Pervert!" they repeated as he walked through the room. On his way out the door, the girls dispersed from Sarina's bunk and ran to their own. From pillowcases, they pulled ammo and pelted Jack's back with Tootsie Rolls and Hubba Bubba. Big Jack slumped his shoulders. He just kept walking.

Candy flying past her, Bitty trailed after her father. She watched him walk down the porch steps and out onto the road. The chants died down as Bitty shuffled forward.

"Bitty," said another counselor, the group leader. "Wait."

Bitty Jack kept still. She fought with all she had to keep from shaking and showing the other girls she wanted to cry. She felt as if the bunk beds were creeping up behind her like a tidal wave. At any second, it would crash down upon her, spilling the other girls like seaweed and shells.

Bitty felt the group leader wrap her arm around her shoulder. She took her glasses off because they pinched her temples. She stared at the floor. She choked her glasses with both hands, her tiny pink nails threatening to break the lenses.

The group leader said, "Let's take a walk."

On the path to the lake, Bitty Jack let the group leader keep her arm where it was. She missed her mother's hugs and holds. Her mama's warmth could calm grief and fear.

Bitty Jack said, "I want my mama."

The group leader said, "I know. But let's give her some time. I bet your father's with her now and the bus for the fair trip will be here any second."

"I don't want to go any fair. I want my mama."

"Come on," said the group leader as they reached the bleachers by the lake. "Let's sit for a second and maybe you'll change your mind."

They sat on the first row, but Bitty Jack knew she would not change her mind. She did not want to go, but she would anyway. She would go and sit next to that boy with a deformed baby's hand. They would not talk, but they would not bother each other either. They would pile off the bus and Bitty Jack and the deformed kid would hang out with the group leader who would rather hang out with the boy counselors, but was too nice to make them stay alone. Bitty would reluctantly have fun on the rides. When she got on the Tilt-A-Whirl, she might not feel like crying. When she rode the Matterhorn, she would scream for more speed. If she was good, she could probably see her mama after dinner. Her mama would surely make sense of it all.

Her mother did her best.

After chicken nuggets and spaghetti, Mrs. Carlson took Bitty Jack to the laundry room on the ground level of the Arts & Crafts barn. They each sat on a washing machine and folded thin white towels in their laps. They stacked them on a butcher's block in front of their knees.

Mrs. Carlson said, "Your daddy wasn't at dinner 'cause he didn't want to start any trouble."

"He didn't do anything," said Bitty.

"You're right. But the owners have their noses out of joint.

Sarina called her mother from the fair. Her mother called the office and the office called us."

"Is Daddy gonna lose his job? Will we have to move?"

"Baby girl, not if we can help it."

Bitty Jack stopped folding. "What should we do?"

Mrs. Carlson said, "Just lay low. Camp ends in two days. From what I understand, that Summers girl is just here 'cause her parents are splitting up. I don't think she'll come back and your father's the best worker those owners ever had. I think if we just keep our heads down, this too shall pass."

"This too?"

"I hate to tell you this, but worse things could happen."

"Oh," said Bitty Jack.

"Oh, what?" said Mrs. Carlson.

"Oh-kay," said Bitty.

"Good, baby. Tell you what. Let's say we sneak into the cafeteria and grab ourselves a leftover brownie."

"What about Daddy?"

Mrs. Carlson smiled at her daughter. She hopped off the washing machine and stretched her arms out like when she taught Bitty Jack to swim. She said, "Jump, baby girl. We'll bring him one too."

Big Jack was upbeat and thanked Bitty for thinking of him. He ate the whole brownie she brought and let her watch *Wheel of Fortune* before he sent her back to her cabin.

During the final puzzle, Bitty said, "Daddy, what'd she say you did?"

Big Jack kept his eyes on Pat Sajak who, with only minutes remaining, spun the wheel of fortune to determine the worth of the remaining consonants. Eighty-five dollars. The audience went *Awwuh!*

Big Jack said, "She said I was spying on her."

Bitty said, "On the pot?"

Big Jack shook his head. He said, "Yeah."

Bitty said, "Oh."

Big Jack said, "Oh, what?"

Bitty smiled, "Uh-oh."

"My sentiments exactly."

Bitty said, "But, you weren't, Daddy. Why'd she get so bent outta shape?"

Big Jack watched Vanna turn over two purchased vowels. He said, "I caught her doing something she's embarrassed about."

"What?"

Big Jack said to the TV, "The kindness of strangers."

The returning champion repeated his answer. The bells went off and Pat shook the contestant's hand.

"Yes!" said Big Jack. He turned to his daughter. "Bitty, I don't know how much you know about things,"

"I know plenty."

"She was playing with herself."

Bitty felt her face turn red. She said, "Okay."

"Well, with something," Big Jack struggled. "I'd ask your mother to tell you, but I couldn't explain it much better to her."

"That's fine, Daddy."

"It's sexual. She was doin' something sexual with a thing not meant for sex."

Bitty stood up and again she said, "Okay."

On her walk back to the cabin, the sun was already gone.

In the cabin, the girls were getting ready for the Friday night disco up the hill on the outdoor basketball court. They swarmed around the wall-length bathroom mirror. They watched each other dress. Coordinating earrings, they moved from bunk to bunk.

On her bed, Bitty Jack felt invisible until Sarina caught her eye.

From the bathroom, Sarina hollered, "You stepped on my bunk!"

Bitty Jack froze as Sarina stomped into the main room.

"You stepped on my bunk!"

"Did not."

"You sure as shit did too!" Sarina marched forward and grabbed Bitty Jack by the ankle. "You put your nasty pervert toes on my bed. You got your daddy's germs all over my sheets!"

Bitty Jack said, "Let go."

Sarina said, "Make me, Pizza Face!"

The girls went, "Ohhhh!"

Sarina gave Bitty Jack's ankle a tug.

Bitty drew back her leg. She kicked Sarina in the chin. Sarina collapsed and hit the back of her head against the bunk beside Bitty's.

The girls said nothing.

Bitty looked down at Sarina. She made the meanest face she could. She stared at that girl for what seemed like hours. Sarina put one hand on the back of her head. She brought her other hand across her chin to cover the mark left by Bitty's tennis shoe. Bitty Jack noticed that Sarina's pinkies were not as straight as normal. She felt bold and blurted, "What'd you do, get your fingers stuck while you were picking your ass?"

Sarina's face reddened. She whipped her hands away from her face. She made two fists, then shot double birds.

The girls went, "Ohhhh!"

The red-headed counselor came in from the porch. She said, "What the hell is going on in here?" She put her hands on her hips and made everyone shut up because she had said the word "hell." She looked at Bitty Jack and said, "Well?"

"She kicked me!" Sarina cried. She stood up and showed off her goose eggs. "Here," sniff, "and here."

The red-headed counselor touched Sarina's bumps. She said, "Bitty Jack Carlson, is this really what happened?"

Bitty Jack lied for the first time in her life. The excuse entered her mind before the redhead had finished asking her question. "It was an accident," she said. And the lie felt good.

"You're going to jail!" Sarina threatened Bitty Jack. "Your father's getting fired and I'll sue you and . . . " She sobbed. "And . . ."

"Sarina," came the group leader's voice, "don't you dare say another word."

"She kicked me!"

The group leader said, "I want all of you ladies to go on up to the dance." She nodded to the red-headed counselor, who held Sarina's face and blew cold air onto her chin. "Go with them." Bitty Jack and Sarina did not have to be told to stay put.

The group leader said, "This is going to end."

Sarina said, "What? That's not fair. I didn't do anything."

The group leader said, "Don't. You've been provoking Bitty Jack since the first day you got here. I'm tired of it. It's going to stop or you're going home early."

"Please, can I?" Sarina said in a baby-doll voice.

The group leader said, "Don't tempt me."

Sarina smirked.

The group leader said, "Get out of my sight."

Sarina scowled. "With pleasure." She ran out of the room.

"Don't run," said the group leader.

Sarina slammed the door and, within that noise, Bitty Jack heard her future. She heard the girls taunt her father for seasons to come. They called him Big Jerk-Off and Jackin' His Box. She heard the owners remind him that he was not allowed to enter the girls' cabins. At cookouts, he had to serve cole slaw and let his wife take over the hot dog grill. Bitty imagined Sarina somewhere distant, somewhere tame.

"I hate her," she said.

"No, Bitty, you don't mean that."

Bitty Jack lied for the second time that day. This one delivered easier by way of the first. "You're right," she said. "I'm sure I'll get over it."

Sarina

When Sarina came home from the hospital, her fingers wrapped like pigs-in-the-blankets, she stayed in bed for three whole days. At noon and at night, she woke to her mother's soft yet insistent touch. Sarina closed her eyes and savored chicken bouillon, French onion, tomato; all these soups spooned from white bowls, gold-trimmed at the lip. She chewed on cold toast. She handed the crusts back to her mother.

Mrs. Summers said, "The outsides make your hair curly."

Sarina said, "Can I have my medicine now?"

Mrs. Summers opened the plastic vial labeled EAT WITH FOOD. She shook a pink-and-blue pill into the flat part of her hand. She said, "Whoops. Last one."

Sarina said, "What?"

"Last one. Get your drink ready." Mrs. Summers held the pill up and took aim.

Sarina opened her mouth and offered her tongue as in communion. Her mother pitched the pill and, in the air, the pink-and-blue flew like the Holy Ghost. Sarina chased it with lukewarm Coca-Cola. She let her mother secure the covers at each side of her breasts. She kept her arms over the comforter because the touch of the sheets hurt her tender little fingers. "Mom," she said, "I don't want to go off the pills."

"Give it time," Mrs. Summers said. "Once you get out of bed, you can watch the soaps."

"I won't have a tan."

"We can buy you a tan."

"Will you bring the TV in my room?"

"No," Mrs. Summers said. "You need to get up. You need to move around."

Sarina snorted.

Mrs. Summers said, "I'll make up the couch for you. We can eat on TV trays."

"Can we have steak and baked potatoes?"

"I'll run to the store while you're sleeping."

Sarina let her head loll to the right. The 250-thread-count was cold from too much air-conditioning. She closed her eyes and listened to her mother move about the room. Sarina knew that she would wait at the door, her hand on the knob, until there was no question that Sarina was out cold. Throughout the afternoon Sarina woke from and sunk into a deep, soggy sleep.

Sarina had made her bed and now she had to lie in it. For six weeks to be exact, until the splints came off. Her fingers had been a nuisance. A sore spot on her otherwise enhanceable body. Over the years, comments had been made. Little jokes. People had touched them without her permission. Last year, Ali Rosenthal had come back from Christmas break with a nose half the size of the one in her freshman photo. After the hunting accident, Bill Pruitt got caps. Why not fix what nature had botched? It had been Sarina's idea. Her mother had been unbelievably supportive.

"If something makes you uncomfortable, we'll change it. One, two, three."

Three years before, her parents' divorce had made Sarina uncomfortable. Her mother did not have instructions for that one. She did, however, have plans for her daughter: summer camp and no more going steady at age thirteen.

"You've got the rest of your life to cater to a man."

Sarina had been crushed. Stewart Steptoe had been out of luck.

The night before Sarina left for Camp Chickasaw, Stewart showed up right on time. He knocked on the front door. He was as punctual as his puberty.

Mrs. Summers said, "There are plenty of rich boys, Sarina."

"But, Mom, I love him. I do! Don't tell me how I feel."

Stewart rang the bell. The chime was quick as if he'd gotten a shock from the smudged white button.

Sarina stomped her feet. "Mom, he's here already!"

"This will be a clean break," Mrs. Summers assured her. "You're going to Chickasaw tomorrow. You'll have a summer romance. You don't need to get serious. The boy's getting fat."

"Is that why? There's hardly anything on him!"

Mrs. Summers said, "Trust me. By the time he's in college, the rest will catch up."

"Admit it," Sarina dared. "You want me to get rid of him because Dad's getting rid of you!"

Stewart tentatively used the big brass knocker. Another minute and he would have scooted behind the hedges and peered into the house through the living room windows.

Mrs. Summers said, "You'd better answer the door or he might leave on his own."

Sarina shouted, "Coming!"

Mrs. Summers sighed, "Really."

"Really yourself."

Sarina did not invite Stewart in as her mother always

insisted. She squeezed out of the house as if the chain was on the door. She shut it behind her like a burglar.

Sarina could see her mother watching through the sheer living room curtains. She grabbed Stewart's face and twisted it to meet her own.

Stewart said, "Your mom."

Sarina kissed him flat on the mouth. She used her lips to open his. She slid her tongue in and drew his out. She pulled his head into hers like when she practiced on a throw pillow.

Stewart broke free from Sarina. He nodded to the door. "She scares the crap out of me." He took Sarina by the hand and pulled her down the walkway. He called nervously over his shoulder, "'Bye, Mrs. Summers!"

As they walked into the neighborhood, Sarina looked back at her house, 1348 Cheshire Way. She saw her summer camp trunk sticking out of the back of the car. Even with an hour left of sunlight, she saw the timer-set porch lights click on. Her father's study was empty. Books off the bookshelves. His graduation tassels untied and taken from the window's metal lock. She saw lightning bugs and chiggers rise off the grass. All this and her mother had not budged.

Sarina turned her attention back to Stewart and pulled his arm around her waist. She snuggled into him as they walked. She had told her mother that they were going to the strip mall. It was twenty minutes by foot with only one intersection to cross. Stewart would take her bowling, they'd play video games, have frozen yogurt with a topping, and come straight home. It was an easy alibi. Good for a few hours. Her mother would not come looking unless she broke ten o'clock curfew.

Sarina said, "Let's go to the woods."

"What, you're not hungry?"

"Who cares if I'm hungry?"

"I care," said Stewart. He turned her body toward him. He pressed his face into the side of her neck.

Sarina said, "Are you burrowing again?"

Stewart nodded and his breath on her skin made her insides light up. She touched his black buzz shaved with a number-two blade for the summer. She could see his scalp. She said, "I'm not hungry."

Stewart kissed her throat and, even at ninety pounds, her slight double chin. He moved his hands into her hair. "Your hair always smells so good, Ree."

Sarina said, "Please. Let's go right now." She pointed to the Kendricks' house, the backyard rounded by a six-foot picket fence. "We'll cut through there."

They did and then they went into the woods.

They sat with their backs against a pine tree and kissed. As it got darker, Sarina let her hands go where she wanted. She touched Stewart's face. She ran her fingers down his back. She put her hands under his rugby shirt. She played with the new hairs surrounding his nipples. Stewart moved his mouth to her ear and whispered things he couldn't say to her face. Sarina liked these things, but became increasingly aware that her mother had not left her. It was as if Mrs. Summers was sitting on the lowest branch of that tree, commentating on her daughter's make-out session like someone off the Discovery Channel.

As our female subject removes our male subject's Eddie Bauer Item #1454E, size L, color Mango, we notice his flesh, peeling and protruding slightly above his belt. With the aid of Oscar Meyer Wieners and his mother's second helpings, our male subject will surely put on ten pounds before his start of Central High West. What is commonly referred to as "love handles" will be only the beginning of his body's descent into the far reaches of Fatdom. To your right, ladies and gentlemen, the city of Can I Finish That for You? To your left, over the horizon, Super Size Those Fries.

As Stewart slid his tongue into Sarina's ear, she kept her hands on his chest and wondered if her mother was right. When he got older, would he have breasts like that boy who drank four milks and sat alone during lunch? Would Stewart's shoulders round and slump? Would he lose his posture? Would he fit between the chemistry table and that old schoolmarm's blackboard? Sarina moved her body closer to Stewart's. She boosted herself onto his crossed legs. She felt his bare feet cradle her butt. She loved that. She straddled him and wondered how long she would be able to get in this position. If he got as big as her mother predicted, Sarina would not be able to get her legs around him. She was not known for her splits. She did not want to be known as the girl who loved the fat guy. *Lard Ass. Wide Load. Mr. Ho-Ho-Ho. Stupid Retard Taking Up the Whole God Dang Bus.* She could hear the other kids cutting him down.

Sarina refused to be taken down with him. She loved Stewart. She had envisioned car rides, spring breaks, surely the prom. They would go all the way when she felt the time was right. Yet that night she saw nothing but a sorry fat chance. It would be difficult to stand by him. Embarrassing. A drag.

She heard her mother say *Dump the porker.*

The next morning, Sarina woke to Stewart's knuckles against her bedroom window. She drew up the purple balloon curtains and said, "I told you it was over."

Stewart said, "You're making such a mistake, Ree, and when you figure it out I'll take you back."

Sarina shut the curtains and wondered how long he would wait in the yard. As she pulled her T-shirt over her head, she thought about starting high school after summer camp. In the shower, she swore she would never stop by his locker. She would invite him to her parties but it would be understood that he should not come. It would be hard, but Sarina would make him disappear. Her mother was right. She would never call him again.

* * *

Three years later Sarina changed her mind.

Coming out of her drug-induced slumber, Sarina heard her mother start the car to go get dinner. With her fingers broken, Sarina would not get her driver's license for weeks. She felt cooped up and wanted to continue taking charge of her life. She wanted to make more things happen. Stewart had his license. Sarina wanted a ride.

Using the palms of her hands, she picked the Princess phone off the nightstand and steadied it on her lap. She remembered the pattern of Stewart's number. She dialed. He answered.

"You said to call if I ever wanted to see you again."

Stewart said, "Your voice sounds weird. And why haven't you been at the pool?"

"Do you want to go out or not?"

Stewart said, "I guess."

"So pick me up at nine. I'll make sure my mom's asleep by then."

"Still sleeps like a big ol' bear?"

"Just show up on time. Park the car down the street and wait for me in the yard."

"Is this the part where I salute?"

"I'm sorry. Just come. I need to see you tonight."

Sarina fell asleep with the phone in her lap.

When her mother woke her she was halfway hysterical. "I tried calling from Kroger's." Mrs. Summers squatted and scooped up the phone which had fallen off the bed. "It's been off the hook. What on earth happened?"

"I must've knocked it over."

"I'll move it to the dresser."

"Mom." Sarina stopped her. "Would you wash my hair?"

Mrs. Summers studied her daughter. She touched the oily

knot Sarina's hair was tied into on the top of her head. She stroked Sarina's hairline where a few wirelike gray hairs were in urgent need of a trip to the beauty parlor. She plucked them instead, then pulled back the covers. Remembering her groceries, Mrs. Summers hurried to the kitchen to put the Fudgsicles in the freezer. Sarina looked at her pallid legs and thought that while at the hospital she should have figured out a way to get the color fixed. She needed to bathe and to put on some lipstick. When her mother returned, Sarina was seated on the toilet lid. Mrs. Summers ran the water and tested the temperature. She said, "On your knees, sweetheart."

Sarina obeyed. She steadied herself on the edge of the tub. The shower curtain smelled funny. She said, "When's Meena coming back?"

"When the splints come off. We don't need any gossip." Mrs. Summers sat on the side of the tub and worked Sarina's hair into wet soapy mounds. "And don't call her that. We call her Will."

The maid's name was actually Willamina, but the whole family thought Will was more manageable. Mr. Summers had hired her to clean house while his wife was busy with Tuscaloosa charities. Willamina was a light-skinned black woman from New Orleans who had been referred by her sister, who cleaned the Hicks' house directly across the street. Mrs. Summers didn't ask Mrs. Hicks. In all the years in Cheshire Way, Sarina had never seen her mother speak to Mrs. Hicks.

Willamina's sister had contracted cervical cancer from the genital warts her husband caught screwing his coworkers on the graveyard shift at the tire mill. When the cancer got ugly, he left her. So, Willamina took his side of the bed and, during the day, took care of the Summers.

Willamina was the same age as Mrs. Summers. Since the first day she'd started, her body had remained a larger version of her employer's. She was heavyset whereas Mrs. Summers was pleasantly plump. Sarina saw both women as comfortable retreats.

When Sarina's parents divorced, Mrs. Summers gave up her charity work.

"Don't you want to see your friends, Mom?"

"They were your father's friends."

Mr. Summers had not fought for custody. He was moving out West with that stewardess from Montana. He settled quickly and forfeited his daughter, the house, alimony, and Will.

Willamina helped Sarina get through her bad times. While her mother was napping, Sarina once stood in the kitchen and called her father fifteen times. She tried his house, the office, his cell phone, the gym.

"What the hell's going on, did Montana close down?"

"Might as well have." Willamina motioned for her to join her at the stove. She pointed to their dinner laid out on the paper towels. "See this?"

"A bunch of raw chicken parts?"

"Back in New Orleans, we'd call that a dead man. Today it's your daddy. Pick up that leg."

Sarina picked it up.

Willamina put her fingers in a cup of water and flicked a few drops onto an inch of oil in the skillet. The water popped and sizzled. "That leg's your father's lack of courtesy. But what do you care?"

Sarina threw it in the skillet. The oil splattered on the stove. The chicken skin bubbled. Sarina said, "I don't care."

"That thigh's his stupid ignorance. Walking off on a such a girl."

Sarina tossed the thigh in. "I don't care. I don't care."

Willamina turned the chicken and made room for some more. Together, they fried Mr. Summers' insensitivity, his lackluster performance, his manners, his taste. "That's right, my sweet girl. Just get rid of what he did."

Sarina reached into the tub to wipe shampoo out of her face.

"Uh, uh, uh." Mrs. Summers gently slapped Sarina's wrist. "You can't get the bandages wet. Wait till I put the sandwich bags on." Mrs. Summers turned off the water and rang out Sarina's hair with several long twists. She wrapped it with Sarina's favorite towel, which was really a beach towel with a beer-bottle print, which Sarina wasn't allowed to take to the pool. She told Sarina, "I'll run you a tub."

The water rose and the mirror began to cloud. Mrs. Summers used rubber bands to secure sandwich bags around Sarina's hands. The rubber bands were soiled from newspapers and they chewed at her wrists.

Her mother left and Sarina's hands began to sweat inside the see-through plastic bags as she unbuttoned her pajama top, slid her bottoms to the floor. She steadied herself against the tiled wall and lowered her body into the bath. She sighed. "It's not hot enough." She turned the hot knob with too much force and the water came hard, splashed her face, and burnt her feet. Sarina pushed her body away and made a wave, which sent the water crashing over the tub, onto the tiles, racing toward the bedroom carpet. Sarina yanked a towel down from the curtain rod and dropped it on the puddle. The water from the faucet roared. The water in the tub wavered at the rim. The overflow hole growled angrily as it failed to swallow fast enough. The plastic baggies stuck to her hands. "Just turn it off," Sarina bullied herself, and with her sticky, sweaty flippers she did.

Sarina looked at the stopper buried in her bath. She looked at her flippers. She drew her knees to her chest and propped her elbows on top. She placed her face into the gummy hollow of her hands. With her toes, she fished for the plug. She thought aloud, "I'm clean enough." She remained in the drainage and lathered her legs, her pits, her pube line with shaving cream. She shaved everything she could reach, then rinsed one part at a time.

She met her mother at the grill.

Sarina's stomach rumbled as Mrs. Summers slapped two steaks over the coals. Sarina said, "While they're cooking, will you roll my hair?" She offered a Ziploc bag full of foam curlers.

Mrs. Summers sat in a lawn chair and Sarina leaned back into the cavern of her thighs draped in a denim jumper. Mrs. Summers put her daughter's hair up in a matter of moments. She tied a kerchief around the pink bones.

As they ate dinner and watched *Entertainment Tonight*, Sarina felt like the Mammy doll Willamina had given her when she was six. Sarina wondered where her mother had put that doll, black lips crusted with Baby Alive's apricot pudding, when she spent that summer at Camp Chickasaw.

Mrs. Summers drank white wine and each time she left her TV tray to answer the phone or get another sliver of steak, Sarina would refill her mother's glass. By eight o'clock, Sarina's hair was dry and Mrs. Summers was ready for bed.

Mrs. Summers said, "I'm ready for bed."

Sarina said, "I'll clean up."

Mrs. Summers pushed herself off the sofa, lost her balance, and knocked the TV tray with her hip. The wine rocked in the glass the way the water had rocked in Sarina's bathtub. Rounding the couch, Mrs. Summers headed down the hall toward her room.

During the next hour, Sarina fought every urge to cry out each time she bumped a pinky. She cleaned the kitchen. She wiped off the TV trays. She took her hair down, did her makeup, got dressed, then waited by the living room window.

Two houses up the block, she saw Stewart walking toward

the front yard. He seemed taller. He sat by the mailbox and, through the peephole, his back looked broader than could be possible. Sarina opened the door so quietly, Stewart did not hear her. With the sprinklers running, she tiptoed through the grass and stood behind him and listened to a Beatles song he sang under his breath.

"All my lovin' I will give to you."

Sarina felt herself blush. It had been a long time since she had been so close to him. He smelled, just as she remembered, of Irish Spring and benzoyl peroxide. She wondered what his face would feel like now that he was shaving. After three years of dating other boys, Sarina was dissatisfied. None of them—Mr. Football, Mr. Sophomore Class President, Mr. We'll-Just-Lay-Here-We-Don't-Even-Have-to-Touch—treated her as nicely as Stewart, the first boy she'd kissed, the one who made her feel like she, alone, ruled. Stewart would do anything for her. All Sarina had to do was ask. Sarina ran the flat of her hand across the top of his buzz.

"Geez!" said Stewart. He jumped to his feet. "You scared the crap out of me. Don't do that."

Sarina said, "Sorry."

"Hey, what's this all about anyway? Geez! And what the hell did you do to your fingers?"

"I didn't *do* anything." She tried to tuck her hands underneath her crossed arms, but that hurt so she held them out in plain view. "It was an accident. I shut 'em in a door. Did you bring your car or not?"

Stewart said, "Yeah." He reached out to touch the gauze. Sarina winced before he got near her, so he pointed up the street toward his mother's station wagon.

"Good," said Sarina. "Let's get out of here."

As Stewart leaned over her body to buckle her seat belt, he asked her if she wanted to listen to the radio or a tape, which tape; he had a portable CD player he could plug into the cigarette lighter if she hadn't started smoking; if she had, that was cool, did she want to stop at the 7-Eleven and pick up some Virginia Slims?

Sarina said, "You talk different. Stop talking so fast."

"You haven't talked to me since the eighth grade. I do a lot of things different."

"You haven't *done* it, have you?"

Stewart put the keys into the ignition. He stared at the darkened speedometer. He said, "That's not your business anymore."

"Come on," Sarina said. "I just want to know. I won't tell. I'll tell you mine."

"Everybody knows yours. The whole school knows you do everything but."

"Who said that? I do not. I've never done," she whispered the word, "oral."

"Well, you never did it with me, that's for sure."

Sarina said, "I used to practice for you."

"What?" said Stewart.

"You're the only one I ever wanted to try it with."

"Shut up. Really?"

"Uh-huh."

Stewart shook his head. He crossed his arms. "Cool."

Sarina said, "So have you or not?"

"Not. In the experience department we're about even."

"Good," said Sarina. "Let's go to the fair."

"That's not till September."

Sarina said, "It's in Birmingham now. Let's go, please, let's go."

On the Ferris wheel, Sarina let Stewart put his arm around her. Forty feet above the fair, they could hear the catcalls from the freak-show tents. Sarina snuggled closer. She reached down his Duck Heads and pulled out his shirt. She reached further down and felt the elastic of his briefs. Without looking, she could tell they were white Fruit Of The Looms. He could not have changed that much. She dared her fingers even further. She coaxed out a few hairs from under his underwear.

"They're curlier," she told him and bent sideways to peer into his pants. "They're darker."

"Quit it," Stewart said, but did not take her hand away.

Sarina could see the sweat start on his stomach. She wondered if that counted as getting her bandages wet. As their seat swung down, Sarina moved her hand in careful, slow circles underneath the teeth to his zipper. When their seat rose up, Sarina moved her hand like madness.

When it was time to get off, Stewart staggered past the ticket-holders' line, tucked in his shirt, and tripped and fell onto the flat wooden monkey whose sign read, "You must be this high to ride this ride." Sarina dropped down on top of Stewart. She balanced herself on the monkey's chipped lips. She kissed Stewart as bystanders whooped and stopped sucking on their hot cinnamon-candied apples.

"Win me something," Sarina teased.

"What?" said Stewart.

"One of those big pigs."

As they made their way through the game booths, Sarina ignored the operators' solicitations. "Hey, little lady!" "*Hello,* gorgeous!" "I got two balls for a dollar!" Stewart pulled blue strands of cotton candy from the paper cone. He tilted his head back to feed himself in a tempting way.

"You want?" he said.

"No thanks."

Sarina noticed overlooked stubble on his Adam's apple. His face was fuller than it used to be. His cheeks stuck out, but they were tan without one freckle.

"How about the basketball toss?"

"It's fixed," said Stewart. "The hoop's bent so you can't see."

"How about the swinging ladder?"

Stewart said, "That's worse than the Flying Dutchman."

"Bear shoot?"

"Fixed."

"Ring toss?"

"Fixed."

"You pick," Sarina said, although she did not know what he would choose. Stewart was the high scorer on the math team. Each spring, he did Olympics of the Mind. He never showed up for any of the other events. The cheerleaders made him nervous.

"There!" said Stewart. "At last. A game of chance!"

Pick a Duck. Before them bobbed what must have been two hundred two-inch-tall plastic ducks. Various shades of Easter eggs, their heads were discolored from years of being snatched from the stream, flipped upside down, and scanned for a number matching a big prize. Currently, the game was surprisingly vacant. Sarina smiled at Stewart. She said, "Go for it."

Fifteen minutes later, they left the fairgrounds. Pick a Duck had not been a successful endeavor. Sarina knew the game was rigged. That ugly bitch behind the counter kept giving Stewart small prizes. Sarina wanted a big pig. When Stewart didn't win one for her, she lost her temper and things got out of hand. Even though that Pick a Duck girl started it, the security guards asked Sarina and Stewart to leave.

On the way to the parking lot, Stewart toted a caramel apple rolled in peanuts. He tried to put his arm around her, but she was angry and did not want the night to end with a wilted bouquet of felt snakes in her hands, their black eyeballs rolling loop de loop in their sockets.

Stewart opened the passenger door for her. Sarina watched him walk around the hood. He dropped into the driver's seat and the car rocked just a little. While he buckled their seat belts, he held the caramel apple in his teeth.

Sarina said, "Let's go to Deerlick."

Stewart said, "I got to get home."

"Come on, it's not even ten. Please, Stewart. Please, let's go."

Stewart looked at her. Sarina knew he was remembering that night before camp, his lips on her puffy nipples, his fingers on her breasts that had hardly formed at all.

Sarina said, "I wear under-wire now."

Stewart started the car.

They drove back to Tuscaloosa. Deerlick Park ran into the woods behind her house. Stewart parked the car in the lot, and he and Sarina wandered into the thick of it. They followed a trail to the shore of the lake.

Sarina remembered the rumors that the area was haunted. Couples had reported seeing ghost legs left over from water-skiing accidents, and not-so-bright brimstone reflected in the water. It turned out to be the local Ku Klux Klan. Sarina did not know which she was more afraid of. But the park was quiet that evening. It was dark and there were stars. Stewart and Sarina slid off their shoes and stepped forward, anxious to feel the water that was indistinguishable from the shore. The lake was quiet and not too cold. They waded in to their ankles.

Stewart said, "It's so good to see you again, Ree. Your skin's so nice. It, like, glows in the dark."

Sarina did not hear him. She was distracted by the possibility of a broken bottle under foot. Plus, she had led him there for a reason. She leaned forward and kissed him, careful to keep her feet planted, fearful that she might lose her balance, lose her nerve, and come home, mission not accomplished, her bandages reeking and stinking of pond scum. She opened her mouth to say what she had rehearsed while laid up in bed. Her voice came out cracked, not at all like she'd planned. "Make love to me."

"Are you crazy?"

"Make love to me," Sarina said, this time more assured, this time a little annoyed that his answer was not immediate, to the point, a resounding Yes.

Stewart said, "Are you on finger drugs?"

"Why are you making this so hard for me?"

"I'm not. I'm confused, that's all."

"Well, don't be," Sarina softened her voice. "It's just sex. I want the first time to be with someone I trust."

Stewart said, "I always knew you'd come back." He looked sheepishly at Sarina. "I hoped you'd come back. And, now, here you are and we're doing all this date stuff and I feel like I just kissed you for the first time and now you want to go all the way. It's weird. It's like too good to be true."

"I know," said Sarina. "But I'm tired of not knowing what all the fuss is about. Aren't you tired, Stewart? Don't you want to find out?"

Stewart's mouth fell open slightly as Sarina led him back to the shore and eased them down to the sand. She straddled him and wrapped her legs around his waist. Between her legs, she could tell that he was not as lean as he used to be. The muscles in her groin strained, but not enough to make her uncomfortable.

"Do you want to?" She kissed him. "Huh? Do you want to?"

Stewart nodded under the warmth of her mouth against his cheek, his jaw, the corner of his nose. He whispered, "I don't know how."

"Me either," smiled Sarina. "That's what makes this so perfect."

As Stewart turned off the ignition two houses from Sarina's, he said, "I'm so glad we're back together, Ree."

Sarina motioned to her seat belt. She said, "Undo me."

Stewart did. He kissed her and Sarina smelled all the sugar

from the night. She felt his semen clotting the breathable crotch of her panties. She wondered if he would fix himself a bologna sandwich before he went to bed. Sarina looked straight ahead. “We’re not back together.”

Stewart said, “What?”

“After tonight, it all goes back to the way it was.”

Stewart whispered, “What?”

Certain that there would be no repercussions, Sarina got out of the car. In her sixteen years, she had learned that not all bad deeds were deservedly punished. Her father got to live with that stewardess-slash-cowgirl. She herself had gotten to leave Camp Chickasaw without coming clean on how she’d treated that maintenance man. And sleeping with Stewart was not the worst thing she could have done to him. It’s not like she stole his virginity. It’s not like he didn’t enjoy it.

As she shut the car door, Sarina leaned through the open window. Stewart looked at her as if she’d just keyed his car. For a second, she felt sorry for him. Then she got over it. She said, “If you tell anyone about tonight, I’ll tell the Kendricks that when I was babysitting Mary Jo, you touched her when I was changing her.”

Stewart said, “But I didn’t.”

Sarina said, “But they’d believe me.”

As she walked away from the car, Sarina looked back through the windshield. Stewart covered his eyes with one arm, reclined the seat, and sank from view. Sarina looked toward her own house. The sprinklers were humming, which meant her mother had not stirred. Water filled the gutter and the grass smelled good. As she stepped onto the welcome mat, she felt taller, wiser, more grown up. She was ready to start eleventh grade. She was ready to compete with older girls. She turned the door knob that she had left unlocked. She snuck inside and left the lights off.

Nicole

FROM HER bedroom window, Nicole Hicks had watched the whole thing happen. She couldn't believe it. In the course of one evening, Stewart Steptoe had been beckoned, then dumped. As Stewart drove his car away, Nicole wondered how far Sarina had let him go. She wondered if he had seen what she, herself, had seen in locker rooms, at sleep-overs, at the peak of games of Truth or Dare.

Nicole imagined Sarina unzipping her pants, untying her shoes, settling into bed, still in her clothes. It was a ritual of hers: to sleep with the smell of the boy who had driven her home. Another ritual was to call Nicole, no matter how late, and tell her what time to come over the next morning. Sarina liked to tell the details of her dates in person. She liked to act things out, to use her hands, to close her eyes and open her mouth, to kiss the air in front of her friend. She liked to make Nicole blush and Nicole liked it too. Nicole waited for the phone to ring.

Nicole said, "If you don't call, I'll kill you."

Nicole checked for a dial tone. Since Sarina's sweet-sixteen party earlier that week, Nicole had not heard word one from her friend. When Nicole called Sarina's house, Mrs. Summers had told her, "Sarina's got mono. She'll call you when she's not contagious."

"But I can't catch it over the phone."

Mrs. Summers had said, "Aren't you sweet."

Nicole dreaded a summer without her best friend. She had seen girls with mono disappear from school for entire semesters.

"Nicole," Sarina had told her, "they're pregnant, not sick."

Nicole wondered if Sarina was pregnant, sneaking out to plan her elopement, then suddenly aware that she wanted none of it. No baby. No boyfriend. No rumors she could never live down. Maybe Stewart's was a consolation call because Sarina was laid up after an abortion. Her mother would have known just by looking at her. Sarina probably never said a word. Mrs. Summers just made an appointment and put her in the car.

This is how Mrs. Hicks tried to operate: mother and daughter as one well-oiled machine. Boom, boom, boom. One, two, three. Like clockwork or coworkers in a monstrous mission mill. But Nicole never could keep up with Mrs. Hicks. She was the monkey wrench in her mother's works.

In the fifth grade, Mrs. Hicks had sent Nicole to the Cheshire Elementary School science fair with a model of the solar system. To craft the universe, Mrs. Hicks had skipped a Tri Delta luncheon and advanced-intermediate yoga for more than a week. She manhandled coat hangers and spray painted Styrofoam snowballs left over from the Girl Scout Christmas-parade float where Mrs. Hicks had been the only mother skinny enough to slide into the chicken wire–crafted Frosty the Snowman suit. Jupiter was orange. Mars was red. Earth was green and blue and took the most time. It had to be perfect. She had to get the continents right. On the day of the science fair, Mrs. Hicks spray painted the round Frosty head silver, plucked its cardboard carrot nose, and topped off her daughter's semblance to Interplanet Janet, the Galaxy Girl.

As Sarina and Mrs. Summers approached the school bus with a poinsettia they had sung to and a poinsettia they had screamed at and kept in the dark on top of the clothes dryer, Mrs. Hicks spit on her fingers and wiped oatmeal off Nicole's tinfoil blouse. She whispered, "We're so much better than that. You can beat her. Just remember what I taught you."

Sarina placed second only to Norvin Roberts, who'd taught one of his mice to scale over six Lincoln Logs when he tapped C-A-T in morse code. Nicole received her first failing grade when, in response to her teacher's flurry of questions, she blanked on her mother's galaxy drills and blurted the only fact she knew to be true.

"The yellow one is the sun! The big one in the middle is the sun!"

Nicole had been sent home with her helmet in her hands. Mrs. Hicks was discouraged from attending PTA meetings for the rest of the year.

Sarina had phoned. "Forget it, Nic. That teacher's a loser. If my flower'd lived with her it would have died from ugly-itis!"

Mrs. Summers had brought over a green-bean casserole.

"Nobody's dead," Mrs. Hicks said and refused to take it. She slammed her front door on Mrs. Summers, her oven mitts and Corning Ware.

Nicole stared at the telephone and used all her mental powers to make her friend call. If Sarina was healthy enough to sneak out with Stewart, she was damned well healthy enough to call her best friend. And no one would ever be as good a friend as Nicole. In all of history, there had never been a better second banana, an orange to her apple, a pea in her pod. Nicole and Sarina were a budding buddy salad. They were a well-balanced meal. They were Cabbage Patch Kids.

Nicole's mother disagreed. She saw Sarina as a choice cut of steak who used Nicole like salt to bring out her flavor. Mrs. Hicks wanted her daughter to be seen as prime rib. Even if that meant putting Sarina through the grinder.

Freshman year, when Sarina convinced Nicole to join her at tryouts for the junior-varsity cheerleading squad, Mrs. Hicks bought a trampoline for their backyard.

"I hear that Summers woman hired a personal trainer for your friend. Now there's good alimony going to waste. Nobody beats this baby." Mrs. Hicks patted the boost-up bar.

After supper, Mrs. Hicks would leave the kitchen window open and turn the television volume up as she and her daughter went barefoot into the night.

Nicole's father was the senior anchorman for the six and ten o'clock Tuscaloosa News. As Nicole bounced, flipped backward, landed hard on her butt, she could hear her father's voice as if he were watching from the house.

"The Dow fell two hundred points today, while Greek hazing at the University of Alabama is at an all-time high."

Mrs. Hicks barked, "Higher, Nicole! You're not even trying!"

"This is Bert Hicks saying good night, Tuscaloosa. Have you talked to your kids?"

"HOW DO YOU EXPECT TO BE HEARD WHEN YOU'RE WINDED LIKE THAT?"

Nicole did not like to be alone with her mother, who watched so closely and expected so much. Mrs. Hicks wanted Nicole to win the top pyramid spot, to have the loudest voice, to be tossed so high she could free volleyballs lodged in the gymnasium rafters. Nicole was good enough be captain. When Mrs. Hicks was a girl, she was on the spirit squad. Being best was like blond hair: passed from mother to daughter like a stick of DNA dynamite.

Mrs. Hicks was right. Nicole was a natural athlete. With

only one month of training, one-handed cartwheels came as easy as breathing. Splits were no problem. She was limber and trim.

Nevertheless, Central High West junior-varsity tryouts were tougher than the Army, Navy, Air Force, Marines. Over the course of three days, girls were subjected to intense choreography and regulation gymnastics. There were weigh-ins and shouting matches. Pom-pom hurls and shows of strength. To claim one of twelve spots on the squad, Nicole had to beat out two hundred hopefuls. To stay close to Sarina, she competed heroically.

Both girls made the squad.

But when it came time for pyramid placements, Nicole did not give it her all. If parents were allowed at practice, Mrs. Hicks would have stormed the cheerleading sponsors and insisted on do-overs. Her daughter was just nervous. Let Nicole try again. With her mother confined to the Central West parking lot, Nicole had the freedom to do as well as she wanted. What she wanted to do was slightly worse than Sarina.

Sarina was so happy when she was ranked number one. Nicole liked to see her happy. From the bottom of the pyramid, Nicole could see all Sarina had to offer. Dropping down from a basket hurl, Sarina's pom-poms rustled like a plume on a bird kept at the pet store behind bullet-proof glass. As she fell, she made this incredible noise, which would not stop until Nicole caught her and placed her gently on the floor.

Sarina said, "You're the only one I trust, Nicole. The other girls would drop me. They're so jealous. They'd love to see me hurt."

"I'd never hurt you."

Sarina said, "Duh!"

Nicole loved the feeling that, to one person, she was irreplaceable. Her parents had her older brother, Rick. Her teachers had an abundance of students. There were always pretty girls. The world would keep spinning whether Nicole lived or died. But Sarina Summers would be empty without her. Nicole supported her soul. She was her spirit's gauge and guide.

On the football field sidelines, Sarina kept Nicole close at hand. Her arm around her waist, Sarina cozied next to Nicole as the squad walked leg over leg and roused the crowd with "*Hey! Hey you! Get out of our way, because today is the day we will push you away!*"

Mrs. Hicks mouthed the words from the alumni section. Her husband shook hands and gave the A-OK sign he gave on TV. Nicole's parents had been sitting in the same spot for years, her mother wearing Mr. Hicks's jacket. Mr. Hicks left with only one of his collection of cardigans. Junior varsity and varsity games were played on different nights on the Central High East campus field. Before Nicole started cheering, they watched her brother, Rick, one of the best high school linebackers T-town had ever seen. When he graduated, Rick got an athletic scholarship to the University of Georgia. Saturdays, he could be seen on TV. He was still the talk during halftime entertainment.

Every time Nicole looked up, her father seemed to sense it. In a split second, he would move his eyes from the field or his fans to her red-and-white uniform in front of the crowd.

After each game, Mr. Hicks praised her banana jumps and Flying Dutchman. He told her that the elocution lessons were really paying off, the cheerleaders had conquered their Southern accents, every word was crystal clear.

As Mrs. Hicks held out sweatpants for Nicole to step into, Nicole would watch the other cheerleaders scamper to the fold-out back door of Mrs. Summers's station wagon. Mrs. Summers always had Cokes and Rice Krispies Squares, cookies that were never burnt, sometimes root beer, sometimes gum. By the time Nicole brought her attention back to her parents, Mr. Hicks invariably wore Memory Lane like a scarf.

"Did you see County High's quarterback dodge that tackle? I'm telling you, Rick could have buried him alive. Remind me, when Rick calls, to tell him that his old team is getting soft."

"Sure, Pop."

"That Rick . . . he was a star out there."

Wrapping a jacket around her daughter's shoulders, Mrs. Hicks would lean forward and whisper, "You could be too. If you'd only try harder."

Try, try again. In the eyes of Mrs. Hicks, being good was never good enough.

This was nowhere more apparent than in after-school study sessions. Every day, after cheerleading practice, Mrs. Hicks would check her daughter's homework. She would use Wite-Out to correct mistakes and fill in the right answers copying Nicole's loopy cursive. Nicole was a below-average student who, under her mother's charge, was pushed into a B-slot.

Sarina Summers was right there with her.

After Mrs. Hicks's many failed attempts at demand and supply *(Memorize these vocabulary words and you can wear that skirt I hate . . . Do these multiplication drills and I'll give you a low-fat Eskimo Pie)*, she accepted the fact that her daughter would not advance without her best friend. So, when Mrs. Hicks held up a flash card, she had to make a game of it. Nicole and Sarina would sit across from her and slap the mahogany table when they knew the answer.

Smack! "Argentina!"

Smack! "George Wallace!"

Mrs. Hicks often made the girls switch seats. If Sarina beat the table in one place for too long, Mrs. Hicks had to remind her it was not good for the wood.

Nicole's mother was the Great Reminder. *Stand up straight.*

Don't chew on your nails. I've already salted that. Could you smile, at least?

Mrs. Summers never uttered anything close. When Nicole stayed over, Mrs. Summers let her do as she pleased. If she wanted, Nicole could eat a whole bag of dill pickle–flavored Golden Flakes. She could pour ketchup on pot roast. Skip brushing her teeth. Mrs. Summers never asked Nicole how school was going, how her teachers were treating her, how she intended to spend the rest of her life.

Sometimes, Nicole would show up when Sarina wasn't at home. Mrs. Summers didn't mind. She'd let Nicole watch TV in her bedroom. Turn off the light and keep the volume down low. Serve her warm milk. Often, not wake her when Nicole nodded off. More than once, Sarina had come and gone while she slept.

Mrs. Summers's response was always the same: "I'm sorry you missed her, but she's gone. Go on home."

"Where'd she go?"

It could be a number of places. To this girl's house, to that boy's house, out for a car ride, back to school to paint posters for pep rallies or plays. Mrs. Summers apologized no matter what. "You're such a sound sleeper, I forgot you were here."

Despite the regularity of such unfortunate mishaps, Nicole found herself going back for more. The Summers' house was such a haven. Mrs. Hicks never knocked, came looking, or phoned.

Unlike at home, where Mrs. Hicks's voice ran rampant and cold.

When Sarina talked Nicole into double-dating (at least once a month), Mrs. Hicks would always bring it up at the breakfast table. "Why don't you let me do your makeup? You're so much prettier than that Summers girl." She'd hold the butter knife to Nicole's eye like an eyeliner. "With a little Clinique, I could bring out your color."

"Her eyes are fine," Mr. Hicks would interrupt.

"But dear, it's hypoallergenic."

"They're brown and she's beautiful." Sometimes, he would pick up the ends of her hair and playfully swat Nicole on the nose. "Do you know what the women down at the station pay to look this natural?"

"Nicole is not a forty-year-old weather girl. She is a teenager and this is the South. We roll our hair and we wear lip gloss."

When Nicole showed up at the Summers' house before their dates, Sarina would gasp, "Oh my God, Nic, you're so much prettier than me. I hate you," she'd laugh. "I really, really hate you."

This sort of reaction made Nicole have to pee. She'd go to the bathroom, then wash off her mother's paint-by-numbers. Sarina never said a word, but when the dates arrived and both complimented her, she gave her approval by saying, "Nicole looks nice too."

With Sarina, Nicole made an effort to play down her beauty. She didn't powder her nose. A zit was like a door prize that she'd never try to hide. Who cared what her date thought? Not Nicole—one single bit. Her unfinished face put Sarina at ease. When Sarina was at ease, she was more attentive to Nicole. She accompanied her to the rest room, to get popcorn, refill their drinks. Anytime Nicole could steal Sarina from her date.

When Nicole got home, she'd find her mother waiting up for Mr. Hicks, who was wrapping up the late local news. Nicole guessed that her mother attributed her blush-free cheeks to a heavy makeout session with Joe Half-Back or Lenny the six-foot-four shortstop. Mrs. Hicks wanted her daughter to be socially toasted, so Nicole never argued with her suggestive smiles or took down the Dear Abby articles about birth control taped to the fridge.

The truth was, Nicole did not care much for the boys they

went out with. They droned on about sports and stereo equipment, other couples, and who had done what with whom and how soon. They wore too much aftershave. They thought passing their driver's test earned them a hand job. Nicole did not know why Sarina was so interested, but she was. And she asked Nicole to stay with her, so she did. Every double date ended the same. Nicole in the front seat, Sarina in the back. Nicole ignoring her date's awkward advances, making sure the boy with Sarina did not go too far.

Nicole wished she had been in Stewart's car this night. If she had, she wouldn't be suffering so much. She would know what had happened, what or who had gone down, if Sarina'd bailed on their elopement, if Mrs. Summers had sucked out the life that boy'd made inside her.

But with daylight approaching, Nicole had a more serious matter to consider.

The weekend before sophomore final exams and Sarina's sweet-sixteen party, Mrs. Hicks sat down to help the two girls study. She'd chosen bright pink flash cards to liven things up. She wore her Tri Delta pendant from that afternoon's brunch.

"First question: what body of water joins the Alabama River to form the Mobile River?"

Smack! "Tombigbee!"

"I'm sorry, Sarina." Mrs. Hicks flipped the card around. "That would be the Mississippi."

Nicole said, "But Mississippi's in Mississippi."

"Nicole," said her mother, "try to keep up."

Sarina readied herself, her palm shaking slightly over the Pledge-polished wood.

"Next question: capital of Alabama."

Smack! "Montgomery! Hey, hey, Montgomery!"

"While I admire your spirit, Sarina, the answer is Mobile."

"Mom, what are you talking about?"

"Alabama history, your first period exam."

Sarina said, "I'd swear it's Montgomery."

Mrs. Hicks said, "They both start with *M.* I can see why you're confused. *Mobile,*" she repeated. "Think auto*mobile.* You need an auto*mobile* to get to the capital."

Sarina whispered, "Automobile."

"Mom, you're wrong."

"It's on the card."

"Card, schmard!"

Mrs. Hicks pointed to the hallway stairs. "Maybe you'd do best with some study-alone time. Your friend seems to be the only one interested in bettering herself."

"But Mom!"

Mrs. Hicks pointed and Nicole went to her room.

Through the vent, Nicole could hear Sarina slap the table. Over the course of an hour, the slaps became fewer, her loud answers far between.

At five o'clock, Mrs. Hicks let herself into Nicole's room.

"Mom, what the hell were you doing?"

Mrs. Hicks held up two sets of flash cards. "The white ones are for you. The pink ones are for that Summers girl."

Nicole examined the cards as her mother seemed to shoot to the ceiling like a beanstalk grown from pride pills. She had written in all capital letters. She'd made cards for every subject. Except for their color, the stacks seemed identical. Until Nicole flipped them over. Her answers were right. Sarina's were wrong.

Mrs. Hicks said, "We're bringing her down a notch."

Nicole said, "We who?"

Mrs. Hicks wrapped her viney arms around her daughter. "We—you and me, of course. Let's get that mother/daughter spirit right this time. Let's show those Summers not everyone gets a free ride. That woman rode her husband into this neighborhood and now that girl is trying to ride you. It's time we show this town what you're made of. It's your turn to shine."

"But I don't want to shine."

"Too bad. It's your turn."

Mrs. Hicks sat down on the bed beside her daughter and scratched Nicole's back like she liked when she was little. Her voice, dull as a lullaby, made Nicole want to sleep. "Your Second Best routine ends today, little one. You've got to do better. Better than everyone. Better than her. Next year, you're a junior. Grades are important. You've got to stand out."

"Shine," said Nicole.

"You want to drive, don't you? You want to be able to stay out till twelve."

Nicole nodded and thought of the places that she and Ree'd go.

"If you help me do this, I'll give you anything you want. When I say she's wrong, pretend that she's wrong." Mrs. Hicks stood and looked down at her daughter. "Otherwise, we'll have to get you away from that girl. Your father can be convinced to take another job. He gets offers every day. He's an excellent broadcaster. How about watching him on the Louisiana News? Would you like to finish school in the Ol' Bayou? Catch an alligator bus? Make friends with the Swamp Thing?"

Unaccompanied, Nicole took the pink cards into the bathroom. She sat on the toilet with a large pair of scissors and proceeded to cut and flush, cut and flush. *Alligator bus.* Her mother was crazy. Like she would really give up Tri Delta and T-town. *No way,* thought Nicole. *No way. No freaking way!* But she would ride piggyback until Nicole finally collapsed. The days leading to exams would be the trampoline revisited. Her mother would hound her and ground her to keep her closely in check. No more oxygen for Nicole, just her mother in her face. And what of Sarina when this effort failed? No pink cards, no pink slip. Mrs. Hicks wouldn't quit. She'd bring out the big guns. *God*, thought Nicole, *what are her big guns?* She bet her mother had a complete collection of If This Doesn't Work, then This Will, then This Will. Her mother would keep slinging until Sarina was reduced to a notch on her belt. *Shit.* What if her mother was a Texas Cheerleading Murdering Mom? What if she was worse? *No way. Oh, it could be. Way*, she thought. *Way!*

After about ten cards, the bowl backed up. The water drained endlessly. Soon, Nicole knew, her mother would question the noise, pound on the door, and push her way in with a cereal spoonful of Maalox. She'd be furious at the bowlful of all her hard work. Having to call a plumber would piss her off more.

Nicole turned the scissors on herself. She traced her life line and her smarts line and, with just enough pressure, cut a trail along her love line which stopped short halfway widthwise across her palm. The blood felt warm and stung her dry skin. It was an excuse to make a fist. She squeezed and felt the wetness push in between her fingers. She watched the blood drip into the toilet and saw her future come apart in the crimson.

During that last week of school, Nicole failed every sophomore exam.

Now report cards were due to be mailed. The principal was sure to call, and Nicole wished Sarina would call her first. She wanted to tell her that flunking out wasn't as bad as it seemed. She wasn't stupid. Everything would work out okay. Sure, they'd be in different classes with different kids, but they'd still live across the street. They could see each other after school. Do homework. Still be best friends.

To stay friends with Sarina and relieve the pressure of competition Mrs. Hicks so actively sought, Nicole had cast off her mother's wet blanket, soaked with maliciousness, poison, and lies.

The morning after Stewart rendevoused with Sarina, Nicole and her mother stood outside the two wide steel doors of Central High West. Principal Jessup had called and the two hurried right over.

Mrs. Hicks looked at her daughter and said, "How the hell are we going to get out of this one?"

Nicole shrugged. She stepped aside as her mother pushed open one of the doors and cut a path to the principal's office. Mrs. Hicks did not wait for her daughter. Her high heels echoed in the dark empty hallways. Her soles left scuff marks for the janitor to mop up.

Mrs. Hicks's voice ricocheted off the lockers. "You're lucky I didn't call your father first."

Mr. Hicks was in Birmingham on special assignment. A zookeeper, distraught over the sudden loss of his arm during the crocodile rat toss, had unlocked eighteen cages before authorities arrived. There were lions on the highway. A gorilla in the midst of Little Five Points South. As last seen on TV, Mr. Hicks was on the trail of a snowy egret last spotted in the parking lot of the Mount Royal Retirement Center.

Nicole followed her mother at a very slow pace. She knew by the time she caught up Mrs. Hicks would be waiting outside principal Jessup's office, tapping her foot, pulling loose hairs from her over-the-shoulder ponytail, which, with the help of Sun in a Bottle, was the same natural color as Nicole's.

Nicole looked into classrooms. The blackboards were clean. The seats lined in tight, perfect rows. She knew what it would be like to repeat the tenth grade. It would be hot. Unless you counted the box in the principal's office, there was absolutely no air-conditioning at Central High West.

Central High East was cool and refreshing. It had water fountains on both floors. It had bigger classrooms, bigger everything. Left over from Alabama's Separate but Equal clause, the high school was divided into two campuses, West and East. The younger kids on the black side of town. The eleventh and twelfth graders on the white.

Nicole rounded the corner to find her mother right where she expected.

"Stand up straight." Mrs. Hicks manipulated Nicole's shoulders so that the blades were almost touching. "You could at least try to look the part."

"What part, Mother?"

"Don't get smart with me." Mrs. Hicks rapped her knuckles on the opaque window. "You're not stupid. Just follow my lead. I'll think of something."

Principal Jessup opened his door. He was tall and thin, but moved like his suspenders supported a barrel. He was known as a strong and silent type. He kept a paddle and a hair pick where his wallet ought to be. Principal Jessup held his door open for the Hicks and, once they were seated, put his hands on the back of each of their chairs. This was not the first time Nicole had been in trouble at school. Due to the elementary school science-fair incident, this young lady had a record.

Nicole said, "I failed. That's all."

Principal Jessup moved between the Hicks. He crossed his arms and sat on the edge of his desk next to the sharp bronze nameplate he forced delinquents to polish with a sock and saliva whenever they mouthed off in class. Nicole could see the warped reflection of her bangs and brows. Principal Jessup stretched his legs out in front of him. "That's all?"

Mrs. Hicks said, "Just what are you suggesting?"

"Mrs. Hicks, when a girl like your daughter does this poorly this fast, a red flag goes up and questions have to be asked."

"What questions?"

"Questions like, drugs, feminine issues, is everything all right at home?"

Nicole shifted her weight in the waxed wooden seat. She imagined the trampoline in the city dump yard. Her body pinned to the mat. Her mother's eyeliner pencil like a knife driven straight through her heart. In Principal Jessup's nameplate, she noticed the golden reflection of her skin. She tried to recognize her father's favorite brown eyes.

"Well, answer the man," said Mrs. Hicks, stamping an exclamation point at the end of her sentence by picking up her chair, turning it away from Principal Jessup to face Nicole, and pushing it into the floor with all 108 of her pounds.

Nicole refused to look at her mother. She would not be bullied. No way. No damned way.

Mrs. Hicks said, "I'll tell you what it is." She put her hand on the arm of Nicole's chair. "Go on." She gave the chair a shake. "Show him your arm."

Principal Jessup leaned forward and Nicole didn't move at all. She was astonished. Her mother was about to fold up all sense of decorum and whip out their dirty laundry.

"Don't dillydally." Mrs. Hicks snatched her daughter's arm and twisted it so that the palm faced up. "Look at what she's done to herself."

Besides the damage she had done to her hand, there were two skinny scabs connecting her wrist to her watchband. Rust-colored lightning bolts. Nicole remembered how she'd put them there when Sarina didn't call. She'd used her mother's cuticle clippers and flushed the blood in the bathroom sink.

Principal Jessup shook his head. "When will you kids learn that things are never as bad as they seem?"

"Oh, for Christ's sake, she didn't try to kill herself!" Mrs. Hicks jerked her daughter's arm higher, bringing the scars closer to Principal Jessup and Nicole two inches out of her seat. "Isn't obvious? They're initials. It's that Summers girl."

"S. S.," muttered Principal Jessup.

"Is there another?"

"Stewart Steptoe."

"Nicole's not interested in boys." Mrs. Hicks released her daughter's arm. "That's the problem. It's all about that Summers girl. Nicole is completely obsessed."

"I'm not obsessed."

"Sure you're not. What'd she do, dare you to flunk out?"

"Mrs. Hicks," Principal Jessup interrupted, "Miss Summers has spent two years in my school. I've been here for nearly twenty. I've known a lot of kids, Mrs. Hicks. I've seen the worst of them. But the one thing I know is that no teenage girl is going to convince another one to ruin her permanent record."

"Are you kidding me? People are killed every day. Don't you watch the news? There's devil worship and Dungeons and Dragons!"

"Miss Summers is a cheerleader."

"Miss Summers is a grade-grubbing—"

"Mrs. Hicks, you need to calm down."

"Calm down? The only reason that girl's still in school is 'cause I help her study. I help Nicole and the only way Nicole will be helped is if I help her stupid cheerleader friend."

Nicole said, "I'm a cheerleader."

Mrs. Hicks said, "You're anything she wants you to be."

"Miss Hicks," said Principal Jessup, "is there any truth to this?"

Nicole watched her mother's face take on the Warrior pose from her yoga videotape. At that moment, Nicole knew that her mother was ready to inhale peace and exhale any demons necessary to convince Principal Jessup that her daughter deserved a second chance. But she didn't want a second chance. She wanted this meeting, this conversation, this moment to be over. So she said, "There's some truth."

Mrs. Hicks let out a sigh of relief so strong Nicole wondered if her mother might finally fit into that size four dress she'd bought at Talbot's semiannual sale.

"So this was all a hoax," said Principal Jessup.

"She'll retake her exams," said Mrs. Hicks.

"This won't go without repercussions."

"Fine, fine. But you'll have to call that Summers girl." Mrs. Hicks's face took on the yoga tape's Prayer to Sun pose. "My vote is expulsion. I'll be happy to tell her mother. We live across the street."

"I have a perfectly good phone right here." Principal Jessup patted the receiver.

"You don't understand." Nicole stood up and, channeling all of her mother's mean spirit, laid both hands over the principal's. She wondered if her wounds would open and her blood ooze out over the principal's knuckles. Her mother would be appalled. Nicole squeezed. She squeezed hard. She'd turn this around. She'd turn it. She'd turn. "You've got it all wrong."

"What's wrong?"

"We're friends, but Sarina had absolutely nothing to do with it. It was me." She let go of his hand and picked up his nameplate. She clenched and pointed it like the last lottery ticket. "And her," she said. "My mother made me do it."

Nicole spouted half-truths as soon as they came to her. She told Principal Jessup that her mother didn't help her study, but still did her homework for her. She hardly ever cracked a book. As soon as she got home, her mother took her assignments and finished them before her father got home. She wanted to see if she could pass by herself. So she flushed her cheat sheets. Call Roto-Rooter, they'd attest. "And I flunked," Nicole insisted. "She's been pushing me so hard, I haven't learned anything."

"Lies!" Mrs. Hicks circled the principal's desk. "Can't you see that? It's that Summers girl."

"Miss Summers finished with a strong B average."

"It doesn't matter!" Mrs. Hicks slapped her palms against the cherry wood. "She's got a hold on my baby! Please." The tears were coming full force along her Cover Girl. "Don't let my child do this to herself!"

Nicole swiftly brought the nameplate to the principal's throat. *Ah ha!* she thought, *Mother. What'll ya do about this!* She shoved the nameplate against the principal's Adam's apple. Once from pure instinct. Twice for good looks.

"Miss Hicks," mouthed the principal, his weight behind him on his hands. "Calm," he choked his words out. "You need to calm down."

"I am calm!" Nicole shouted, her eyes fixated on her mother, who was rocking heels to toes, Nicole imagined, primed to pounce. *You're not going anywhere*, Nicole warned her in her brain. *Sit, Mother. Stay. Or we'll never get away.*

"Keep me back," she told the principal. "I deserve to be held back." If true confessions didn't work, she would flunk out for attacking a well-respected school official.

Mrs. Hicks was hysterical. Rocking, rocking, teeth clenched and bared. She lurched forward in what Nicole thought was a faint. Her stomach hit the desk blotter, but then she scrambled and grabbed Nicole's short sleeve. She tugged and she tugged, but Nicole would not be ceased and arrested.

Suddenly, Principal Jessup took hold of Nicole's dissected wrist. He let her keep the nameplate in place, but held her firmly enough to let her know that this was a threat that would not go any further. He said, "Name Alabama's four Indian tribes."

Nicole said, "I can't."

"What's the Pythagorean theorem?"

"E equals MC squared?"

"NO!" Mrs. Hicks scrambled across the desk and rammed her body in between them.

The nameplate hit the floor and Nicole took a nosedive.

She tried to snatch the nameplate from underneath her chair, but behind her, she could hear her mother talking gibberish, interfering, begging "Please!"

Mrs. Hicks had her fingers around the principal's lapels. "Let us come back next week and you'll see! I swear, you'll see! You can ask her anything! She can go to summer school! There must be something! Be reasonable! Please!"

Principal Jessup looked over Mrs. Hicks's shoulder at his once apt pupil now down on all fours. "Nicole," he asked, touching his throat gingerly, "tell me, will you, what is our fiftieth state?"

In her head, Nicole knew the answer just like she had known Choctaw, Chickasaw, Cherokee, Creek and $c^2 = a^2 + b^2$. But she did not say Hawaii. She said Nebraska and, for the third year in a row, reserved a spot in Central West's yearbook.

Bitty Jack

On the night that Sarina took Stewart to the Alabama State Fair, Bitty Jack Carlson was temporarily stationed at the Pick a Duck Pond. She was sixteen and, in order to spend a summer away from Camp Chickasaw, had taken a job in one of the freak tents. The fair would tour three Southern states and wind up back in Summons County by the end of August. Fair folks appreciated the Chickasaw field trips. So, the fair made two stops: one in May to pick up summer help; one in August to pick up the tab. Home-schooled, Bitty Jack was allowed to cut out early to take the job. The Carlsons saw it as Bitty's shot to see the world. Bitty Jack was put in charge of hosing down Johnny Iguana.

Johnny Iguana was eighteen years old and not nearly as cool as his name made him sound. His real name was Mason Potts. He was six-foot-four, with a slight slump to his shoulders. The Freak Boss made him wear a helmet-hard black wig and cutoffs to pay homage to John Travolta in the beach scene from *Grease*. But that "Chang, chang, chang-e-tee, chang shoo-bob" riled up the crowd, so the Bee Gees were played when Johnny took the stage. He always went shirtless to show off his skin. On tour, four years earlier, the Freak Boss had found him busing tables in a Yazoo City Denny's.

"The poor kid was sweating up a storm," the Freak Boss told Bitty Jack on the day she arrived. "That pot-bellied, chain-smoking manager had him in pants and polyester. Had him in a bow tie. The kid was clearing my table and I took a good look. He was all red faced and working with his eyes halfway shut.

"I said, 'What's wrong, boy?'

"He said, 'Nothing.'

"I said, 'Don't lie to me, boy.'

"He said, 'I itch, that's all.'

"I told him to have at it. Have himself a good scratch. What's stopping him? Or was it the crabs that had him? That I'd understand. That kind of business, you got to take care of in private, you know what I'm saying?"

Bitty Jack nodded and made a mental note to look up crabs in the dictionary. It had to be slang for something.

The Freak Boss said, "So, I said, 'Is that it, boy? Crabs got you your first time out of the gate?'

"The kid said, 'No sir, I got it all over.'

"I said, 'Whazzat?'

"He said he didn't know. So I said, 'Let's see.'

"I could tell the kid was nervous that his boss would toss him out on his ear for any old reason, so I told him to give me a signal when he took his fifteen. I tell you, I haven't been back to Denny's since then. That cross-eyed manager worked him for most of the night. I sat there and sucked down Grand Slams and coffee and Coke till I thought I would bust. The waitress thought I was flirting with her, but I can tell you, I was not. Once you find a woman like my wife, everyone else pales in comparison."

Bitty Jack blushed. She thought of the Freak Boss's wife. She imagined him on top of her in bed. All six breasts supporting his weight, moving him in and out of her like a factory conveyer belt.

The Freak Boss said, "So, around quarter to one, the kid gives me the signal. I leave my money on the table and follow him out to the parking lot.

"The poor kid rolls up his sleeve. It was awful to watch. The kid didn't know what was wrong with him, so he'd all but bathed in calamine lotion. The lotion made his shirt stick to his skin and I told him to pull it up quick like a Band-Aid. He did and I thought the kid was gonna cry. Hell, I'll be honest. I thought I'd cry myself. The kid had scales. Patches on his forearms and, turns out, his back and his butt.

"I said, 'It must be a bitch to take a dump.'

"And the kid just shook his head. The whole thing was so pitiful. I took a good look at his skin and I knew what it was. A good old practical joke of nature.

"So, I told him I could get him out of this stinking job. I said, 'Son, I'm a businessman. I run a very profitable organization. I sponsor unfortunate cases such as yourself. You get to travel. You get three squares a day. You get friends for life. A family. In return, you let the public take a peek. You become a performer, an oddity of nature that people will pay top dollar to see.' I told him I wasn't going to cushion the job. 'I run a freak show,' I said. 'And you can come with me and be a star, or you can take cold baths and try to fix the unfixable and remain a nobody in this godforsaken town.'

"The kid said, 'Yazoo.'

"I said, 'Who knew?' "

Bitty Jack laughed like she knew that she should.

"So, I said, 'What'll it be, son?' And the kid said what all of them say.

" 'Take me away.'

"And I did. He's been with me for four years. He's still one of the new ones. Tambourine Man and Little Miss Horse and Pony joined last July, and there's a guy who wants to try out when we reach Mobile. Says he can eat whatever you give him. Says he ate a bicycle once. I'll see him when we get there, but I doubt he'll outdo my night at Denny's. Besides, my freaks are special. Everybody's seen a bearded lady. Everybody's seen the guy shove nails up his nose. Albinos. Two-headed babies. Been done.

"Johnny's a nice kid. Real cooperative. Never given me a minute of trouble. He'll be a good one to break you in. You just hose him off between acts. Don't get his hair wet, but his jean shorts are okay. Pardon my French, but he's got quite a bulge and the ladies like that, scales or no scales."

Bitty Jack said, "Shorts are okay, but not on the wig."

The Freak Boss said, "You'll get along fine with him. I can tell. You wouldn't be here unless you was an ugly duckling once yourself."

Bitty Jack said, "I'm no swan."

"You're not chicken shit, either. Pardon my French. Besides, around here, you'll be the belle of the ball. Excluding my wife, of course."

Bitty Jack said, "Really?"

"Sure," said the Freak Boss. "What you got? Glasses. Skin that'll clear up sooner or later. Freckles. You're skinny, but you're nothing to turn your nose up at. You'll give Johnny the thrill of his life. You two are about the same age. Most of my freaks are older. Thirty and up. Little Miss Horse and Pony's twelve, and you know that's no fun for anyone. It'll be nice for Johnny. Nice for you. You don't mind the sight, right?"

Bitty Jack said no and wondered if she would.

At supper, the Freak Boss took Bitty Jack into the mess tent. Johnny Iguana waved to them from his picnic table. He smiled, stood up, and pushed the bench away with the backs of his knees.

The Freak Boss said, "Johnny Iguana, this here's your new partner, Miss Bitty Jack Carlson. Miss Bitty, this here's the one and only Johnny Iguana."

Bitty Jack thrust her hand out as her father had told her to do.

"Bitty," her father had said, "you be kind to them freaks. I can't see that it's easy what they do. I don't care if the guy's name is Mr. Pus Boil, you shake his hand and make the guy feel okay."

Bitty Jack had said, "Yes sir, Daddy."

Johnny Iguana shook Bitty's hand and looked at her like she'd kissed him full on the mouth. Beneath her fingertips, Bitty felt the smooth of his skin. He wore a T-shirt and the scales on his arms did not look as she expected. They were far from slick and slimy. They were diamond shaped. A real sweet shade of green. Bitty Jack wondered if they would sparkle in the sun.

The Freak Boss strolled away from them toward his wife, who sat in her bathrobe, her long, black hair in a pony tail spouting off the top of her head like whale's water. She waved to her husband with a fried chicken leg.

Johnny said, "Show starts in ten minutes."

Bitty Jack started toward the tent flaps she had walked through earlier.

Johnny caught her by the elbow. "Hold up. Not that way."

"How come?"

"Only Regulars use that way."

"Regulars?"

"You know, regular-looking ones like you and the Freak Boss. Summons help."

Bitty Jack slowly put it together.

"I can't just walk around like I'm you. Nobody pays to see Bitty Jack Carlson. They pay to see the ones who aren't let out of the tents. You know," he whispered, "freaks."

Bitty Jack said, "Right."

Johnny Iguana led Bitty Jack to the back of the mess tent,

past the grinning Freak Boss, his arm around his laughing wife. He held the flap open and Bitty Jack walked through. To her left were woods, guarded by a high wire fence. To her right was a wall of ten-foot canvas draping. She could hear the deejay in the operation booth on the Matterhorn that she rode every year. The Matterhorn was a ride that was just like its name suggested: tight, fast hills surrounded by a mural of ski slopes and skiers the likes of which the riders would never see.

The deejay boomed through a deep drum beat, "DO YOU WANNA GO FASTER?"

She heard the riders scream, "*Yeeeaaah!!!*"

"I SAID, DO YOU WANNA GO EVEN-STEVEN, MONKEY-BEATIN', STOP-YOUR-LOVIN'-HEART-FROM-CHEATIN' FASTER?"

The riders screamed, "*Yeeeaaah!*"

"OKAY THEN, LADIES AND GENTLEMEN, BACKWARDS IT IS!!!!"

"*Oh my Gaaaaawd!*"

Bitty Jack touched the canvas draping. "To keep people from seeing in?"

Johnny said, "For free, yeah."

When they reached the tent he performed in, Johnny showed Bitty Jack his area behind the stage. Tacked to one of the tent walls was a queen-size yellow waterproof sheet. An identical sheet was tacked to the ground.

It reminded Bitty Jack of her childhood Slip'n' Slide. Every time she slid and yelped "Rock!" her father would get on his knees and flip over the Slip'n' Slide. No matter how small a pebble he picked out of the grass, his response was always the same. "My princess found a pea."

Pulling her Miss Piggy one-piece swimsuit out of her crack, Bitty Jack would say "Daddy!" and march back to the front of the Slip 'n' Slide.

Johnny said, "I don't need one of the lit-up mirrors like the others."

Two vanity tables lined the connecting tent wall. Bitty Jack examined postcards and pictures stuck in the creases where the lightbulbs met the glass. She was happy not to find the Freak Boss's wife in any of them. Hers was the one show Bitty didn't think she could sit through.

Johnny said, "There's not much to my act. Between shows, one of the Regulars lets one audience out, then lets the next audience in. You can't see them from back here, but believe me, on the other side of that curtain the Freak Boss packs the house. Anyway, while that's going on, I stand on the tarp and you hose me down. In the summer, the tent gets incredibly hot. It's hard on my skin. Besides, the water makes my scales shine."

Johnny pulled his wig off a faceless Styrofoam skull on the corner of the nearest vanity table. He kept the wig in his hand as he tugged his T-shirt over his head. Scales covered his back where hair might sprout on an old man's body. He said, "It would help if you took care of my wig and threw me a towel during the breaks. If I get Little Miss Horse and Pony wet, she'll have a major cow. She spends a lot of time on her tail and if it gets wet it frizzes or something."

Bitty Jack said, "No problem."

"I know it's kind of gross, but I swear I'm not contagious. If it makes you feel better, there's some gloves in Little Miss Horse and Pony's top drawer."

Bitty Jack opened the top drawer, expecting to find a pair of Little Miss Horse and Pony's gloves, white lace with elastic ruffles at the wrist. What she found were the dish-washing variety as yellow as the slicker sheets. She said, "I don't need any gloves."

The back tent flap opened and in came the other performers. Little Miss Horse and Pony smelled like Miss Breck. Tambourine Man jingled all the way. Johnny made the introductions and Bitty Jack shook their hands.

"Ladies and gentlemen," the Freak Boss called from outside the tent. "Step right up! Form a line and see what nature never intended! Take a look, folks! Bring the kids! Six tickets and you've got dinner conversation for the rest of your lives! Six tickets to see what your mothers always warned you about!"

Two minutes later, there was standing room only in a tent with no chairs.

Behind the curtain, Bitty Jack heard the crowd buzz and hush their kin. She whispered to Johnny Iguana, "What happens now?"

"We wait for introductions."

"Sorry I'm late, guys," a Regular said as he opened the back tent flap. He held a boom box in one hand and sat on the ground behind the curtain. He turned the volume up and pushed Play. The Freak Boss's voice came out of the box.

Johnny said, "The boss moves around and gets people to buy tickets. He only emcees his wife's show live and she just gives one at ten-thirty at night. You might want to watch the Regular work the tape recorder. He might get sick. You never know."

Bitty Jack crouched beside the Regular. She watched him turn the tape off and on depending on the audience's response. Throughout the night, she memorized each performer's introduction and stage comments. She hosed Johnny Iguana off like she was taught, and while he was onstage, she watched his silhouette against the curtain. He moved so everyone could see.

"He had the grace of Vanna White," Bitty Jack would later tell her father. "But not like a sissy."

While the fair was in Summons, Bitty slept at her house, but most of her waking hours were spent at the fair. She ate breakfast with the freaks. Lunch and supper with the freaks. She spent all her free time with Johnny Iguana. If he wore jeans and a button-down, no one recognized him on the fairgrounds. When he wasn't performing, the two of them went on rides, ate junk, played games. With all her hosing experience, Bitty Jack got real good at shooting the water gun into the clowns' mouths. She won a big pig for Little Miss Horse and Pony. She won big pigs and pink giraffes and medium-sized bears for Camp Chickasaw's upcoming Carnival Day. The owners told her parents that they were extremely impressed. Bitty Jack got good at most of the game booths, but refused to play Pick a Duck after the first time she tried it.

"There's no skill involved. It's totally boring."

Johnny said, "Can you think of something you'd rather do?"

The Matterhorn deejay boomed, "ARE . . . YOU . . . READY?"

The safety bar secured across their laps, Bitty Jack and Johnny Iguana looked at each other while the riders screamed "*Yeah!*"

Johnny Iguana nudged Bitty Jack's elbow with his own. As their seat began to creep forward, he gripped the safety bar and made his show face, like Elvis. "Uh, huh-huh!"

Bitty Jack said, "I love this so much."

The deejay boomed, "HOW YOU FOLKS DOIN'? ARE YOU READY TO GO FASTER?"

Bitty Jack and Johnny Iguana joined the chorus. "*Yeaaah!*"

"I SAID, ARE YOU READY TO LOSE YO' LUNCH?"

The riders screamed "*Yeaaah!*"

His eyes hidden behind sunglasses the size of Moon Pies, the deejay boomed, "WELL, ALL RIGHT! HOLD TIGHT! LET'S GET READY TO RUM-BLE!"

As the ride took off, spinning fast, faster, faster, the deejay pumped the music louder and the centrifugal force pushed Bitty Jack toward the outside of the seat. She crushed Johnny

Iguana. "I'm sorry!" she yelled and tried to pull her body away from his by hand-over-handing the padded safety bar.

"HEY, HEY, HEY! I DON'T THINK YOU FOLKS ARE SCREAMING LOUD ENOUGH. I CAN'T HEAR YOU! HOW'S ABOUT I SEND YOU MOTHER-PLUCKERS BACKWARDS?"

The riders screamed "*Nooo!*"

Bitty Jack laughed and tried to pull her body off Johnny's. Hand over hand. She yelled, "I'm squashing you!"

Johnny yelled, "Don't worry about it!"

"NOW, COME, COME, LADIES AND GENTLEMEN! WE ALL KNOW THAT NO MEANS YES! I CAN SEE IT IN YOUR EYES! LET ME ASK YOU ONE MORE TIME. DO YOU WANNA GO BACKWARDS?"

Some of the riders screamed "*Nooo!*" Some used that reverse psychology they had seen on TV. They screamed "*Yey-yas!*"

Bitty Jack screamed, "I can't get off you!"

The deejay boomed, "BACKWARDS IT IS!!!"

Johnny screamed, "Let go! It's okay!"

The riders screamed, "*Oh my Gaaawd!!*"

Bitty Jack allowed her body to cram itself into the nooks of Johnny Iguana. As the ride jerked into reverse, Bitty Jack's hair blew across her face. She stopped worrying about hurting Johnny Iguana and hollered at the top of her lungs. Her excitement made Johnny laugh. His laugh made Bitty Jack laugh. When Johnny put his arm behind her, across the back of their seat, Bitty Jack took his hand and pulled it over her shoulder. Wrapped up in the speed and direction and her wild, messy hair and the extra warmth of his arm on that hot summer predinner daze, Bitty Jack felt what was given to her. She stroked the scales that lay under his long sleeved shirt. They felt soft. Surprise, surprise. She lay her head back against his muscle and let the tears roll out from too much laughing and making noise.

Johnny Iguana kissed her temple and, all out of words, Bitty Jack squeezed his hand. Then both of them let go of the safety bar and wrapped their arms around each other. They were quiet and shut their eyes. They got lost and dizzy in the darkness and the speed.

The deejay boomed "LOOKS LIKE WE GOT A COUPLE UH LOVEBIRDS!"

The riders went "*Oooooh!*"

"WHAT'S SAY WE GIVE Y'ALL AN EXTRA MINUTE ON THE MATTERHORN! SEE IF WE CAN'T THROW 'EM OFF. TEACH THOSE TWO TO HOLD ONTO THEIR SAFETY BAR!"

The crowd went wild and Bitty Jack and Johnny held their grasp, contemplated breaking every safety rule, and wished that the ride would never come to an end.

Bitty Jack was soon more than Johnny Iguana's personal assistant. All the freaks knew it. Their summer romance was the talk of intermissions.

The night before the fair moved from Summons, Bitty Jack brought her parents to see Johnny Iguana's show. They had been asking to meet her boyfriend. It was the appropriate thing to do.

The Freak Boss took the Carlsons into the tent personally. He made his way through the crowd. "Coming through, ladies and gentleman! VIPs, here. VIPs."

Mr. and Mrs. Carlson smiled weakly at everyone as if apologizing for their status. They stood center stage, no heads to look over, no fitful babies to ignore. The taped voice of the Freak Boss came on behind the curtain.

Mr. Carlson whispered to his wife, "The great and powerful Oz."

The voice behind the curtain introduced Little Miss Horse and Pony. She trotted out and the audience hushed.

Someone said, "Holy Ta-moh-lee."

Mrs. Carlson whispered, "She has such a pretty face."

Little Miss Horse and Pony showed off her hooves at the ends of her arms. She turned to let her tail grandiosely sweep the stage. When the audience applauded, she smiled to show her big, big top teeth. The voice behind the curtain continued to compliment her features until it sped up, scrambled, then stopped. Little Miss Horse and Pony quit smiling. She looked over her shoulder. Even though she knew that the tape recorder had eaten the tape, she hissed, "What's wrong?"

The crowd began to murmur. Mrs. Carlson took her husband's hand and they stood as if they were bride and groom before a tent full of witnesses who all had objections and were just there for the cake. "Where's Bitty?" she asked.

And then, there she was. Bitty Jack parted the curtains as Little Miss Horse and Pony galloped past. Her tail slapped Bitty Jack's bare knees and she resisted bending past her shorts to touch her skin growing redder under the spotlight. Bitty Jack said, "May I have your attention?"

Besides her parents, no one paid attention.

Bitty Jack remembered the Matterhorn deejay. She boomed, "LISTEN UP, PEOPLE!"

Her parents turned to face the crowd. They helped with "Shhh!"

Bitty Jack recited the Freak Boss's tape. She said, "Coming to the stage next, this guy is straight out of the swamp! His daddy was a crocodile. His mama was a disco queen! Please put your hands together for the one and only Johnny Iguana!"

Johnny Iguana parted the curtains and bounded onto the stage. Without the *Saturday Night Fever* medley, Bitty Jack did her best to go on with the show. She flipped the light switch on and off. She looked at audience members as if they'd gotten their money's worth.

Bitty Jack heard her mother say, "Oh dear Lord."

She saw her father wrap his arm around her, give a squeeze,

then nod to Bitty to keep up the good work. As Bitty Jack spoke, she noticed the audience she'd never seen before. Behind the curtain, only Johnny's silhouette existed. Now she saw faces and overheard snide remarks.

"That guy's fucked up."

"Wonder if he's got a little lizard dick."

"Wonder if he's got one at all."

"Yeah, maybe just a gill down there like a woman."

"Gross! Shut up, I'm trying to see."

To ease their daughter, Mr. and Mrs. Carlson put on two happy faces. Bitty Jack kept on with her speech. The audience grew rowdy. Mrs. Carlson's eyebrows moved farther up her forehead. Her lips pressed into what looked like no lips at all.

"Show us your dick!"

"You got scales on your dick? You got lily lizard balls?"

Johnny smiled at each ticket holder personally. He pivoted. He turned. He took a bow, then walked off the stage.

Bitty Jack introduced Tambourine Man and the audience applauded. Mrs. Carlson did not. Big Jack nudged her and tried to clap for the two of them, but Mrs. Carlson could not be swayed. She tugged her husband's arm. She said, "Let's go."

As Bitty Jack sang along to Tambourine Man's homemade music, her father mouthed, "We'll see you at home."

Bitty Jack didn't know why they were leaving until Mrs. Carlson looked over her shoulder and uttered the word that answered her question.

"Remember."

And Bitty Jack did. Camp Chickasaw, Cabin 11, the day her family's world was threatened by such catcalls. She heard the campers taunt her father. She saw Sarina Summers egging them on.

After the show, Bitty Jack picked up the hose and asked, "Is it always like this?"

"Pretty much," said Johnny.

Bitty Jack sprayed his shoulders and stomach, his thighs to

his feet. "I never knew." She tossed him a towel. He patted himself down, then swapped the towel for his white button-down. Bitty Jack looked away while he slipped on fresh boxers, khakis, socks, and sneakers. When he put his hand on her hip, Bitty Jack turned to face him. She kept her eyes on the ground, but Johnny tilted her face toward his. "Really, it's not that bad. It doesn't get to me." He drew her body close. "Come on," he said, "I'll buy you a Squishee."

He did. Red cherry for her. Blue raspberry for himself. They lay down under a table in the deserted mess tent. They kissed, their lips stained the colors of clowns'.

The following morning, the fair pulled up stakes and caravanned five hours to Birmingham, Alabama. Feigning sleep in the back of the truck, Bitty Jack heard the Freak Boss counsel Johnny Iguana from the driver's seat.

"Don't get too attached. She's only sixteen. You're both too young. Your life's on the road."

Johnny said, "I've got savings."

The Freak Boss said, "You'll see her next year. Besides, maybe she'll have grown some nice titties by then!"

"That's not funny."

"Think about it, son."

Bitty Jack tried to breathe like she was sleeping. She could feel their eyes on her from the rearview mirror. She imagined extending her stay past the summer. Traveling to more places. Staying with him. And, of course, there was the more immediate excitement: where she would sleep when the fair closed that night.

By the time the gates opened, there was trouble in Birmingham. Food poisoning had hit employees who'd chosen beef over chicken. Half the staff was throwing up. There was something wrong with the Sloppy Joes.

Bitty Jack agreed to help out in one of the game booths and

followed the Freak Boss through the crowd to Pick a Duck. A tarp covered the window. They entered through the back door to set up shop. The Freak Boss started the water flowing through the circular stream. The plastic ducks bobbed. Bitty Jack watched them float.

"Which one's the big pig?"

The Freak Boss pulled the winning duck out of the flock with ease. He turned it over and showed off the numeral 3 scrawled with permanent Magic Marker. Number ones were snakes, which could pass for carpet samples. Twos were stuffed puppies with black plastic ears. Threes were for big pigs. There was only one three.

"How'd you do that?"

"I take it you're not a card player."

Bitty shook her head.

"The duck's marked." The Freak Boss pointed to the tail. There was the slightest chip. "Nobody looks at the tails. They all look at the heads. I've heard all sorts of theories. The ducks whose heads are worn clean through are small prizes. The duck with paint chipped off its nose is a mark for a big pig. There are only a few blue ducks, so obviously that's a signal. What else? Oh yeah, my favorite.

"Some lady in Montgomery thought a pink one that got stuck against the far side of the pool was the big winner. She reached for it and fell in. She must have weighed three hundred pounds. Had her face in the water. Had her legs four feet off the ground. Thought she was drowning like a two-year-old off *Rescue 911*.

" 'Shatner!' she kept screaming. 'Get Will Shatner! Call 911!'

"She was flailing around like a pig in shit. Pardon my French. I had to get two strong men to pull her out. Poor ducks were stuck in every crevice of her body. Ducks in her cleavage, in the pockets of her dress. There was no courteous way I could ask for my property. I had to forfeit what must have been twenty ducks and, still, she didn't walk away with this little beauty." He patted the plastic duck with the chip in its tail. He set it swimming into the current.

"Someone got the whole ugly incident on camera. Won ten grand on that goddamned embarrassing video show. Beat out a slew of wedding takes."

"Throwing up at the altar?"

"Yeah." The Freak Boss chuckled. "I saw that one. Looking back. I wonder if that Montgomery woman staged the whole thing."

Bitty Jack said, "No."

"Miss Bitty, you'd be surprised at what people will do."

Customers poked the tarp with their fingers and fists. "Brawk, brawk!" they insisted.

"They're getting restless," said the Freak Boss.

"But those are chicken noises."

The Freak Boss said, "They want the ducks.

"You'll be fine," he continued. "Two picks for a dollar. Keep the money in this apron. One pocket for change. One for dollars. You'll get nothing more than a fiver. When the weight gets too much, dump your change into the lockbox. Never take your eyes off the ducks. Never take your eyes off the customers."

Bitty Jack nodded. She ran her hands over the front of her apron, the right side lumpy with quarters, nickels, and dimes.

"If you're not comfortable calling for customers, use the blow horn. Talk normal and even your boyfriend will hear you on the other side of the fair." He took hold of the draw string and gave it several good yanks. The tarp rose and exposed a crowd of eager duck pickers. He walked out of the booth.

Bitty Jack faced the crowd and, with every ounce of courage, said, "Who's first?"

Twenty hands shot up in the air.

Bitty Jack picked a grandmotherly type who brazenly squawked, "Four tries!" then leaned over the counter to work eight quarters out of her bra.

As the night went on, Bitty Jack became more comfortable. She gave good banter. She made correct change and tossed fuzzy snakes. No one picked the big pig. No one caused a fuss. When the Freak Boss passed by, he smiled and clapped his hands. She was getting the hang of it. She could do it. She was sure.

At 11:00 P.M., Johnny showed up and snuck into the back of the booth. He sat on the floor, hidden by the counter. He stroked her bare legs which made Bitty Jack smile which made everyone think she was happy to see them. Her sales increased. It was a very good night.

Until Sarina Summers entered the picture.

She was clinging to a boy, resting her head against his shoulder. They walked straight toward Bitty Jack. Bitty Jack stiffened.

"What?" said Johnny.

"Stay down there," she said.

Bitty Jack put the blow horn on the counter and gave a snake to the last person who tried. Now no one was at the counter and Sarina Summers and her boyfriend cut a clear path toward Pick a Duck.

Bitty Jack said, "Will we get in trouble if we close the place down?"

Johnny said, "I'll get in trouble. You'll get fired. Is there a drunk? Is someone fixing to start trouble?"

"I don't know. Just, please, no matter what happens, stay down, Johnny, stay down."

Sarina held her hands behind her back. She leaned over the pond as if trying to find room among the ducks for her reflection.

"Two for a dollar," Bitty Jack said and waited for Sarina to look up and recognize her.

As she'd told the Freak Boss, Bitty knew she was no swan. Her beauty wasn't storybookish: no dragon returns to find Bitty's face morphed into a pot of gold. She still had to wear glasses. The shower was a war zone against combination skin. But she wasn't the same girl she was at thirteen. Bitty knew she had bettered. She looked different, but not that different. In a matter of moments, Sarina's insults could fly. *You're Big Jerk-Off's kid! You're nothing! You're no one!*

What Sarina said was, "Is this a big pig or not?" She pointed to the bottom of the duck her boyfriend offered with brown, eager eyes.

"No," said Bitty Jack. "Sorry."

Bitty Jack handed Sarina's boyfriend an orange snake. She took the duck from him and set it drifting with the others.

"Don't pick that one again," Sarina advised. She licked her Lip Smackers that made the booth stink of strawberries. She examined her prize. "Stewart," she said, "make her give me a purple one."

Stewart's attention was on a pink duck with a dent in its head. Without taking his eyes away, he asked Bitty Jack to make the exchange.

Bitty Jack knew that this was a legitimate request. *Keep the customers happy*, the Freak Boss had told her. *Keep the suckers at your booth.* Bitty Jack did not want Sarina Summers at her booth. So she said, "No switching prizes."

Johnny thumped her shin.

Stewart shrugged and snatched the pink duck from the stream.

Bitty Jack pulled another snake from the barrel. This time, a red one. She handed it to Sarina, who crossed her arms in protest. "Give me a purple one."

Bitty Jack dangled the red snake by the tail, its eyes rocking brainlessly above the duck-ridden water. Stewart took it and slung it over his shoulder.

"Hey!"

"Ree, do you want to try for a big pig or not? This is the only game where I've got half a chance."

"Fine." Sarina kept her arms crossed, her stiff pinkies standing tall.

For a moment Bitty Jack forgot about the ducks. She took her mind off her money, off her customers, off her snakes. She stared at Sarina's fingers spun in gauze, set in splints.

Sarina said, "What?"

Stewart held out a blue duck. Blue ducks were always small prizes. Bitty Jack swapped it for a green snake without ever taking her eyes off Sarina's white bandages.

"What's your damage?" Sarina said. "What's the big goddamned deal about giving me a purple one?"

Stewart lowered his head to watch the ducks, who seemed to be swimming faster, laughing as if they could. He began to grab at random. He yanked each duck with increasing desperation. Bitty Jack traded each one for a snake. Yellow duck. Green snake. Blue duck. Red snake. Pink. Green. Blue. Another red. Within minutes, Sarina stood like Medusa's maid of honor. A wilted bouquet of bold-colored snakes drooping from her grasp.

Stewart peered into his wallet. "I think we're done here."

Sarina said, "She didn't even look at half the ducks!"

Bitty Jack refused to utter one word. Sarina didn't recognize her. She probably didn't even remember what she had done. Bitty Jack's fear was eaten by anger. She kept her eyes dull and made Sarina squirm.

"Quit looking at me!"

Stewart took her elbow.

"Let go of me!" Sarina grabbed a duck. "I need to teach this girl some manners!" She hurled the duck and the duck bounced off Bitty's neck. It fell to the sawdust that covered the ground.

Johnny Iguana stood up.

Sarina said, "What the hell?"

"Ma'am. You need to simmer down."

Sarina said, "She won't play fair!"

Stewart said, "We got to go."

Sarina said, "Hell, no!" She grabbed ducks fist over fist. She threw each one at Bitty Jack. Less than two feet away, Sarina hit her every time.

The ducks did not hurt, but Bitty Jack fought back. With each try, she aimed a duck at Sarina's precious face. She bet that girl had never shed tears, never felt lost, been left out, been sad. Maybe if Bitty's ducks took off her makeup, Sarina's boyfriend would see that she was flesh, just skin on bones. Maybe he'd leave her. Maybe she'd cry.

Stewart and Johnny tried to hold the girls back. Sarina shrieked, screeched, and screamed. Bitty hurdled the stand. A crowd gathered as pastel ducks flew. The fight stopped when a shot was fired.

The Freak Boss lowered his starter's pistol. "You two, break it up!"

Sarina said, "She started it! She wouldn't play fair. Fire her! Fire her or I'll . . ."

"Little lady, I will tend to my employee. Do I need to call the authorities to escort you and your gentleman friend off the fairgrounds?"

"No, sir," said Stewart. He led Sarina away.

The Freak Boss told Johnny Iguana to take a walk, then looked at Bitty Jack sterner than her father ever had. Bitty Jack turned away from him to discover a booth with no players, money scattered like ticket stubs, strewn from her apron.

The Freak Boss told her that this night would be her last. Even though she was a good worker, she had to be the example. She had fought with a customer and turned her back on Pick a Duck. Unlike Johnny Iguana, who could not be replaced, no offense, Regulars like Bitty Jack were easy to find. Besides, their relationship was getting too serious. He bet her parents would agree. He would drive her to the bus station. She was banned from the fair.

Nicole

FOLLOWING WHAT Mrs. Hicks was already referring to as the Report Card Incident, Nicole spent the evening locked in the upstairs bathroom. It was a safe place for her. Hospital clean with no windows.

Her father had returned from the Zoo Mania coverage. Nicole knew he was in the house. She had heard the car pull in. She had heard him call, "I'm home!" Usually, when Mr. Hicks returned from assignment, Nicole would rush to meet him, open his briefcase, and rummage through papers for a little something brought back for her. Usually, it was a pencil with the logo from whatever event he had covered printed on the side. Special Olympics. Alabama Pledge Week. Nicole owned a clay pot full of them. It once housed a cactus Nicole had watered like a geranium.

Nicole knew what her mother was doing. She was downstairs telling Mr. Hicks her side of the story. Her version would involve lies and scandal, plots and schemes, a manipulative best friend and a wishy-washy daughter. With enough persistence, Nicole's mother could make her husband believe anything. After all, for sixteen years, she had made him believe that she knew best for their daughter.

Nicole opened the medicine cabinet. She saw her father's electric razor stationed between her mother's pastel cans and cloudy jars. She picked it up and felt its weight. For as long as she could remember, she had heard its buzz every weekday afternoon. She had heard her father complain that it was in his contract to keep a clean shave. She wondered if her mother missed his beard. Nicole had seen it in photo albums. It was red even though her father's hair was jet black. But she couldn't be sure this was true anymore. On the top shelf, three boxes of Grey Be Gone sat at the ready.

Nicole hadn't thought of what her flunking out would do to her dad. At the time, it had seemed such a logical choice. Mom versus friend. Friend wins in the end. Now, here she was: hidden away. Soon to be a family embarrassment. And, still, Sarina was playing hard to get.

Nicole opened her mother's makeup drawer. She struggled with clasps and camouflaged locks. She ran her fingertips over muted eye shadows. She toyed with mascara wands. She twisted lipsticks out of gold ribbed containers and brought them to her nose. Everything smelled rosy. She wondered how long she could stomach this quiet, lonely place.

She went for the eyebrow tweezers. She picked out a pair of cuticle scissors. She opened cabinets and more drawers, slid back the sliding door to the bathtub, and gathered a sharp bouquet of instruments. There was so much to choose from: orange sticks and nail files, safety pins and pink plastic razors, hair accessories and hot roller clips with the rubber ends bitten off.

In a way, the tools were beautiful. So many points and slick edges begging to be touched. It was a pleasure she doubted anyone else could understand. In this room, Nicole could appreciate the good stuff.

* * *

Nicole had cut herself for the first time when she was twelve. She caught her brother masturbating. It was an accident. It really was.

She went to Rick's room to get him for supper. She knocked on his door. His stereo was blaring. She thought she heard "Come in." So she opened the door and there he was: naked on a towel, humping his football. Rick opened his mouth, but was at the point of no return. His body rocked in spasms. His cream came uncontrollably all over the pigskin.

Nicole ran to the kitchen and, for want of distraction, offered to open a can of corn for her mother. As the can turned beneath the electric opener's round, pronged blade, Nicole let her finger travel too close. It was just a nick, but the blood went everywhere, in the corn, on the counter. Mrs. Hicks went ballistic and sent Nicole to her room.

That night when her father brought her a dinner plate, Nicole refused a second helping of Tylenol. Left alone, she removed the dishtowel that she was supposed to use to apply constant pressure. She studied her cut. She spread its mouth and let the blood start again. She let one drop drip onto her comforter. The air-conditioning burned the wound, but Nicole treasured the pain. It released all anxiety, all embarrassment, all the fear that Rick would never forgive her, never talk to her again, never pal around. It was a fair trade. She wore that scar like a badge.

When Nicole left the bathroom, she found her mother camped on her double bed, her back waffled against the blue wicker headboard, the bright flowers on the bedspread twisted in her fists.

"Your father and I have discussed it. He thinks you've punished yourself enough by ruining your future. I disagree. I've taken your license. No car privileges for a year. You want to be a tenth grader so bad, you can be one whole-hog."

"But Mom—"

"Don't But Mom me. No telephone. No TV."

"But I have to call Sarina."

"Nicole, don't try me. Say that name again and, I'll ground you till you're grown!"

Over the course of the summer, Mrs. Hicks came close to keeping that promise. She let her daughter out of the house only to get the mail and take out the trash. Nicole wore down the driveway. Every time she got to the end, she would linger at the mailbox, staring across the street for any sign of her friend. Sarina was never there. No glimpse of her in any window. No front-lawn acrobatics.

Nicole knew that Sarina had called. She'd heard her father greet her by name. She'd heard her mother remind him of the conditions of her punishment and tell Mr. Hicks to hang up the phone.

So Nicole reverted to the girls' old tactics. She shone a flashlight out her bedroom window. She called the Summers and let the phone ring half a ring. When she took out the trash, she raised the metal mailbox flag. Anything to signal Sarina that it was safe to sneak out of her house and into the Hicks' kitchen and up the stairs to Nicole's bedroom.

But Sarina never showed. Between their two houses, Cheshire Way was always bare. No sign of a young girl running shoeless so as not to be caught. Sarina, it seemed, had little time for childish ways. Nicole, however, had all the time in the world.

By the end of the summer, Mrs. Hicks had washed her hands of Nicole. She was more self-involved. She was doing her thing. While other mothers took their daughters to the pool, Mrs. Hicks kept tan by lying out in her backyard on the abandoned trampoline.

She said, "I don't want to explain myself to those women at the club."

Nicole said, "Why do you have to explain yourself?"

Mrs. Hicks slid her feet into purple-soled orange flip-flops. "Because that's what good friends do." She crammed a paperback into her straw bag and gathered her beach towel, still warm from the dryer. "Now, let me alone before the sun moves to the front yard."

Mrs. Hicks spent her free time with her husband, who did not know what to do with a daughter who simply sat in her room. Without the activities her mother pushed her into, there was nothing for Mr. Hicks to attend. No football games, no PTA. With no distractions, Mr. Hicks lavished attention on his wife.

One afternoon, Mr. Hicks came home unexpectedly. From where Nicole sat on the stairs, she could survey his corner of the den. He sat in his reading chair by the fireplace that had never been used. He crossed his legs, an inch of pale skin peeking out from between his cuff and sock. He took the rubber band off the newspaper and laid it over his lap. But he never looked down. For over ten minutes, he stared through the sliding-glass doors, into the backyard. At one point, Nicole crept to the window in Rick's bedroom to see what exactly captivated her father.

Mrs. Hicks lay on her back on the center of the trampoline. Her sunglasses covered the tops of her cheeks. Her stomach browned like baked Apple Betty. She touched the bun on the top of her head. She ran her fingers over the oil on her arms which were so thin, Nicole thought they might possibly be hollow.

Mrs. Hicks picked up her water bottle lodged between two springs. She swirled it and doused her chest with the backwash. Tucking her towel around her waist, Mrs. Hicks got to her feet and wobbled to the edge of the trampoline. She swung her body to the grass and, as she went toward the house, Nicole returned to her spot on the stairs.

Nicole heard the glass door slide open and her mother exclaim, "Well, this is a surprise!"

Mr. Hicks patted the arm of his chair.

Mrs. Hicks hesitated. "You must be joking."

Pat, pat.

Nicole watched her mother secure the towel and sit where Mr. Hicks had asked. From under the newspaper, he produced a small gray velvet box. When he popped it open, Mrs. Hicks gasped, lost her balance, and toppled onto the carpet.

"I know that it's gold, but why wait another twenty-five years to give you this?"

Her mother got to her feet and plopped her bottom on top of that paper. She took the cocktail ring from the box and pushed it down her index finger. The diamond it sported looked too big to be true.

Mrs. Hicks whispered, "We can't afford this."

"What we can't afford," said Mr. Hicks, "is to see you so unhappy."

Mrs. Hicks kissed her husband and Nicole held her breath as she waited for them to break apart like decent parents did. When she finally took in oxygen, Nicole felt lightheaded. Her parents were arm in arm, lips still locked, walking dazedly toward their bedroom. The reading light shone on the empty box on the chair. The towel that hugged her mother's waist lay deserted on the floor.

When school started, Nicole's mother drove her to the Central West bus stop located in the parking lot of Central High East. For the past two years, Mrs. Hicks had split car-pool duty with Mrs. Summers. This year, Sarina would be driving herself. For her repeat performance, Nicole would be in her mother's charge.

Mrs. Hicks flicked the automatic lock from her side of the car. "I hope you realize that your actions affect everyone. I have to miss my early mornings at the gym. When I go at nine, it throws my whole day off."

"You could give me my license back."

"Get out of the car, Nicole."

Nicole jerked her feet up off the floor mat and felt September's heat suck her out into the day. She felt so tired. So unprepared. Before Nicole let go of the door handle, Mrs. Hicks gunned the engine and doubled out of the fifteen-mile-an-hour school zone. Alone in the crowd, all Nicole could think about was finding her friend.

Sarina was nowhere.

Nicole walked toward the bus stop where kids were packed under the aluminum shed. They were scattered in clumps in empty parking spaces. They looked older than she remembered. They made a lot of noise. As she got closer, she recognized the new tenth-graders. Last year, they were the ones who tried to muzzle in as she and Sarina walked through the halls. Now they were the first to tell new kids exactly who she was. *Here comes Nicole Hicks, a flunkie, a retard, a loser held back.* Nicole hugged her spiral binders, one for every subject, close to her body. She waited for a miracle.

Sarina skidded to a stop to answer her prayers. She honked her horn and, with one hand on the steering wheel, pushed the passenger door open and waved. As Nicole slid inside the gift Sarina's father had delivered by way of the same moving company that transferred him out of the Summers' house after the divorce, the other kids gawked.

Sarina said, "Let's roll!"

"Where are we going?"

"I'm taking you to school, Nicole. With your mom pulling that Rapunzel crap, this is the only way I can see you."

Nicole was astounded. Thrilled. Chilled. Too-good-to-be-real-ed. She flung her arms around her friend.

"Hey." Sarina squirmed. "I'm driving here."

"I'm sorry, Ree." Nicole wiped away tears with her wrists. "I'm just so glad to see you." She rubbed her eyes and regained focus. "You're . . .you're like a dream."

Sarina merged into the two-lane main road. She turned the radio way up. She poked the seek knob. As morning drive-time teams teased the winning caller (*"Oops, I don't know, Bob, seems like this is number 99 not 100." "Naw, Jerry. You sure?" "Oh, Gawd, don't hang up, don't hang up!"*), Sarina said, "Yeah, yeah, I love you too."

For months, Nicole had imagined what this moment would be like. When she finally had Sarina back. When she at last, once again, had Sarina to herself. But now Nicole was unable to say anything. It was an awkward silence that lasted close to five miles.

Sarina said, "I know you probably don't want to talk about it, but do you think it's dyslexia?"

Nicole stared out the side window. She recognized the Central West bus route. There goes Krispy Kreme. There's one, two, three Bridal Boutiques. Amoco. Texaco. British P. Gulf. As soon as she smelled the bread from the Sunbeam factory, the West campus would be just around the corner. She said, "You're born with dyslexia."

Sarina leaned toward Nicole. She checked her lipstick in the rearview mirror. She said, "Well, I don't know. I'm just trying to help. Oprah had on kids who were totally messed up from the chemicals their schools used to wipe the blackboards. One girl's breasts were bleeding because the vents were shut for like a hundred years."

Sarina stopped the car outside the barbed-wire fence that surrounded the parking lot of Central High West. She offered information about varsity cheerleading practice that had started two weeks earlier. "People think we have it easy, but it's worse than JV. Look at this." Sarina twisted in her seat, pulled out her blouse, and lifted it to show Nicole a large bruise above her hip.

Nicole tucked her hands under her thighs. She wanted to reach over the stick shift and touch the black-and-blue, kiss it and make the bad colors go away. She chewed the inside of her lip. "You're so pale, Ree."

Sarina stuffed her shirt back under her waistband. She shook her chocolate curls as if trying to shoo the comment out of the car. "Way to remind me."

"No," said Nicole. "In a good way. You're like a doll."

Sarina's face reddened.

"I don't mean to embarrass you. You know you're good-looking."

Sarina said, "I'm not embarrassed."

Nicole felt embarrassed. She felt that way all day.

When the last school bell rang, Nicole left under scrutiny. She was all anyone could talk about. Teachers wanted to be shrinks. Students wanted to get the skinny. Everyone wanted to know how a good-enough kid could flunk out of school. Everyone wanted to be the one to make her crack.

All day long, Nicole had kept her mouth shut. She chose a locker at the end of the hall. She ate lunch at the corner of the science nerds' table in the cafeteria that stunk of gossip and Tater Tots. She wondered why anyone gave a rat's ass. It wasn't like she had a baby in the bathroom. It wasn't like she'd killed someone.

When she got off the bus at Central High East, her mother was waiting in the car, her sunglasses on, reading an oversized magazine. She asked, "Was it all that you remembered?"

"It was fine," Nicole said and buckled her safety belt.

But it wasn't fine. It was far from fine. Nicole had somehow found her way into a place where she was the last person anyone wanted to be friends with and still the center of attention. She was not happy there. But she was happy with the thought of tomorrow morning and of Sarina's door-to-door and of fifteen minutes in a place where she would be giddy and grateful and could sleep easily if given the chance. All the way home, Nicole tried to figure out how she could spend more time with her friend.

During the next morning's commute, Sarina came up with the answer. "Tell her you have to stay late. Study hall. Extra credit. Tell her Jessup's watching you. You know, he wants to make sure that you pass."

Mrs. Hicks did not doubt it for a minute.

The fall semester continued this way. At the beginning of each school day, Sarina picked Nicole up where her mother dropped her off. On the afternoons that Sarina did not have cheerleading or Key Club, she took Nicole places where they would not be seen.

"If we went to the mall, your mom would totally kill you."

Nicole knew that was true and allowed Sarina to tuck her away anyplace she saw fit.

Sarina was great when they were alone. At times, Nicole thought, she was better than when their friendship was public. Sarina seemed more interested in what was on Nicole's mind. How the West campus was treating her. If there were any junior-varsity cheerleading terrors who need to have beer spilt in their hair after the pep rallies. Was there anyone in particular who was making her life miserable? Sarina could take care of it. Accidents could happen.

But Nicole just laughed at Sarina's tough act. She hugged her own knees and rocked on the trunk of Sarina's car wherever it was parked. Behind the Dumpster at the Piggly Wiggly. In the woods along the train tracks. Wherever. Whenever Sarina made time.

* * *

A week before Christmas break, Nicole knew something was wrong.

"It's nothing," Sarina said.

"It is too something. Look at you. You're all twisted in your seat."

There was a chill in the supermarket parking lot. Sarina had the car heater running and the windows were fogged.

"Is it that obvious?"

"Just tell me."

Sarina uncrossed her legs, took her clasped hands from between her thighs, touched the front window, and made five fingerprints. She admitted, "The Stewart thing has me all screwed up."

Nicole felt the heat rise to her face as it had when Sarina had told her about that one night at Deerlick. She hated to think of Stewart on top of her, breathing out of order, toes in the sand, trying to get his footing. For the first time, Sarina had told her very little about what had happened. Nicole had not pressed her. But she had wanted to. Real bad. She'd wanted to ask if Stewart knew the way Sarina liked her feet rubbed, the way she liked her hands played with, her scalp scratched where the roots met her neck. Did he know that the way to get Sarina to agree to anything was to point out how very pretty she was?

What Nicole pointed out was, "Look, you asked for it."

"Nice," Sarina said and reached for the keys hanging idle from the ignition.

"Wait, I'm sorry. Tell me. Is it that you're still in love with him?"

"I'm not in love with him. At least, not like when I was a kid." Sarina drew a plus sign with her knuckle on the driver's side window. She traced the capital letters of her name on top of Stewart's. "If we got married . . ."

"You'd have the same initials."

Sarina wiped her hand over the inscription. "Not a surefire sign of love."

"So what is it?" Nicole whispered. "What is it? What's wrong?"

"Once you've had sex, everyone expects it."

"Everyone knows about you and Stewart?"

"God, no. He's the captain of the math team." Sarina turned toward Nicole. She tucked her feet beneath her. She put her back against the door. "Everyone knows about me and *someone*."

"Someone," Nicole repeated.

"Someone in college. A college boyfriend."

Nicole could picture Sarina in the locker room, all the cheerleaders rallied, eager for details from her long-distance love affair. Each girl wanting a man, not a boy. Each anxious to grow up. To be like Ree.

"So you made him up."

Sarina nodded. "This way, I can still talk, but don't have to go all the way with guys after the games. You know, it's all just tits and tongue."

Nicole cringed. "Isn't that cheating on Mr. Big Man on Campus? Which college did you say he's at?"

"Georgia. And it's not cheating unless you really mean it."

"So what's the problem?

"Geez, Nic. The problem is the prom. I've just got to find some college guy to take me. None of the high school guys will ask me. I'm spoken for, remember."

Nicole said, "If it makes you feel any better, there's no prom for me, either. No one's going to ask a flunkie. Looks like we both screwed ourselves out of a date."

"I figured I could set you up. Get someone to ask you. We could go together like we planned. Do the hotel thing, the whole nine yards. There's got to be a college boy. You've got to help me think."

With those words, Nicole was transported to a place without punishment. Her privileges weren't stolen. The grounding surrendered. She would go to the prom and double-date like the old days. She would store the corsage in the fridge, pull it out and smell it if she was ever chastised again. Nicole had to make this date a reality. She had to think of a plan.

She did. “What about Rick?”

“Your brother, Rick?”

“He even goes to Georgia.”

“You’re right,” Sarina clapped. She reached out and practically fell on Nicole. Her hair covered Nicole’s face and Nicole remembered the scent of her pillows after Sarina slept over. Cheek-to-cheek, Nicole felt her skin vibrate as Sarina spoke. “He’s perfect.”

Thus, the plan was laid out in a parked car between two girls. They would convince Rick to take Sarina. Sarina would convince an East Campus guy to invite Nicole. They would be together like last year. In pretty dresses and high-heeled shoes.

Sarina

IT WAS NOT part of Sarina's plan to have Nicole approach her brother. She could get Rick all by herself, no assistance necessary. But the opportunity was there. Christmas vacation was well under way and Nicole's parents had a day planned at the University Mall. So when Nicole called and told her to come over quickly, the coast was clear, Sarina could hardly refuse. Nicole was so sensitive. If she didn't feel needed, she was no use at all.

Sarina stopped in the carport. She touched Rick's bitchin' Camaro. Just back from Georgia, the hood was still warm.

Rick was in his room.

"Be cool," Nicole pleaded.

Sarina said, "Sure."

At the top of the stairs, Sarina could see that his door was wide open. He was unpacking his suitcase, sorting his clothes into two piles. Bed and floor. Clean and dirty. When he looked up, he found them standing in the door frame, Nicole switching her weight from foot to foot, Sarina with her arms crossed, feeling feckless and more juvenile by the second. Before Nicole said word one, Rick put his hands in the air like a convenience store clerk under the gun. He said, "No way."

"But you don't even know what the question is."

"Whatever it is," Rick told his sister, "there is no way I'm doing it." He ran both hands through his tall blond hair. He caught some of it in his fists and stared at the dirty laundry like it was the greatest burden he could possibly bear. He pressed the heels of his hands against his eyes. When he opened them, he said, "You're still here?"

Sarina gently pulled Nicole into the hallway. "Don't worry about it," she said. "I'll see him at Tracey Hinkle's party. I'll take care of it."

"What if he says no?" Nicole grabbed Sarina's wrists a little too tight and Sarina noticed the skin eaten away at her cuticles. Nicole's fingers were red, purple almost from the pressure she applied.

"Jeez, Nic. Let go." She tried to twist free. But Nicole's thumbs were white now. "He's not gonna say no."

That night, Sarina followed Rick's car to Tracey Hinkle's house. Tracey was a varsity cheerleader and hers was the first of many parties that would go on over the break. The same crowd would move from house to house depending on whose parents were out of town. It was the same clique Sarina hung with at school, plus alumni, plus anyone else who had the gumption to crash. The parties got big. They filtered into backyards. The music could be heard before drivers parked their cars on neighboring lawns. The cops were always called. The drunkest always stepped forward, volunteering to play sober.

Sarina got out of her car and met Rick as he stepped out of his. She took him by the hand, careful not to let her sleeve fall back to expose the marks Nicole had left. She teased, "You're my new boyfriend."

Rick reached through the open car window. He took his wallet off the dashboard and stuffed it in his back pocket. "You think so?"

Sarina pinned his elbows against the roof of the car. She let her body get close enough so that her breasts barely touched his sweater. She whispered, "You know you've always had a thing for me."

Rick said, "You're still a kid."

As she followed him into the party, Sarina said, "Prove it."

Throughout the evening, Sarina kept after him. She poured vodka, smuggled from the Hinkles' liquor cabinet, into the Coke in his blue plastic cup. She helped him get wasted. Boys love that. What resistance he had was lost. Before his buddies drove him home, Sarina took Rick to the backyard, took off her panties, and pushed them into the front pocket of his jeans. She said, "You're my new boyfriend."

"Whatever you say."

When he woke up, Rick would find Sarina's party favor, remember grubbing behind an ivy bush, then call a friend to confirm. Everyone he called had seen the two of them together. Seen them go out to the backyard. Seen them stay out there long enough.

"Did you do it?" one would ask.

"What do you think?"

"Dawg!" his friend would say. "You dawg!"

Sarina knew how it would go. She would follow him to the next party. She would get into the host's parents' private stash of booze. Smile when Rick confronted her. Nod when he said, "Do you want to get out of here?" She would refill his plastic party cup. Kiss him till he couldn't recall. Go along with whatever he could summon the next morning, what his friends could come up with, what she could imagine they might have done if the circumstances were different.

The day before Rick went back to Georgia, Sarina called him during her lunch period. She told him that as her new boyfriend, come May, he owed it to her to drive home and take her to the prom.

Rick said, "Come over while I'm sober and then we'll have a deal."

Sitting in the wooden phone booth outside the Central East cafeteria, Sarina traced a slut's phone number carved into one of the panels. For a good time, she thought, trust no one.

"Mars to Venus," Rick's voice came through the receiver. "Come in, Venus."

"One more time and then you'll take me?"

Rick said, "I swear to God."

Sarina knew Rick would break that promise. Boys were taught by *HBO After Dark* to expect adult content and nudity on prom night. No cum shot, but definitely dyed-to-match silk shoes scuffing up the car's interior. That, Sarina thought, she could handle. She'd spike his punch and watch him struggle with his cummerbund and his fly, his pesky penis too pickled to perform.

Sarina cut out of school early.

Pulling into her neighborhood, Sarina thought of the things people said that they did. She wondered if Rick really believed they went all the way. That he stuck it inside her. That it had been so easy.

Stewart Steptoe was the only boy she had ever made it easy for. In the Central East hallways, he looked at her and she knew he remembered. Wet sand. Her hair tangled. Candied apple breath coming close to his ear. The whole night and everything that happened.

Walking to the Hicks' front door, Sarina assured herself that sex was the way to get what she wanted. She thought, *If Rick challenges me after this, I'll tell everyone he can't get it up.* "Just do it," she whispered. "Do it and get it over with."

But Rick wanted more from her. He wanted some romance. He opened the front door and led her to his bedroom. The desk light was left on and the shades were drawn.

The clock radio was playing something slow where the singer interrupts the chorus to utter something provocative.

Rick smiled at Sarina like the boyfriend she told him he was. He eased her down onto the carpet, on top of an electric blanket laid out like a picnic. He pulled two pillows from the head of his bed. He placed them at the satin seam. "The bed makes too much noise. My mom might come home."

Sarina kicked her shoes off. "So how do you want to do this?"

Rick said, "It's not surgery."

Sarina let him kiss her. His lips felt firmer than when he was drunk. He was more intent. Focused on feeling her out. When he was drunk, he kept his hands at his sides or dormant on her hips. Now, he was touching her, stroking her, tugging at her clothes. "You know," he whispered, "you were right about me having a thing for you."

Sarina began to enjoy herself. She kissed him back. She let him lie down and draw her down beside him. Her pelvis to his hip. Her breasts pushing into his right rung of ribs.

"Touch me," said Rick.

"I am."

"Not like that."

He moved her hand from his cheek to the lump between his legs. He kept his own hand over hers and drew a sharp breath as he helped her massage himself out of rhythm with the radio. "Will you do it one more time?"

Sarina was not sure what he meant until he let go of her hand and unbuckled his belt. As if racing, he undid his button fly. Without any help from Rick, his penis popped out. He closed his eyes, tucked his hands under his butt and waited.

Sarina had never taken a good look at a penis. She had felt her fair share. She had felt Stewart's as it went in. But she had never had one laid out like an autopsy. It was redder than Rick's skin. She touched it. It moved.

"Do it right," Rick said. He put a hand on the back of her neck. He guided her head toward his hot, sweaty crotch. When she resisted, he pushed harder.

"Okay," said Sarina. She pried his penis off his stomach. It was warm and oozed at the tip. She put the head in her mouth and the taste made her gag. Sarina's eyes stung as she held her breath for another try.

Five months later, Sarina held out her prom dress, ran her fingers down the length. It was black with velvet trim. It had a deep V-neck.

"It's too old for you," Mrs. Summers had said in the store.

Sarina insisted, "It's what I want."

Sarina held the dress up to her in front of the mirror on the back of her bedroom door. She stuck a leg out and noticed the slight sparkle from her midnight-sheer pantyhose with the panties built in. She folded the dress over her arm and leaned forward to examine the cleavage enhanced by her strapless bra. The electric rollers were still hot in her hair. When her mother called, Sarina put on her robe and secured the tie. She wondered if black heels really did match everything. It was a week before the prom and this was the dress rehearsal.

Sarina opened her bedroom door to find her mother with the camera hung around her neck. The idea was to take a series of photographs of Sarina with her hair done different ways. With different level heels. Her mouth painted an array of colors. This process could stretch well into the night. Mrs. Summers had sent Willamina home early, ordered a pizza, and set the den with soft 60 watt lightbulbs. She was very excited. She had already bought an oversized picture frame for the best of the bunch. She had written Sarina a late note for the next day of school. Mrs. Summers tugged the belt of Sarina's robe twice. "Hup, hup. Hop to it."

Sarina backed up to let her mother in. As she went into the bathroom, Mrs. Summers sat on the end of the bed and hung her legs over the frame like a kid. Sarina rummaged through her lipstick drawer.

"Stay away from the red," Mrs. Summers said. "If you dance, your face will flush and red lips will only draw attention to it."

Sarina knew she was right. She twisted the Cherry Bomb back into its tube. She applied a frosty pink.

Mrs. Summers said, "Do you want help with your hair? I could put it up for you."

Sarina imagined her hair in a French twist, her earrings dangling down. She would look incredible and her mother would do a better job. Sarina sat sidesaddle on the toilet and motioned for her mother to come in. With great effort Mrs. Summers pushed herself over the bed frame. As she walked toward Sarina, the camera bounced against her bosom. She picked up a brush and a can of White Rain. With bobby pins pinched between her lips, Mrs. Summers smiled a prickly smile. She handled her daughter's hair like a pro. Careful not to inhale while the aerosol was in the air, Mrs. Summers spun yarns about her prom and what she wore and the sequence of forks Sarina should use at dinner.

Sarina could see through her mother's cream blouse. She noticed that her camisole had birds in the lace. Their beaks were open as if to say Peep, peep, peep. Sarina said, "I'm sorry about how mean I was when you were getting divorced."

Mrs. Summers put the White Rain on the back of the toilet. "Sweetheart," she said, "why on earth would you bring that up?"

"He cheated on you, didn't he?"

Mrs. Summers began to shove bobby pins into her daughter's hairstyle. Behind the ear for working Saturdays. At the nape of the neck for working late. The French twist was fastened for cash withdrawals he could never seem to account for. At a medical examiner's pace, Mrs. Summers semicircled her daughter. She examined her work. She gave Sarina a hand mirror, and Sarina stood and checked out her do from every conceivable angle.

"You were never mean," Mrs. Summers told her. "Carolyn Hicks, now that woman is mean."

"Why do you hate her so much?"

"She's a liar. She'll say anything against anyone for no reason at all."

Before Sarina knew it, her mother was gone. Probably in the kitchen, pulling a little something from the fridge to wash a bad taste out of her mouth. She was always doing that. Pulling a little something.

Sarina let her robe fall onto the black-and-white tiles. She took her dress off the hanger and stepped into it. She pulled the zipper up her back. She saw that she did indeed look older. Maybe twenty. Maybe twenty-five. She looked better than a beauty pageant contestant. Better than those actresses who played college-age parts. The University of Alabama Homecoming Queens always made the front page of the paper. None of them were half as pretty as Sarina felt right now. Sarina imagined Rick ringing her doorbell, pinning the corsage, honoring the woman she was determined to become.

Sarina met her mother in the living room. She let her arms go loose but not limp as her mother placed them in different positions. On her hips. Click. At her sides. Click. One on the mantel, one behind her back. She looked good. In her heels, Sarina stood nearly five foot eleven.

Mrs. Summers said, "So how did you get away with going with your ex-friend's big brother?"

"She's not my ex." Sarina tilted her head in the direction her mother was pointing. Down, at an angle to hide her slight double chin.

Mrs. Summers said, "I'm surprised she didn't ask if she could tag along."

Sarina said, "She did."

Mrs. Summers stopped snapping snapshots. She sat down on the sofa. "Well, you certainly said no, didn't you?"

Sarina tugged at her panty hose that were puckering behind her knees.

Mrs. Summers said, "I know she's been a friend to you, but that girl is not well. It would be one thing if she was bulimic. But that girl is self-destructive. Don't think I haven't seen the scars on her arms."

Sarina wiped off the frosty pink lipstick and applied a sheer beige.

"You didn't invite her, did you? Tell me that you didn't invite her."

Sarina sat down in the leather La-Z-Boy her father had left behind and her mother had consequently recovered with a pale, creamy shade to match the living room curtains. She pulled out the foot rest. She told her mother the truth.

"You did what?"

"Mom, don't worry about it. I just told her she could come so she wouldn't freak out about Rick."

"So what, you're double-dating? Who on earth did you get to go out with her?"

Sarina said, "No one."

Mrs. Summers began to fan herself with her 35mm camera. She reached for the end table where Willamina always placed a coaster for that glass of white wine. Mrs. Summers brought the half-empty wine glass to her forehead. "Tell me." She shut her eyes as if imagining the Prom Under the Stars gymnasium photograph. "Tell me it's not just the three of you."

Sarina had to laugh. "Mom, come on. I'll take care of Nicole. Trust me. My reputation is safe. Next week, it'll only be me and Rick."

"Rick and me," Mrs. Summers corrected.

"Rick and me," Sarina agreed and pushed herself forward, her lips like Spring, the La-Z-Boy back in position for a sitting-down shot.

Initially, Sarina had toyed with the idea of accompanying Nicole to the prom. After all they were best friends. There was nobody else who she'd have as much fun with. Nicole was good that way. She did not mind tagging along. Whatever Sarina wanted to do, to try, wherever she wanted to go, Nicole had always been right there with her. Nicole had always been very supportive. She could sense when things weren't right. Sarina never had to say she was feeling fat or insecure or depressed or not like talking. Nicole always knew. And she knew what to do. She said the right things. Noticed a new outfit. She could sit with Sarina in front of the TV and never say a solitary word. Nicole let Sarina live out her cold funks. She was happy just to be with her and expected nothing in return. So as her pinkies healed and Mrs. Summers wrote the book on bedside manner, Sarina had come up with a plan. She would seduce Rick. Mrs. Hicks would fold when he informed her he was coming home for the prom. Mr. Hicks would convince his wife that their daughter had been grounded long enough. The prospect would give Nicole a few weeks of happiness. Something to look forward to. A dream. Some time well spent.

Sure the other kids would gawk, but Sarina's excuse would be Rick. When Sarina told Nicole she had lied about dating a college guy, she wasn't telling the whole truth. From the very beginning she had claimed the guy was Rick. At separate campuses, Central East gossip would never reach Central High West. Even if it did, no one talked to Nicole. That was the beautiful part. She could hang with Nicole under the carpooling circumstances. She could tell those who judged her that she was doing her boyfriend a favor. Being nice to his kid sister. Giving an old gal pal a break.

But the school year hadn't worked out as Sarina had planned. Her classmates weren't behaving like an *After School Special.* In their minds, Nicole had cut herself out of their circle of friends. She had cut herself out of the mold they'd all known. No more cheerleading. No more clubs. No classes together. No parties. No fun. Nicole had sunk to the bottom of the popularity food chain. Below the potheads and headbangers, Special Ed and the dykes. She might as well have shaved all her hair off and pierced her face a million times. Nicole was no longer a girl to be seen with. Not without a damned good excuse. While Rick had served as an adequate explanation, his mileage wouldn't take Sarina from car service to the biggest high school spectacle of the year.

In a way, she was grateful for the prejudice of her peers. Since she'd introduced the prom plan, Nicole had gotten weird. Weirder than the obvious failure of tenth grade. Weirder than the additional grabbing she had done since that day outside Rick's bedroom. Nicole had started passing her notes. Notes really wasn't the word. They were ten-page letters, backs and fronts of spiral paper. The edges were frayed and so was her handwriting, her diction, her cursive to caps, cursive to certain words scrawled out in crayon. Every letter was complimentary, full of metaphors for her eyes, lips, and skin. They were the love letters she had dreamed of receiving from Stewart, from Rick, from a real college boyfriend.

Sarina never knew what to say in response. What could she say other than thank you? But that was certainly enough for Nicole. The notes kept on coming along with Home Ec–sewn pillows and Wood Shop–sawed key racks. And every time she gave a gift as minor as a stick of Trident, Nicole leaned forward to receive a hug that always lasted longer than Sarina would have liked.

But Sarina ignored how uncomfortable she felt. She reasoned Nicole was just going through an emotional phase. She was her only friend. Nicole's appreciation was natural. Besides, Sarina did not want to risk hurting Nicole. God forbid she tell Rick and for once he play the part of protective older brother. If Rick dumped Sarina, the prom would not be such a victory. But if they took Nicole to the prom, the night would be disastrous.

So Nicole had to be clipped and Mrs. Hicks had to be the one to do it.

Mrs. Hicks had always had it in for the Summers. Sarina didn't know why. She really didn't care. She liked Mr. Hicks. She watched him every night on the ten o'clock news. He was handsome and spoke in the sincerest of voices. Sarina felt sorry for him. To guarantee that Nicole be re-punished, Sarina had to tear his family apart.

Since Nicole had given her the third "Ree Ree" nameplate, Sarina started plotting to push her out of the prom. Sarina knew where the school year would take them. To this very moment: the Kelly brothers' pre-prom party.

There were four Kelly brothers, each two years apart. They were blond and funny and sexy and smart. The last week of April, their parents always went on a ski trip. That weekend, the brothers hosted an out-and-out free-for-all. The whole school came. They had a huge house with an even bigger backyard and a lake. There were illegal firecrackers their father always "accidentally" laid out on the kitchen table as their mother started the car. They had a tree house and a hammock, a pool table and Foosball. It was better than any bar. It was the party of the year.

The night of the Kelly brothers' pre-prom party, Sarina would make two phone calls. One to Nicole. One to the police. There was no way things could go wrong. It was the master of her master plans.

At midnight the party was reaching its peak. The place was packed, kids everywhere. Through bodies and wine coolers, Sarina pushed her way into the youngest boy's bedroom. In the darkness of the room, she saw the shapes of science-fiction action figures, books and magazines, clothes on the floor, clothes all over everything. And yet, the twin bed was made like a soldier's. Sarina sat down. She picked the phone up off the floor and dialed Nicole's number, which she still knew by heart.

She let the phone ring half a ring. That was their signal. She counted *One Mississippi, two Mississippi* until she reached sixty. She called back and Nicole answered the phone before the ring was even finished.

"Ree?" Nicole whispered.

Sarina kept her mouth shut.

"Ree?"

Sarina could hear the panic squeezing Nicole's voicebox. Sarina squeezed her own voice by imagining being blind. She put herself in a wheelchair, a paraplegic, blowing herself down the street with a tube. What if she got her face sliced with a box cutter? What if she tripped and knocked out her front teeth? Sarina felt her throat close, her eyes start to sting. "Nicki," she choked, "Nicki, it's me."

"Where are you? What's wrong?"

Sarina was amazed at her ability to cry. "I'm at the Kellys' house. You've got to come get me."

"Ree, I don't have a license. I don't have a car."

"Nicki, please!" Sarina hung up the phone.

Sarina sat still in the youngest brother's bedroom. She knew what was happening a five-minute drive away. Nicole was scared to death. She was racing for the car keys and climbing into her father's new convertible Jeep. She probably didn't even take off her pajamas. She probably didn't bother to drive away quietly.

Sarina called 911. She said there was a party and she gave the address. She said there was underage drinking and firecrackers and about a thousand stupid kids disturbing the peace. Yes, this was an emergency, some kid could get killed.

The operator said, "Officers are responding."

Sarina hung up the phone. She left the party. She kept the radio low as she drove the long way back to her house.

The police and Nicole should arrive at the same time. Even if they didn't Nicole would be the one person there they'd be able to catch. Everyone else would scatter when the cops rang the doorbell. Nicole would be found searching for her friend. In her pajamas. Without a license. Behind the wheel of a car Sarina would now call and report as stolen. The daughter of Tuscaloosa's local news celebrity in apparent disarray. It was sure to hit the papers. NEWS ANCHOR'S DAUGHTER ARRESTED DELIRIOUS. Maybe Nicole would hit a parked car. The Hicks could be sued. Their insurance rates would double. There were endless possibilities. But all had the same result—Mrs. Hicks would be humiliated and Nicole's prom privileges revoked.

PART TWO

Through the Looking Glass

Bitty Jack

Since Bitty Jack was ousted from the Summons County Fair, Johnny Iguana had come back for her two years in a row. The first time the trailers rolled in, Bitty Jack knew he would call before the tents went up. In his letters, he had promised that he loved her, he missed her, he wanted to see her as soon as he could. But the freak show kept him traveling, and the Carlsons kept Bitty Jack from leaving Camp Chickasaw grounds.

"Letters is one thing," Big Jack had said, "going after what you can't have is entirely another."

So Bitty Jack wrote more letters. Often two a day. For the few weeks the fair was in town, the mail lady delivered those envelopes to one of twenty P.O. boxes at the Summons County station. Johnny Iguana read every one. He told Bitty Jack that he kept them in a waterproof bag so he could bring them backstage. He called her sometimes, but he stayed away from Camp Chickasaw. He respected the Carlsons' wishes and valued his job. He didn't want to make trouble. He would not try anything until Bitty Jack turned eighteen.

The second summer the fair returned, Bitty Jack was a counselor and old enough to do what she wanted.

What she had done was become a sort of patron saint of persecuted campers. Geeks, spastics, four-eyed cry babies. Girls who wet the bed so often that by the time Bitty Jack discovered the fitted sheet it was rung with stains resembling the inside of a ten-year-old tree. They wore headgears. They were soft-spoken, shy types who came close to hemorrhaging each time they were up at bat at mandatory softball games. But Bitty Jack made time for them. She played catch after dark, tried to teach them how to shave their legs. She did what she could. She let them sit out on the porch with her when she sat "On Duty."

OD meant lights out, campers in bed. One counselor at each cabin until the others got back from Trinka's, the only bar in a sixty-mile radius. Trinka's never carded. If counselors could get off campgrounds, they could get into Trinka's. On most nights, the Chickasaw owners provided a van for a staff who did not realize life might get better than cheese-filled pretzels and three-dollar pitchers. The owners wanted to keep their counselors happy. Gas money was a small price to pay.

Bitty Jack wasn't much of a drinker. She wasn't the best at the social scene either. So she sat OD for other counselors whenever they asked. She was comfortable in the night. The woods in front of her. A few of her favorite campers reading quietly at her side.

It was a peaceful summer. Uninterrupted, until Johnny showed up.

He came out of the trees in front of the cabin. He was more muscular than she remembered, but wore the same brand of khakis. On the narrow road in front of the cabin, the light from the porch cast his shadow for yards.

The girls drew their breath in, but stifled their screams when Johnny Iguana called their counselor by name. They huddled a little closer as Bitty Jack walked quickly into his arms. She kissed him like the girls were not even there. Her heart popped as Johnny whispered promises in the crook of her neck. He held her as if she were impossible to break. He held her until she told him good-bye.

Later, the girls told her it was the longest hug in history. They asked her to tell them the whole entire story. Who that young man was. And why she let him go.

"He wanted me to go with him," she quietly explained. "I can't go. I've got college."

"So go to college later!"

Bitty Jack looked into the faces rallied around her bunk eager for romance to hurry up and start. "It's not that easy." She touched one of their friendship bracelets. "I got a scholarship. There's no way I can pass that up."

"But what about him?"

Bitty Jack looked over their heads to the front door of the cabin. She imagined Johnny walking through that door, ignoring her good sense and carrying her back to the fair, to the Matterhorn, to an easy life where the only choice was him. Maybe they'd make love for the first time in the air castle after everyone went home. Maybe they'd get married. Live out their days together in many towns.

Bitty Jack remembered how proud her parents had been when the notice of scholarship had come from the University of Alabama. She herself had been genuinely excited. Hopeful with such a chance. She had worked so hard. Driven two hours to take the SATs. Written a brilliant essay on which historical figures she would have dinner with if given the chance. They were ordinary steps to a not extraordinary college. But Bitty Jack could get an education in Tuscaloosa. Maybe find a peer group. See another part of the world, even if that world was still enclosed in Alabama. Summons was not a town that people left. Once the roots were planted, it was too easy to not weed.

She thought of all the Summons girls who got married as

soon as the law would allow. How most of them moved back with their mamas after the babies had come and their husbands stayed late at the bar. How her parents were the exception to the rule that young love was destined to fail. What were the odds that Bitty Jack and Johnny would have that same special kind of luck?

Bitty Jack looked back into the faces of her frustrated faithful campers. She told them the truth before she turned out the lights. "I'll miss him," she said. "And the carnival too."

During the last week of Chickasaw, Bitty Jack said good-bye to her campers. She spent her last night in Summons in the cabin instead of her house. She snuck the girls brownies that her mama had made for the bus ride to Tuscaloosa. She let them use swear words. She let them stay up all night long.

In the morning, she sent the kids off to breakfast. When the last one was out of sight, she heard the family Ford roll up behind her. Her parents got out of the truck and her father walked straight to the porch. He put one hand through the canvas straps of his army duffel bag and Bitty Jack worried that she had packed it too full. Before she could ask, her father swung that bag into the back of the truck as if he were turning one end of a jump rope.

Mrs. Carlson said, "I packed a smaller suitcase for you. Put a coat in. Put in some pants."

Bitty Jack nodded and took a step toward her.

Mrs. Carlson stepped back. She squeezed her crossed arms closer to her chest. She shook her head vehemently. "I love you, baby girl, but if you get any closer I won't never let you go."

"Bitty," said Big Jack, "your mother needs to make this short and sweet."

Bitty walked past her mother, scared to touch her, scared to say anything at all. She got in the truck. Her father got in too. As they drove by Mrs. Carlson, Bitty Jack got to her knees and put her hands against the back window. Her mother was walking as if the pavement had melted. She was staring back at Bitty, shielding her eyes, the gray patches of her hair lit up in the sun. Mrs. Carlson's lips did not move, but in Bitty Jack's mind she could hear her voice over the engine and the radio and the noise coming out of the mess hall. Her mother was calling over birds, wind, and sky, "Good-bye, baby girl. I will always be here."

Pulling into the Greyhound bus station in downtown Tuscaloosa, Bitty Jack marveled at how short the trip had seemed. Aided by Dramamine, she had slept the first three hours, awakened only by a pee break at the Montgomery highway rest stop. There she bought a Coke and a Kit Kat, which kept her awake for the rest of the ride. She counted VW Bugs. She got to thirty-three bottles of beer on the wall before getting bored. As the bus cruised along I-65, she quickly appreciated that, on her map of Alabama, one inch really did equal one hundred miles.

The Greyhound station was stuffy and deserted. The fans mounted high in each corner of the waiting room buzzed and gave Bitty Jack the creeps. As she searched the phone book for a taxi cab company, Bitty Jack sat on the suitcase her mother had packed and anchored the duffel bag with her ankle through its straps.

The taxi, which was really a station wagon in disguise, dropped her off on campus at Tutwiler Hall. Bitty Jack had read that you could judge a place by its tallest building. In Summons County, the narrow jail stood three stories high. Tutwiler stood fourteen. It was a single-sex dormitory, for girls only. Double-room capacity. No suitors past the lobby.

Bitty Jack had arrived one week before classes to search for work. Her father had called her the Early Bird Special. Her scholarship covered tuition, but not books and not room and board. She had savings from her Chickasaw salary. Plus two hundred dollars her parents had promised for every semester. Still, that wasn't enough. She had to find a job. More than part-time. More than minimum wage.

When she got to her dorm room, Bitty Jack found the bed by the window already taken. Makeup bag spread open, curlers and pins on the floor like a moat. By the end of the week, Bitty Jack would learn to live with this. Her roommate was from Florida. She had come early for sorority rush. She was blond and pretty and pledged Tri Delta. She was never in their room and, for Bitty, that was fine.

Through the job-search board, Bitty found a job at the Fifteenth Street Bakery. Tom Bradley was the owner and paid minimum for bakery work and waitress-minimum for his catering business because the clients always tipped.

Beside the swinging glass doors to the bakery, there was a small room with a wall-size window facing Fifteenth Street. Bitty Jack often found herself there, three ovens behind her and a counter in front, level with her hips. This was the cookie-baking room. The job wasn't so bad, except that Tom insisted his bakers sport tall paper hats. When Bitty Jack sweated, the rim left a rash. Catering was okay, but the real money was made in the "private" bakery. Unbeknownst to his best catering clientele, Tom ran a cake and party service geared toward bachelor parties, stripper conventions, and any general blowout with a sweet tooth and pornographic needs.

Often, Bitty Jack found herself in the windowless back bakery frosting arm-length penises or strawberry-and-cream-layered D-cup breasts. She boxed edible underwear. She placed tiny naked dolls into lime green Jell-O molds. On the overhead shelf, there were two books of reference: *Betty Crocker's Cakes and Pastries* and *Kama Sutra for Dummies*.

Sure, it was embarrassing, but for her steady hand and attention to detail, Bitty Jack got paid twice as much as she did in the cookie room, where she had all eyes on her.

In the afternoon, crowds gathered. They wandered toward the cinnamon-sugar smell or the peanut butter smell or the idea of chocolate chips. They liked to watch Bitty Jack place the walnuts in the dough. When she pried open glue-sealed plastic bags, they knew the raisins or Goobers were fresh. Some of them licked their lips. They tapped on the window. They eyed the plain cookies Bitty Jack set aside. It didn't take a genius to figure out what was eventually bound for frosting. They peered over the counter, squeezed in from the sides of the window. There were old eyes and young eyes. Blue eyes and some whose irises were indistinguishable from their pupils. Sometimes the eyes had on too much mascara. Some mornings they were bloodshot. But one pair stood out. They were blue and in the middle of the crowd every day.

They belonged to Stewart Steptoe, a 250-pound freshman who got all the answers right in her science elective.

The "Tuskegee: And Other Contagious Diseases" course was continually hard for Bitty Jack to follow. No matter where she sat, Stewart put his books on the chair in front of hers. Gingerly, he'd squeeze himself into what, with him in it, looked like a vise. One thigh stuffed between the chair and the small, screwed-on desk. Half his butt hanging off the seat. Bitty Jack felt too sorry for him to get up and move. So she scooted her seat slightly to the left or slightly to the right and tried to crane her neck around Stewart's stoic form. But parts of the blackboard were always blocked. More than once, Bitty Jack resigned herself to just listening to the lecture and staring at the stubble of Stewart's soft buzz cut.

At every class, Stewart wore clean shirts, possibly ironed. He had more than one belt and new books, not used. Bitty Jack guessed that he must come from money. At least three dollars a day went to Bitty Jack's baked goods.

Her first week on the job, Tom had pointed Stewart out. "He's got to keep his weight up. Smile at him when you get the chance."

"He's a football player?"

Tom said, "He's better than that."

Stewart Steptoe was Big Al, the University of Alabama's beloved mascot. Big Al was an elephant who rode the waves of the Crimson Tide. He was six feet and gray, naked except for a red T-shirt with BAMA spelled out in white capital letters. He had a short tail and a floppy trunk he could spin to distract the opponent's best player. No matter who blocked which tackle or which cheerleader was losing the elastic in the crotch of her bloomers, he was the star out there. Turning cartwheels, goosing the coach. All the fans loved Big Al. Very few knew the Stewart inside him.

Bitty Jack was curious. When he asked her out, she was curiouser still.

Catching her after class, what he'd said was, "Do you wanna study together?"

Bitty Jack agreed, but she could read those blue eyes. They said *Come a little bit closer. I could take care of you. You can depend on me.* Johnny Iguana had blue eyes. They were familiar and full of promise.

So Bitty Jack met Stewart in the food alley of the Ferguson Student Center.

It was still hot in late September, so Bitty Jack wore shorts. Her legs held the tan from her summer at Chickasaw, yet the freckles were everywhere, all over her knees. Bitty Jack was thankful that Stewart did not buy small sizes in hopes of denying his weight. He must, she thought, shop strictly at Big & Tall. His pants did not gather or rise at the crotch. His belt was not hooked on a custom-made loop. He seemed so soft and cruelty-free. In the line at TCBY, Bitty Jack noticed how the air-conditioning hit his shirt and blew it slightly at the sleeves.

When he got back to their table, Stewart took a bite of yogurt topped with crushed Oreos and broken Chips Ahoys. "I eat a lot of yogurt. It's good for you." He broke off a piece of waffle cone, took a scoop, and offered it to Bitty. "Start with Black Death and work our way to smallpox?"

"Sounds good," Bitty Jack said and tasted the flavor of two cookies together.

Stewart himself was one smart cookie. Better than that, he was an excellent study partner. Bitty Jack had never had someone to study with. With the nearest school district two hours from Summons, the Carlsons' only choice was to teach Bitty at home. They ordered the state curriculum textbooks. They followed the letters as Bitty spelled aloud. They kept the kitchen table clear for Bitty's notes and chapter outlines. When her father ran errands, he'd bring back Hi-Liters. Maybe a ruler. Anything that looked as if it might be of use.

Stewart was always just a little more prepared than she was. He could sketch the prongs of a virus at a moment's notice. He could talk about syphilis as if it were an uncle. He was always laughing. Cheerful. Joshing around. No matter how serious the case study, Stewart could find something to break Bitty's unease. It sometimes was as simple as the way he pronounced a body count. Like Tweety Bird, he might say, "Dee Bwack Puh-weg. Too Tow-zand Wost!"

Their study sessions soon became a regular thing. Twice a week and sometimes a movie. Sometimes Bitty Jack would let him treat her to popcorn. Sometimes she'd share his over-iced Coke. But they never held hands. In the light of the silver screen, they were considerate with the arm rest.

It seemed to Bitty Jack as if every time she got comfortable, Johnny would materialize like a dead usher's ghost. He would walk up the aisle and shine his flashlight on Stewart's shoulder where Bitty Jack was tempted to rest her weary head. She felt guilty sitting in the dark with such a nice, thoughtful boy. So they stayed friends. Neither one brave enough to make a first move.

Until November, when Stewart invited her to Homecoming.

"A date," said Bitty.

"You can't sit on the sidelines, but my parents are like major alums. You can hang with them in the president's box."

"There's nowhere closer I can sit?"

"What?" Stewart grinned. "You don't want to meet the folks?"

The game started at two o'clock, but Big Al had to be there at noon to warm up the crowd. So Bitty Jack's options were to be picked up at the bakery and go early with Stewart or, right before kickoff, meet his parents at a tailgate party and walk in with them.

Stewart said, "You can't miss `em. Their Jeep's got a sticker that says 'Dr. Steptoe Knows the Agony of De Feet' then gives his number. You wouldn't believe how many patients he gets from that sticker."

Bitty Jack said she would believe it, but decided she'd rather go with Stewart than his mother and Tuscaloosa's leading podiatrist.

"Besides," she told Stewart, "I want to see your Before and After."

The morning of Homecoming, the bakery was busier than Bitty Jack had ever seen it. Every group on campus seemed to be sponsoring a brunch. Bitty Jack's roommate was on the Tri Delta/Kappa Alpha pregame party committee. She'd bypassed calling in an order and asked Bitty personally to take care of five trays of cinnamon buns.

"Please," she'd asked her. "I'll get fined if anything's stale."

"Don't worry about it," Bitty told her. "We make everything fresh."

At quarter to five that morning, Bitty Jack passed her roommate in the Tutwiler lobby. Her roommate was coming in from working on the Tri Delta/Kappa Alpha Homecoming float. Bitty Jack was on her way to the bakery and accepted the cup of cold coffee her roommate passed off to her. On the Fifteenth Street bus, she drank it as if each sip brought her closer to a reasonable hour.

From five to eight, she worked the ovens and prep. From eight to ten she was stationed at the cash register. At ten, Tom pulled her cash drawer and hurried her through customers to the private back bakery.

At 11:30, Bitty Jack started to get nervous. She had to finish decorating the booty cake before she changed out of her work clothes. She could get away with a sloppy frosting, but the blue sugar letters had to be lined up evenly across the biggest butt she'd ever seen. The blue dye kept coming off on her fingers. Every time she touched the booty cake, she left blue spots that turned puke-green on top of beige frosting. She had to remix small batches of white and chocolate. Just the right shade to smooth over her mistakes. *Everybody has to be tan*, Bitty Jack thought as she spackled. *God forbid anyone have a white ass.*

The phone rattled in the room filled with only Bitty Jack and cold stainless steel.

Stewart said, "You ready?"

"Almost," said Bitty Jack and slid the booty cake into a box.

In the rest room, she untied her apron strings and used her eye teeth to remove the frosting caught under her fingernails. She picked dried frosting from the lenses of her glasses. She looked in the mirror and picked it off her cheeks and chin. She debated the lipstick in the side pocket of her purse. She put in on. Wiped it off. Put in on. Wiped it off. She changed into a black skirt and white sweater and jumped when Tom knocked twice on the rest room door.

"Your date's here," he shouted. "You Cinderella yet?"

In the parking lot, Stewart patted the front of Big Al's Mascot Mobile. "I use this during the games. Hope it's not too embarrassing."

Bitty Jack took a walk around the van. It was white with the back three rows of seats pulled out at the screws. Along the sides, Crimson waves were painted across the doors. The back windows were covered by a mural of Big Al, his hands on his hips, looking tough but kinda cute. Stewart opened the passenger door and told Bitty Jack how great she looked.

Bitty Jack could not help herself. She whispered, "Do not."

Stewart shut the door and leaned in through the open window. With two fingers, he combed away a hair caught under the bridge of her glasses. He smoothed it behind her ear and repeated. "No, really, you look good."

At Bryant-Denny Stadium, Stewart flashed his pass and the security guards let them walk into the players' tunnel. One of the guards called after Stewart, "Hey, be sure to do that thing you do. My kids love it. I mean, they really love it, man."

"You got it," Stewart shouted and led Bitty Jack to the locker room.

The locker room was empty, but the lockers were set. Down either side of a row of long red benches were open stalls, helmets hung top and center, uniforms on hooks, pads on shelves. The team was playing Texas A & M and the Bama Boosters had painted banners and hung them across the opaque windows. By the coaches' office, the Coke machine hummed. The showers had been scrubbed and the fresh pine scent of generic disinfectant overpowered Stewart's cologne.

Stewart pulled out his keys and led Bitty Jack to his own private dressing room. "It used to be a utility closet, but now it's all mine."

Bitty Jack asked, "Why keep it locked?"

"Other teams used to steal the costume. You know, run it up the flagpole, burn it to get people psyched before the games."

"Has anyone ever tried to steal you?"

"I'm way too heavy to drag off the field."

"I'm sure that's not the only reason you got the job."

Stewart said, "I dance good too."

The first thing she saw when Stewart opened the door was Big Al's head resting bodiless on a swivel chair. His eyes were lifeless, his trunk draped over one ear.

Stewart said, "You can sit there if you don't mind holding him."

"I don't mind," said Bitty Jack and let Stewart lift Big Al's head off the chair and place it carefully on her lap. Big Al's head was the weight of two three-layer booty cakes. His ears dangled by the outsides of her thighs. His trunk swung slightly between her legs spread for balance.

Stewart kept his back to Bitty Jack as he stripped down to his undershirt and boxers. The rest of his costume was stored in a large wooden crate. As he fiddled with the combination lock, Bitty knew he wished he'd opened the crate before he undressed. The back of his neck was turning bright red. He got the combination wrong at first, then pulled out the costume and held in front of him like a sheet.

He started with Big Al's feet because once Stewart was inside the elephant's body, he could not reach past his knees. Big Al's legs were held up by suspenders. A hoop kept his waistband perfectly round. When the band played the fight song it gave him that certain swing. Baby powder prevented chafing. A padded vest softened Stewart's taut chest.

Stewart said, "It's the same stuff Santa uses at the mall."

The largest piece of the costume consisted of Big Al's Bama shirt, his arms and front feet. The front feet were stumplike, no fingers apart from the palms. Inside the costume, Stewart held on to them by easy-grip elastic bands. He did have the option of wearing white gloves. But he thought it was unrealistic: a rootin' tootin' elephant with tiny man hands.

Bitty Jack helped zip and Velcro the back seam of the suit. Inside Big Al's body, Stewart looked smaller, almost petite.

Stewart said, "We can wait for the head."

"It must be really hot in there."

Stewart nodded, the first signs of sweat starting to surface.

There was little help with heat inside the dressing room. No paper, no programs. No Kleenex, no battery-operated fans. There was a narrow steel sink, but Stewart was already dressed. Two pairs of lockers lined the right and left walls, but Bitty was scared to go searching inside. She imagined any number of things springing out at her like snakes from a fake can of peanuts. Within minutes, Stewart's face was a faint shade of pink.

Big Al's head back in her arms, Bitty Jack approached Stewart, stood on her toes and blew cold air onto his throat. When Stewart closed his eyes, Bitty Jack blew on his forehead and face, behind his ears and along the hairline along the back of his neck.

Stewart whispered, "That feels so nice." He opened his eyes and put his front feet on Bitty Jack's hands which held Big Al's head by his two pudgy cheeks.

By the look in Stewart's blue eyes, Bitty knew what was coming. She had seen that look before. That look that said kiss. Up until now, there had only been Johnny. Up until now, Johnny haunted her every day. But the dressing room was too small to house both memories and new interests. Bitty Jack leaned forward despite the mascot's head, Stewart's extra padding, and her own quickening heart that up until now had belonged to another.

Before kickoff, Stewart led Bitty Jack up the steep stadium aisle to the president's box. With Big Al's head secured over his own, Stewart disappeared and Big Al came to life. He took the cement stairs by twos, slapping five with eager fans, doing the

Rocky routine with his arms overhead in a victory *V.* He was working the crowd. Bitty Jack followed, but nobody noticed. All eyes were on the elephant. In the Crimson Tide spirit. Roll Tide Roll Tide, Roll.

When they reached the president's box, Stewart waved through the glass windows, and his parents, along with everyone else, waved back.

Mrs. Steptoe raised her hand and pointed as if to ask, *That her?*

Stewart nodded his heavy gray head. He nudged Bitty Jack with his fat, felt elbow.

Mrs. Steptoe made her way through the hotshot alumnae. She pointed out the cute couple to everyone she maneuvered around. Through the soundproof glass, Bitty Jack could read her lips.

"*Hah-loo,*" she called. "I'm coming! Hah-loo!"

A security guard held the door open as Mrs. Steptoe fell into Stewart's elephant arms. She was five foot two. She lay her cheek against his extra-extra large T-shirt. "I love him like this," she shouted over the noise. "Call me Tootsie. Everybody does."

In the president's box, Mrs. Steptoe introduced Bitty Jack as "Bitty." In a room full of Missies and Bootsies led by a Tootsie, Bitty Jack's name seemed cultured and sane. Mr. and Mrs. Steptoe mingled and let Bitty Jack sit at the front long narrow table and watch their son make the whole town proud.

During halftime, the Million Dollar Band marched onto the field. They spelled BAMA with their bodies, the guy with the tuba dotting the twelve-man exclamation point. The drum major's feathered hat blew easy in the breezy. Stewart held a megaphone and mimed cheers with the cheerleaders. He charged at the refs. He hexed the other team's goal post.

Mrs. Steptoe sat down next to Bitty. She took her hand and seemed to slowly pet it. "You're a nice girl, I can tell."

Bitty Jack said, "Thank you."

"You'll take care of him when he needs it?"

Bitty Jack said, "Sure."

"He's our only one," Tootsie said and squeezed her fingers. "You know what that's like. You're an only. I can feel it. Your parents love you like we love Stewart. To us, you onlies can do nothing that's not right."

The game continued and Alabama won. Bitty Jack said goodbye to the Steptoes, said she'd see them again. She waited for Stewart in the Big Al Mobile. He had given her the keys. Promised something special after their kiss.

He took her to the Alabama Museum of Natural History located in Smith Hall to the right of the library.

"Won't it be closed?"

Stewart said, "Skeleton key." He jangled his key ring and separated a long brass suspicious-looking one. "Job perk."

"What for?"

"Tradition. You know, from one Al to another."

As Stewart unlocked the front door, Bitty Jack played lookout, increasingly ill at ease as if spotlighted by the past. Smith Hall was built entirely of yellow bricks. A former president's wife had grown tired of a campus made of redbrick, but her efforts never reached further than the end of Capstone Drive. There were cars parked, but the drivers were elsewhere, caught up in post-game Homecoming festivities. Music drifted overhead from fraternity backyards. The street lights drew moths and Stewart fumbled with the skeleton key. When the lock clicked out of place, Bitty Jack wondered how many other study buddies he might have brought here before her. She wondered what else might be a mascot tradition. If stories of conquests were passed along with that key.

As if reading her mind, Stewart said, "I've never done this before. I was half scared the thing wouldn't work."

Inside, the darkness caused Bitty Jack to instinctively reach out and take his hand. It was meaty and warm. Tight, padded skin covering palm, thumb, and fingers. Bitty Jack was suddenly comforted. At ease in the grasp of such a great, sturdy man.

Stewart flipped a switch that lit up ten glass cases along the walls of the circular Indian artifact room. Beneath the soft glow of 40 watt voltage, Bitty Jack and Stewart looked at arrow heads and sharp sticks and shallow bowls for crushing corn. There were photos covering the backs of each case: Chocktaws sharpening spears, Cherokees nursing babies, the Creeks rowing down the Black Warrior River, Chief Tuskaloosa telling stories to his tribe.

Bitty Jack stopped at the Chickasaw case. She noticed how different the Indians were than the ones painted on the mess-hall mural back at summer camp. There were no photos of the wild-eyed warriors she had grown up with. No red-skinned men with white stripes across their faces.

Every single case displayed one shrunken head after the next.

"Pretty cool," said Stewart and wrapped his arms around her waist.

Bitty Jack allowed herself to lean back against Stewart's stomach. He was much wider than Johnny. He was as solid as a wall. Bitty Jack felt the static in her hair ignite against his shirt pocket. She tried to stare into the sewn-shut eyelids of the Chickasaw shrunken heads. But they were gray and puckered and made Bitty Jack turn away. She laid her cheek against Stewart's oxford shirt and breathed in the fresh scent of his laundry detergent.

She said, "Mama uses Tide."

Stewart said, "Oh, yeah?"

Bitty Jack nodded, Stewart's cool cotton shirt heating up from the friction of her skin so close to his. She tried to make her fingertips touch behind his back. When she failed, she squeezed him as if she could make him shrink to fit. She couldn't, but that didn't matter. Stewart felt good. So close, breathing at a rate two beats slower than her own. She considered going to sleep, standing up, right there in his arms.

Stewart kissed her before she had the chance. He cradled her so snugly, she just let her body go. His bottom lip was fuller than the top, so as he repositioned each kiss, Bitty Jack felt the conflicting sensations of pink skin and mustache stubble. Her glasses bumped against his face, but still it was easier than it had been before the game.

"I could get used to kissing you," Bitty said before she realized she had said it out loud.

Stewart said, "Oh, yeah?"

"I don't know," she managed, "I don't know. I'm just rambling."

"Ramble on." Stewart grinned and, like a fireman, picked her up and carried her to the next room, to a bench, by the reconstructed saber-toothed tiger.

Nicole

As Nicole spooned sugar over the grapefruit half her mother had set out for her, Mrs. Hicks sat down at the kitchen table and said, "I've got something to tell you."

Nicole ran her thumb back and forth across the serrated edge of her grapefruit spoon. Feeling that familiar itch where her skin started to tear, she wondered if she could saw that spoon all the way to the bone.

Mrs. Hicks didn't give her the chance. "Don't be so melodramatic." She snatched the spoon and rapped it on the table. "You're eighteen, for God's sake. It's good news. Eat your breakfast."

"I get to live in the dorms?"

Mrs. Hicks said, "No. I've signed you up for rush."

Nicole frowned. "Give me back my spoon."

Mrs. Hicks tossed the spoon onto Nicole's quilted place mat. It landed with a tiny thwup. Mrs. Hicks leaned forward and wrapped her hands around her daughter's wrists. While she spoke, she pumped Nicole's arms as if she was trying to get water from a dead, dried-up well. "Listen to me." She tightened her grip. "The decision is made. You're going with me to a pre-rush party at Tootsie's. You'll wear your black sundress. The one with the daisies." She sized up her daughter. "And my white cardigan to cover those scars."

Nicole crossed her arms to hide the welts she had created with a sharp No. 2 pencil. She knew better than to fight her mother anymore. Since the Kelly party fiasco, Nicole had been doing her best to get out of the house on good behavior. Her grounding had become like a debt. Each time she talked back, raised her voice, or gave her mother a hint of trouble, Mrs. Hicks added interest to her punishment: another week, two more months, or, as she was prone to put it, "Whatever I damn well feel like."

At Central East, there had been no more late dates with Sarina after school. As soon as the last bell rang, Mrs. Hicks could be found in the pickup semicircle, the car in neutral, her hands steady at the wheel. Ready. Set. Go. She hired tutors to account for Nicole's time at home. Whenever Mrs. Hicks had plans, Nicole had a tutor. As a result, Nicole's grades legitimately improved, and Mrs. Hicks was free to join the likes of Tootsie Steptoe at monthly alumnae meetings of the University of Alabama chapter of Delta Delta Delta.

As far back as Nicole could remember, her mother had been a dedicated Tri Delt alum. Since joining the sorority, she had been best friends with Tootsie. So much so that it was she who had given the Steptoes their nicknames back in college. Mrs. Steptoe was Tootsie. Dr. Steptoe was Footsie. Nicole didn't know if the name had anything to do with podiatry. But every time his name was mentioned, whoever heard it would nod their head and concur, "Good old Footsie!" But only Tootsie caught him. And Mrs. Hicks took full credit for setting the couple up.

In regard to her sorority, Mrs. Hicks nabbed credit for just about everything. She was the Standards Chair and, each year, she sponsored the Tri Delta Poker Play-Off. It was held at the Hicks' house the Sunday following pledge initiation. Tri Delt alumnae from six Southern states tried to win their way in through their chapters' qualifying tournaments. The event went under the guise of charity and good fun, but there was a small side pot no winner would be embarrassed to take home.

Tootsie and Footsie lived in Lakewood, two houses from the Kellys, just ten minutes from Cheshire. The street was silent for the most part. As quiet as Nicole's friendship with Sarina had been since her panic attack in the cul-de-sac.

Pulling up to the curb, Mrs. Hicks told her daughter, "You're doing the right thing. Letting me help you like this."

Nicole let her gaze fall into her own lap. She surveyed the sheer pink nail polish her mother had insisted she borrow after breakfast.

Mrs. Hicks said, "Tri Delta can change your life. It's still the best house on campus. So stay close to me and let everyone know that you're my daughter."

Nicole felt funny in her mother's good graces. It was almost nauseating. Nicole was so anxious that she did not notice the blue Prelude at the end of the driveway. It belonged to Sarina, a second-year Delt.

The party was just as Mrs. Hicks had described. Finger food and handshakes. Alumnae and sisters staying in Tuscaloosa over summer vacation. The alumnae were there to push the local girls; the sisters to check out that new crop of daughters and the sweethearts of certain sons. When official rush started one week before school, the Tri Delts would see more than one thousand high school graduates. They picked fifty to pledge. It was crucial that Nicole stand out in their minds.

"You'll stand out because you're an easy cut," Mrs. Hicks whispered as she poured the last of the punch. "You've got your looks, but you are far, far from the pick of the litter."

"Oh, she's not that bad!" said Tootsie as she pushed her body between the Hicks to dump a fresh ring of rainbow sherbet into the punch bowl. The sherbet had been packed and refrozen in a pound-cake pan. In the champagne pool, it floated and spun slightly like the last inner tube at the end of the world.

Mrs. Hicks said, "I'm just being honest."

Tootsie wrapped an arm around Nicole's shoulders. She pulled Nicole's hair away from her ear and whispered loud enough for her best friend to hear, "Your mom's a little worry-wart." She pinched Nicole's waist in a way that could force a giggle out of anyone.

Mrs. Hicks said, "Tootsie, be serious!"

"Now, now." Tootsie reached down and took Nicole's hand. "I see the natives approaching. Big Chief Toot Toot know cold sky in bowl bring tribe to buffet table. Me see-um now."

Mrs. Hicks said, "Nicole, hold your shoulders back."

Tootsie said, "Relax. You're making *me* tense. Go do your thing. I'll take care of Nicole."

Mrs. Hicks relented and walked away from the buffet and straight toward Sarina.

Sarina was by the living-room picture window. Nicole had not noticed her because she was surrounded by the Macon triplets, driven down from Birmingham to spend the weekend with their Great Aunt Gertrude, who, every year, turned her four-acre front yard into the Tri Delta Christmas Tree Auction for the crack-baby wing at Druid City Hospital. Old Gertrude liked to piss off the Boy Scouts and their puny trees. The eighty-nine-year-old lady was a Tri Delta supreme.

With one motion, Mrs. Hicks managed to touch all three of the backs of the Macon triplets' necks. She said something like "More punch?" and the Macon girls came barreling toward Nicole as if the ice would melt as soon as they exhaled.

Tootsie said, "Whoa! Slow down. It's not going anywhere. Is it?" She released Nicole's hand and offered her the ladle. "Is it, pumpkin?"

Nicole shook her head and tried to get the punch into the cups without spilling any on the white lace tablecloth. It wasn't easy and it was even harder to concentrate with her mother and Sarina holed up in the living room corner.

"Relax," Tootsie told her. "You're doing just fine."

Nicole nodded and appeased the Macon triplets and five girls from Georgia and some of Tootsie's friends and the pledge director herself. Tootsie introduced Nicole to every person she served.

"Nicole," she said, each time as naturally as the first, "is the Hicks girl. Isn't she a sport helping out on no notice? It's my tennis elbow again. Call me crazy, but I just can't keep my hands off the doc-tah's fuzzy widdle bawls!"

Without fail, whoever heard this would laugh and swat the air. "Oh, Tootsie, you are so bad!"

Tootsie would follow with the sincere note "Nicole is most definitively an RTP."

Rush to Pledge was serious business. An RTP had better get in.

That afternoon, Tootsie and Mrs. Hicks were able to campaign for Nicole. Once official rush started, they would be practically powerless. Alumnae were not allowed on campus. The active sisters ran the show. Although it did not happen frequently, legacies could be rejected. Once cut, there was no second chance. A girl was left with very few choices. If she wasn't cut from rush altogether, she could pledge a lesser house or do the extreme: leave Tuscaloosa and rush Auburn two weeks later. Maybe the girl would make Tri Delt there. But everyone knew that wasn't as good. It was an agricultural college, for crying out loud. At the Alabama-Auburn football games, those girls were known as Delta Dogs.

Mrs. Summers was an Auburn Tri Delt. Nicole wondered if her mother was currently rubbing that in Sarina's poreless face.

"She's just telling it like it is." Tootsie took the ladle away from Nicole and gently let it sink into the remainder of the punch. "Come." She motioned to an empty window-seat. "Sit."

"What's she doing?" Nicole asked. "What's she want with her?"

Tootsie moved a few throw pillows aside, sat down, and made room for Nicole. She looked out the window into the neighborhood laced with cars. "I miss our Jeep," she said wistfully. "Stewart took it for the summer. He's a Black Foot at Camp Chickasaw. Do you know it? Black Feet paint the cabins and keep up the grass."

Nicole waited for the answer to her question. *What's my mother want with my Ree?*

"His girlfriend's parents run that camp. She grew up there. Can you imagine? Making your way out of the middle of nowhere. Working through college. That girl is a trouper."

"What house did she pledge?" Nicole tried to be cordial, but *My mother, what's she want?* ran rampant through her brain.

"She's too poor to pledge," Tootsie said sort of sadly. "But Stewart just loves her. We think she's the One. Her background doesn't matter. If Stewart were a girl, I'd be much more concerned."

"Mrs. Steptoe. My mother?"

"Sure, sure. I'm sorry, pumpkin. Your mother. Your mother's making sure you get a bid next month. She's talking to your old friend. Telling her to push for you from inside the house."

Nicole remembered the car rides to Central West, the prom plans laid out, Sarina's call for help made to her over anyone else in the whole damned school. She felt terrible that she had let Sarina down. By the time she arrived at the Kelly pre-prom party, Sarina had been forced to find another way home. Nicole had ruined everything. Poor Ree. Poor, poor Ree. In the wake of such a disastrous rescue, Nicole understood why Sarina snubbed her at Central East the following year. Then came college, which kept Sarina on campus, too far from Cheshire to reach out for Nicole.

Nicole thought of how much closer Sarina would be to her if their lives were parallel. If they both lived at Tri Delta. If they were again cheering for the same home team. She told Tootsie, "I think Sarina would help me anyway."

Tootsie said, "If there's one thing I've learned, you can never be too sure what young girls will do."

She took Nicole's hand again. It was a habit of hers, taking people by the hand. Nicole had known Mrs. Steptoe all of her life, but the habit never ceased to catch her off guard. Mrs. Steptoe's hands were always lotioned and toasty. Nicole tried to wiggle her fingers, stiff and seizured in Tootsie's like a stroke.

"Relax," said Tootsie. She massaged Nicole's hand. "I can see things about you, just as I can see Stewart's girl could be his wife. She's got strong hands."

Nicole felt pins and needles in her fingers. She squirmed from the pressure that Tootsie applied.

"You're confused," said Tootsie. "I know you're confused. You don't want to rush because your mother wants you to. You do want to rush because you could be with Sarina."

Nicole didn't say anything.

"You have feelings for her. I know. You can't help it. I know."

Nicole felt very tired. She stared across the room to where Sarina crossed her arms and her mother kept on talking.

Tootsie said, "She's telling her about what her mother did when we were in college, you know, before the wheel."

Tootsie laughed at her own joke, then took a moment, then said, "Did you know Sarina's mother went to Auburn 'cause we didn't let her in?"

Nicole shook her head.

"She got blackballed because of what your mother found out."

Nicole knew that she should ask. "What'd she find out?"

"That Sarina's mother was a thief. When we were juniors, your mother and I, she was the Tri Delta pledge director and I was a Rho Chi. Rho Chis take the rushees around. We're incognito. Tourguiders-slash-counselors made up of girls from all the sororities. We're supposed to remain impartial. Help the rushees. Absolutely no contact with our houses. But your mother and I couldn't help ourselves and she asked me about a girl in my group."

"Sarina's mother."

"Exactly. She said there was something about her. She was too friendly or too weird. I can't even remember. But she kept getting called back. She was prettier then. Not as heavy as she is today."

"So what happened?"

"So, on Serious Night, your mother planted my engagement ring in the rest room and that woman took it. Your mother stopped her as soon as she came out. It was right in her hand, ready to walk out the door."

"How do you know she wasn't giving it back?"

"We knew."

Nicole pulled her hand free from Tootsie's ever-tightening hold. "So what does this have to do with anything?"

"Your mother is the Standards Chair. She held her tongue when Sarina rushed last year. Sarina got in so that she could help you get in. If your mother wanted to, she could let the Summers' secret out. Make the other girls think stealing runs in the family."

"So she's threatening her?"

"It's worked before. Didn't you ever notice that Sarina's mother never makes it to the poker play-offs? She made it once. Placed third at Auburn semifinals. But when your mother found out she marched right across the street. Told her to forfeit her spot or she'd let the rumors fly. She'd have no cheaters in her house. How could your mother keep her eyes on the cards, when she had to watch the silverware, her jewelry, the kitchen sink—"

"She wouldn't steal the sink. Plus Sarina loves me."

"Sweet, sweet pumpkin. You are blinded by that girl. Believe me, if there's one thing I've learned, Sarina Summers is not the best seed in the pack. I've held her hand. I've seen how deep her selfishness goes." Tootsie stood up, but when Nicole did not join her, she bent over, face-to-face, and whispered, "To the core."

On the first day of rush, Nicole stood with her group on the lawn mower–streaked grass of the Tri Delta front yard. For more than social rank, Tri Delta stood out. It was a modern round building—sort of like a big birthday cake. She looked down Sorority Row at the other clusters of sixty girls teetering on the lawns of Alpha Chi, Phi Mu, Kappa Kappa Gamma and other houses she could not recognize far off in the distance. When the clock hit 11:00 A.M., Nicole would attend the first of fifteen introductory parties.

Ice-water teas were not really get-to-know-yous. Mrs. Hicks had briefed her on what really went on. On the surface, the parties lasted two days and only ice water was served. They were fifteen minutes a piece, with fifteen-minute breaks for the Rho Chis to get their girls together and get them to the next house. Most girls thought that these parties were their chance to put their best foot forward, to make a good impression, to become something they never were in their hometowns of Not As Popular As She'd Like To Be. But they were wrong. The truth was that before the first rushee stepped into an Alabama sorority house, every decision as to who would be kept and who would be cut had already been made. For the past two weeks the sisters had gathered in their sorority basements or rooms where the windows were blacked out with construction paper. GPAs were examined. Class activities tallied. The pledge director ran a slide show where every rushee's picture was flashed and pros and cons were thrown out in the dark

"She screwed her high school principal!"

"She throws more leg than a stable full of horses!"

"Boob job!"

"Boob job!"

"I hear she has an eating disorder."

When Nicole's picture came up, Sarina had been instructed by Mrs. Hicks to say, "Nicole Hicks. Rush to Pledge." The pledge director had been instructed by Tootsie to second the vote, surely cinching a Tri Delta bid.

Before Nicole knew it, Sorority Row was filled with clamor and commotion. Sisters cheered and filed out of each house. They sang. They moved their hands in unison. Some of the sisters took a rushee by the hand and led her into the house while the remaining girls clapped.

Inside, the rushees were traded among teams of five Tri Delta sisters. The sisters were very polite. They were full of Coke for breakfast. They asked Nicole questions and really seemed interested in her answers.

Nicole was relieved that no one mentioned the report card incident or her police record for causing a public disturbance. She hardly had to talk at all. Everything seemed choreographed. One smooth-moving machine that had been tinkered with by her mother.

When it was time to go, she was passed to Sarina.

"It's okay," said Sarina. "I want you to join."

Nicole felt Sarina lace her fingers between her own. They joined a double line of optimists and sisters that moved through the receiving room like the largest bridal party ever.

"I want us to be friends again," Sarina whispered as the other girls sang *Go TRI Delta, Ba-Dum-Da-Dum!* "I'm really sorry I haven't been around much. It would be so much easier if you'd pledge Tri Delt."

Nicole looked at Sarina from the corners of her eyes. Her lips seemed fuller. Her lashes even darker. She was still so put together. So well groomed. A perfect vision. Nicole let Sarina hug her as she sent her out the door.

Back on the Tri Delta lawn, Nicole saw only Sarina as all the girls waved from the windows, then shut the shutters to do whatever they did until opening their doors to the next group of girls.

Nicole knew what they did. Her mother had told her. As soon as the doors were shut, clipboards were pulled out from under sofa cushions, from inside of drawers. Notes were made. Votes were taken by method of Heads Down, Hands Up. All the girls stood with their eyes on the carpet. When a rushee's name was called, all hands shot toward the ceiling. Fingers spread for yes. Fists equaled no. The greatest amount of cutting took place after the ice-water teas. Some girls were cut from rush altogether. Others were requested by every single house. On the third day of rush, the Rho Chis gave their rush group a list of sororities who had invited them back for skit nights.

Skit nights were half-hour parties, where the rushees were served punch and cookies. The houses put on shows to keep everybody interested. There were four parties per night. Alpha Chis did Alice in Wonderland. Zetas did Snoopy and the Gang. The Deltas were the best because they did Motown. Sisters wore tailored tuxes and long sequined gowns. They sang "Ain't too proud to beg." It could be quite inspiring.

During the course of these parties, the real judgments were

made. The rushees were scrutinized. They were grilled on cold smiles. At some houses a girl's character was reduced to What Her Daddy Does and Who Her Mother Was.

In Nicole's case, her own doings overshadowed her parents' accomplishments. Even if her daddy did anchor the news, no one wanted to give a bid to Nicole. So while the other girls in her rush group hurried from lawn to lawn, Nicole sat in the Hicks house and waited for 10:00 P.M. on the second of skit nights when she was expected at Delta Delta Delta, the only house to ask her back.

On Serious Night, the rushees went to only three houses. The parties lasted an hour and a lot of crying and confessions went on. At the Tri Delt house, Nicole touched the pearls her mother had fastened around her neck. They had belonged to Mrs. Hicks' mother and they were not imitation.

"They'll scare the other girls," Mrs. Hicks had whispered giddily. "You can relax now. You're a shoo-in."

On Squeal Day it turned out that her mother was right. Nicole got her bid in the courtyard of the Ferguson Center. The Rho Chis gave them out and once the girls got them in their hot little hands, they went running toward Sorority Row. It was a half-mile run, but Nicole ran with them—past the Natural History Museum, through the quad—faster and faster toward the houses that chose them.

Nicole and forty-nine others stopped at Tri Delta. Sisters were everywhere, screaming "Find your pledge sister!" The pledges streamed into the sorority house. It was the first time Nicole had been past the living room. She ran through the dining room, through the kitchen, straight upstairs. She searched for her name on every sister's bedroom door. When she found it, spelled out in bright cardboard letters, she pounded hard against the wood.

"Who is it?" came a grandmotherly voice.

"Nicole Hicks!"

"Who?"

"Nicole Hicks!"

"Say it right."

Nicole thought for a second. Should she use her middle name? Should she say Miss Nicky? Then she understood. She called, straining to raise her voice over the other pledges going berserk on every side of her, "It's me! Pledge Nicole!"

Sarina swung open the door and, in one swift yank, pulled Nicole's shirt over her head. For about two seconds, Nicole stood in her bra in the hallway. Sarina jerked her into her room. There were framed pictures everywhere. Sarina and other girls pressing their cheeks to one another, saying cheese for the camera, holding out see-through plastic cups full of beer for proof of party.

Sarina rooted under her reading pillow. She produced a blue T-shirt with SQUEAL DAY ironed onto the back. Delta Delta Delta was spelled out in white and gold on the front pocket. "Put it on!" she said, beaming. "Put it on! Put it on!"

Sarina grinned as Nicole pulled the T-shirt over her head.

"Tuck it in, tuck it in!" Sarina yanked Nicole's belt off its hook. She unzipped her shorts and stuffed Nicole's shirt in, her nails slightly scratching her waist and her hips. Sarina bounced like she had in their cheerleader days. "Let's go!" she said. "Lake Party! Let's go!"

The lake party was the first of many. Nicole had fun because Sarina never left her side. The SAEs crashed and Sarina introduced them. They got Nicole drinks. They flirted. They joked. All the girls congratulated Nicole and she congratulated the other pledges.

"It's going to be tough," Sarina said over margaritas. "But once pledging is over, the pressure's off."

"What pressure?" Nicole said as one of the SAEs took off his jeans shorts and sprinted butt-nekkid straight into the shallow part of the lake.

"Just trust me," Sarina told her. "Promise me, you'll do what I say."

Nicole looked at Sarina, her white shoulders pink from SPF 6, her tank top loose from too many washes. She tried to remember the last time they had stood this close in public. The last time they were seen as sisters. Although Nicole had never seen them as sisters. It had been years. But the years were now just a memory. "I'll do anything," Nicole said. "Just tell me what you want."

A month later, pledging was halfway through. Nicole's class was the first pledge group to pledge for only eight weeks. From Sarina's class back through history, pledging had lasted the entire fall semester. But there had been too many lawsuits over so-called hazing. So the Greek Council had cut the pledge time in half. The sisters and alumnae were not very happy.

Sarina had said, "It's too little time to really get to know a girl."

Mrs. Hicks had told Nicole this would work to her advantage. "It gives you less time to screw up. You can hold out for eight weeks."

"Sure," Nicole had said, but a month later she was totally exhausted.

School was in full swing and Delta Delta Delta insisted on organizing her whereabouts. She was to eat lunch and dinner at the house. Attend study hall four times a week. There were fund-raising projects for local charities. Carnivals for Cervical Cancer. Marathon Walks to sponsor Juvenile Diabetes. There were pledge meetings and miscellaneous meetings and fraternity swaps at least twice a week.

And then there was Homecoming. The pledges did all the work. They painted the banners and posters and the faces of each other. They built the float. They rode it and threw candy at the faculty's kids. They went in droves to the polls to vote for Homecoming queen, who had been picked for this fall's win the past spring by the Machine.

The Machine was the secret white Greek political party (the six black Greek houses were set on the edge of campus on West Fourth Street and equally distant from the machine). The Machine told members who to vote for in every conceivable category. Even though independents outnumbered Greeks six to one, the Greeks ran the university because they were organized and cast their ballots. Each school year, the Machine rotated its houses through important positions. The Homecoming queen was always a Greek. So was the student body president. The Golden Key Captain too. Once the university president had to overthrow the election for *Crimson White* editor. The independent candidate had been a *Tuscaloosa News* columnist for three years running. Since she was thirteen, she'd interned with her dad, who was the top crime reporter at *The Birmingham Herald.* For fun, the Machine put up a bruiser from the dregs of ATO. His nickname was Dick Brain. Guess which one won.

Throughout all Homecoming activities, each pledge was given a goldfish.

"If it dies," Sarina told Nicole, "you don't get in. If it dies, even legacy can't save you."

Nicole brought the fishbowl to eye level. The bowl was the size of a Florida orange. The fish bobbed unconcerned under the water.

Sarina said, "Be sure to keep its water clean."

Nicole looked through the bowl at her friend. The glass made Sarina's eyebrows warp into one.

"Did you hear me?" Sarina said. "Don't let it die."

"I won't." Nicole looked at the fish, and the fish, lacking eyelids, had no choice but to look back. "I'll name him Jeepers Peepers."

"Whatever. Just make sure he doesn't end up in the toilet."

Nicole kept the fish with her wherever she went. In the car, she put the bowl in the coffee cup receptacle. In the tub, she set Jeepers Peepers on the porcelain edge.

Mrs. Hicks said she'd watch Nicole's fish. Nicole could leave him with her and pick him up when she needed him.

Nicole declined. Like the other pledges, she brought Jeepers Peepers to every meal at the Delta house. Mixed in with the gravy boats and salt-and-pepper shakers, goldfish swam at every table.

"This is getting gross," said one of the seniors.

Another one said, "If I did it, they're doin' it. You know it's tradition."

Always first to go for seconds, sometimes thirds, Nicole reached around Jeepers Peepers and poured gravy over her pot roast, mashed potatoes, even her corn.

After Homecoming, the pledges were taken to a cabin in Deerlick Park. They were blindfolded and arranged in five rows of ten. They were pushed to their knees, their hands tied behind their backs.

Nicole was at the end of the front line. She knew she should be scared when Mary Lou Jenkins began to cry. What had begun as a nervous giggle soon catapulted into high-pitched hysterics.

"I can't," she spat out through sad, sorry sobs. "I can't. You can't make me!"

Nicole shook her head in hopes of loosening her blindfold, but the knot was secure and she only saw stars.

"Just do it," said the pledge director. "It's not like we're branding you."

"I can't!"

"Yes you can. You can and you will."

Whatever it was they wanted Mary Beth Jenkins to do, she finally did and seemed to take pleasure in watching everyone that followed her do it. Her dolphinlike laugh could be heard over the other pledges' giggles or shrieks or *No Ways!*

When Nicole's blindfold was removed, it took a few hairs out of the back of her head. She turned around to see who the culprit was only to realize that all the Tri Delts and nine knowing pledges were staring at her. Nicole turned her head front and center. Fifty pledge sisters held goldfish bowls. Nine of those bowls held nothing at all.

Sarina stood in front of Nicole and held out Jeepers Peepers like a snowman in a snow globe about to be shook.

Nicole said, "You're kidding."

Sarina twisted her head from side to side. She clenched her teeth so hard the bleach job showed. She brought her fishbowl to her open lips. As the cupful of water ran down Sarina's chin, it soaked her shirt and Nicole could see that her bra clipped in the front. When the water was gone, Nicole saw Jeepers Peepers through the bottom of the bowl. He slapped against Sarina's smile. With one quick motion, Sarina turned his body with her tongue. She clamped her teeth down on his tail. She took the bowl away and brought her face to hover over Nicole's.

Nicole knew what was expected.

In the moments before she opened her mouth, Nicole thought of what it meant to be a Tri Delt. Social acceptance. A new lease on life. She considered the silence that she'd once known too well. She smelled Sarina's lipstick. She thought, *One, two three.*

As she took Jeepers Peepers into her mouth, Nicole knew she should swallow him like an oyster, but she didn't. She bit into him with her molars and tasted the sweet, salty pop that went off in her head.

Before the pledge meeting the following week, Nicole asked to be excused. She told the pledge director that she had left her pledge book in Sarina's room.

The pledge director said, "If you're late, that's a fine."

The more fines a pledge was given, the worse her chances.

Fines were given for tardiness and absences, giving lip or having an attitude. The pledge book was the Tri Delta bible. When they weren't studying for freshman algebra or Chem 101 or washing their hair for the Thursday night swap or playing guitar at the local orphanage or teaching tire factory workers how to read, pledges were memorizing the pledge book. At any given moment, the pledge director could spring a question on them.

"Who were the five founding sisters?"

"When was the Alabama chapter established?"

"What's our flower?"

"What's our house mother's maiden name?"

If a pledge answered incorrectly, she got a fine. Five dollars for a true not a false. Thirty for being late. Fifty for truancy. There was a big bulletin board by the dining room. A Polaroid of each pledge was placed in the starting square of a grid that stretched the length of the tallest girl there. Whenever a fine was issued, the pledge director Magic Markered a red *X* on the grid. Mary Beth Jenkins had been the perfect pledge until the moment she bucked the goldfish. Now, she had six. Nicole had eighteen. Twenty fines put her on probation. Twenty-five and she was out.

The pledge director told Sarina to keep an eye on her pledge sister.

In her room, Sarina said, "Nicole, you've got to get it together. You're really close to getting kicked out."

Nicole said, "How do they expect me to have time for all this? It's like the Citadel."

"Is not."

"Is too."

Sarina said, "It's not like we're forcing you to get drunk and streak through a frat party."

Nicole said, "Did you see Vicki Capshaw at the Kappa Sig 'Round the World?"

"She can't handle her liquor. That's not our fault."

"But she wouldn't have been there if she wasn't a Delta."

"She wouldn't have a social life if she wasn't a Delta."

Nicole said, "Please tell me you don't really believe that."

Sarina said, "I didn't see you having such a bad time with Jimmy What's-His-Name."

"He wouldn't leave me alone."

"Why should he? People socialize."

Nicole took Sarina's arm. She squeezed tighter with every syllable. "Why can't it be just you and me?"

"Because we're not married at the hip."

"But we were once."

"We were kids."

Applause from the meeting pushed through the carpet. Someone must have won something. Made the Dean's List. Gotten engaged.

Nicole picked up her pledge book. She said, "The pledge director's driving us too hard."

Sarina looked past Nicole. She scanned the pictures on her windowsill. "So take it," she said and left Nicole in her room surrounded by frozen faces of girls Nicole would never accept as substitutions.

At Sunday breakfast, Nicole confided in her parents. "It's really hard. I barely sleep. I feel like I'm drunk three nights a week."

Mrs. Hicks said, "So control yourself."

Mr. Hicks said, "Be careful."

"I am careful, but I feel like I'm losing it."

Mr. Hicks said, "It's all part of growing up."

Mrs. Hicks said, "Nicole, do you really need that much syrup?"

Nicole shrugged and put Mrs. Butterworth back on the table.

Mrs. Hicks said, "I've got something to show you after you finish."

Mr. Hicks said, "Girl stuff?"

Mrs. Hicks reached across the butter dish and put her hand on her husband's. The diamond on her index finger slid toward her thumb.

Mr. Hicks said, "Should we get that resized?"

Mrs. Hicks smiled at her husband, then turned to Nicole. "Let's go to my room."

Nicole followed her mother. Behind her, she heard her father stacking the breakfast plates, carrying all three glasses in one hand by their rims.

Mrs. Hicks pulled a white dress out of her closet. She lifted the dry cleaning bag. She said, "I want you to wear this on Pledge Promise Night. It was the dress I wore when it was my turn."

Nicole held the dress up. She looked at the puffy short sleeves in the full-length closet mirror. "It's beautiful," she said, "but you're so much smaller than me."

"Nicole, you're not overweight. We're just talking ten pounds." She pulled a package of over-the-counter diet pills from a shoe box on the top shelf of her closet. She handed them to her daughter. She said, "It would mean so much to me."

Nicole said, "You want me to starve myself?"

"I want you to get your letters. I want you to show up at my poker party wearing your Tri Delta pin."

Nicole said, "Where's your pin?"

Mrs. Hicks bent her elbow, bringing her hand to her face. The diamond on her hand made her eyes sparkle. "This ring is my pin."

In one hand, Nicole felt the weight of her mother's dress. In the other, the pills felt like nothing at all.

Mrs. Hicks said, "You've only got a week left. Do this for

me. Do it for yourself. I swear," Mrs. Hicks pulled the dry cleaning bag back into place, "at the poker party, you can finally relax."

For the next week, Nicole took a diet pill whenever she got hungry. Her mother fed her breakfast. She halved the grapefruit and took the sugar off the table. At the Delta house, Nicole ate salads. She followed Sarina down the salad bar and took half of whatever she tonged onto her plate.

Sarina said, "It's good to see you taking care of yourself."

Nicole said, "I'm trying."

Nicole got by on three hours of sleep. She went to all the parties. She swallowed kamikazes. She studied on a beer buzz and used her pledge book as a pillow. By the night of initiation, she had lost enough weight.

Nicole tried to catch her breath as her mother pulled the zipper up her back.

"You're sweating," said her mother.

"I'm nervous," said Nicole.

Mrs. Hicks said, "I'm proud of you."

Nicole murmured, "What?"

Driving, Nicole watched the other cars seem to speed by her. The night was blurry. The Burger King looked like McDonald's. She parked her car on campus and made her way to Sorority Row. It was Pledge Promise Night for all the sororities. Girls in white dresses roamed through the trees, across intersections, up walkways like ghosts. Nicole was so wired, when she got to the Tri Delta lawn, she sat on the grass.

"Nicole," said a pledge, "you're ruining your dress."

Nicole wanted to lie down and feel the wet blades of grass flatten beneath her face. She wanted to curl up in a ball and roll off the sidewalk and spend the night under a car. The Volkswagen Cabriolet with the Miss Amy vanity plate seemed awful nice. It looked cool under that car. It looked safe and oh so quiet.

Nicole was pulled to her feet as soon as the front door was opened. The Tri Delts came out. They wore black dresses and thin gold chains with Tri Delta pendants. They sang sweet songs that intermingled with the others down Sorority Row.

Sarina found Nicole and took her inside. On the way up the porch stairs, Nicole tripped, falling into her friend.

"Nicole," hissed Sarina, "what the hell is wrong with you?"

Nicole shook her head, sending the living room chairs somersaulting like children.

"Take your place," Sarina told her and steadied Nicole in line with the other pledges.

The lights were out. They were each given candles. In front of them, their pledge sisters also stood with candles. Behind them, the juniors and seniors were holding candles too. The sisters began to sing. They circled the pledges. They blew out their candles. They kept on singing. They kept on getting closer. "Smile," they whispered, "smile. You're a sister. You're one of us. You're in."

Nicole very much wanted to be by herself. But that was not allowed. She was hot. She could feel her mother's dress pasted to her armpits and back, her bra glued at the under wire, sweat pooling beneath her breasts. She felt dizzy. She felt sick. She wanted to go upstairs and crawl into a closet.

But the girls kept her up all night. They poured her champagne. They toasted and toasted. Their voices were shrill. They never shut up.

Around four in the morning, Nicole grabbed Sarina. "Take me home," she begged. "Take me home. I feel sick."

Sarina said, "Snap out of it. It's a party. Would you just chill?"

Nicole took off toward the stairs.

Nicole knew the pledge director would see this and disapprove. She'd send Sarina after her. She'd say she was responsible.

Nicole locked herself in the upstairs bathroom. There was no one else around and she was prepared to wait all night to be rescued. But Sarina showed up right on her heels. She put her back against the door and Nicole heard the lace on her dress drag against the wood as Sarina slid down into a sitting position.

Nicole was impressed. *She must really love me.*

"Nicole," Sarina called, "what the hell is your damage?"

Nicole crouched down and touched the material from Sarina's black frock sticking under the bathroom door. She gathered a fistful and tried to gather the rest of Sarina by tugging her, tugging her under the half-inch gap.

"Quit it!" Sarina said, yanking her dress back.

Nicole repeated the words that had become her anthem. "Why can't it be just you and me?"

Sarina did not answer.

"Ree?"

Still no answer.

Nicole got on her stomach and peered under the door. She saw nothing but carpet, the beginning of an empty hall. "Ree?"

Not a word. And then, as if Sarina's voice came from some small compartment within Nicole's heart, *I can't believe I let your mother talk me into this. I'm through with you. We're done.*

Nicole went for the faucets. There were cosmetic bags everywhere. Plastic, canvas, some with fold-out locks. Pink ones, travel-sized, even stuffed with trouser socks. Nicole jammed her hands into zippered mouths. She pulled out anything that bit at her fingers. In her fists, the instruments looked like the prongs of two rakes.

With wide, circling swipes, she tore at her arms. The blood came quicker than it had in the past. Maybe her cutting was deeper because of the booze and the pills and that long empty hallway. Maybe laughter from downstairs pushed her tolerance through the roof. She was frenzied and careless. Dazed, until she saw the blood gliding quietly down the length of her dress.

"Ree!" Nicole cried.

She stumbled for the door. The blood made the handle slippery as she struggled with the lock. Turn it left? Turn it right? Push or pull? What, damn it, what?

"Ree!"

When Nicole opened the door, she fell onto the carpet. Blood dropped onto the creamy wool blend, and Nicole got to her knees to mop with the hem of her mother's souring hand-me-down.

Sarina came out of her room as the other girls came up the stairs. By the time Sarina reached Nicole, the hallway was humming with Tri Delta sisters, all pushing forward, toward Nicole's mental breakdown.

Nicole got to her feet and reached out for her friend. Sarina stepped back, so Nicole wiped her hands on her dress and reached out again.

"I'm clean," Nicole whispered. "You can touch me. I'm clean."

"You're crazy," Nicole heard, and then there was nothing but the floor.

Nicole regained full consciousness in the communal bathroom of Delta Delta Delta. She was laid out on the tiles, her stocking feet propped above her head on a chair. She itched and she was hot. She wondered where everybody had hurried off to. At first, she thought she must have passed out, hallucinated, and had her Tri Delta pin torn off by mistake. But soon the mid-morning sun held her face and said No. Nicole fought the four wool blankets wrapped around her like a straitjacket.

Leaning against the row of sinks and flipping through a magazine, a nurse said, "Good. You're awake." She plodded to the door in her fat-soled shoes. She stuck her head out and called, "Yo! We got a live one!"

Nicole tried to get to her feet, but there was no release from the tight woolen blankets. Her balance was off because her legs were wrapped together. Her arms were bound to her sides. Nicole began to panic.

"We sewed you in, honey," the nurse chuckled, then followed with the motions of licking a thread and pushing it bull's-eye smack dab through a needle. "Hold on. We'll cut you loose. Just wait two secs till the girls come up."

"Does my mother know?"

The nurse said, "Just wait two seconds."

There were just a few of them: the pledge director, the Tri Delta pres, the VP of Etiquette. No Sarina.

"She's not here," said the pledge director. "It's in your own interest."

"Did she go home?"

"That's what you're going to do."

Nicole was rolled over onto her stomach. She heard the scissors cut the thread laced up her back. She read the minds that accused *You ruined our party.* When the blankets were folded away from her, she could smell the dried blood before the girls pulled her to her feet.

"Campus security is driving you home. Get your purse from downstairs and get ready to go."

As she took her first few steps, Nicole realized she was stitched and sedated. For the first time, she had cut too far. Skinny black tracks criss-crossed along both arms. They hurt like hell, but she had to lift them and reach out for the walls to move ahead and maintain her balance. Through the hall and down the stairs, Nicole strained to hear some sound particular to Sarina.

Not a peep.

In what seemed like moments, Nicole was handed over to two campus security officers, packed into the backseat of a Night Ride minivan, and driven through the side streets of Tuscaloosa to Cheshire Way.

The Poker Play-Off was on.

Cars were parked along the curb and up on the lawn. There were Greek triangles pasted on every single bumper. This year, Mrs. Hicks had hired a valet. Professional dealers were bused up from Biloxi. It was her best tournament yet.

As campus security escorted Nicole to the front door, she could see the alumnae through the windows. She knew Tootsie's back by the lucky cardigan she wore every year. It was red with a splayed royal flush sewn between her shoulder blades. She fanned her neck with a napkin. Despite air-conditioning, it got warm with so many people in the house. Floor fans were set at every table to cool the ladies' stockinged feet without mussing their well-managed hair. A good hairdo was part of a bluff.

There was little talk with seven-card stud. The players kept their eyes on their cards or the others seated at their gray foldout tables. They didn't look up when the caterers brought their drinks. They were serious. Matching wits against wits. The swift patter of shuffles rose right out the chimney.

When one of the officers rang the bell, a caterer answered. She was young with black-rimmed, unstylish glasses. Obviously not the lady of the house.

Nicole grew impatient as the caterer wiped her hands on her apron and lost all color at the sight of the brown, crusty maze decorating the front of Nicole's once-white dress.

"Just let me in and tell my mother I'm home."

"She needs water," said one of the officers, "so she don't get dehydrated."

Nicole pushed past the caterer and steered clear of the

tournament. All she wanted was some juice. Some juice and more sleep. She made her way to the kitchen where her mother was supervising.

When Mrs. Hicks laid eyes on her, she slapped her hand over her own mouth. Her eyes got as wide as her mouth might if she allowed herself to let out that scream. She shook her head as if the ruined image of her daughter might just disappear. As Nicole continued on her path toward the fridge, Mrs. Hicks immediately shooed away several caterers.

"Circulate the shrimp puffs. I'll call you when I need you."

Mrs. Hicks pushed her daughter against the refrigerator. Nicole could feel the plastic pea pods and carrots digging into her back.

"What the hell is going on?" Mrs Hicks grabbed at the dress. She inspected the damage. She rubbed the material against itself. She let out a loud guttural sigh. Like a magnet, one hand pinned Nicole to the refrigerator. With the other hand, Mrs. Hicks picked up a cold cup of Taster's Choice. She forced it on her daughter. "Drink this, for God's sake. Pull yourself together."

Nicole thought she could vomit enough to fill the Mr. Coffee pot. She gagged on the backwash and started to cry.

Mrs. Hicks said, "If your father saw you."

"He'd help," Nicole managed, then pulled up her hem to wipe the sweat off her face. Mrs. Hicks gasped at the sight of her daughter's Maidenforms bunched beneath her pantyhose. She jerked the dress down, grabbed a dish towel, and started scrubbing at the pickled blood.

"This will never come out!"

The caterer from the front door peeked in and asked if everything was okay.

Mrs. Hicks barked, "Could you give us a minute? Meaning, get the hell out!"

Tootsie stood behind the caterer. "What is it? Oh, no."

"Get her out of here!" Mrs. Hicks shouted and threw the coffee cup to force a scare.

The cup shattered, coffee covering the caterer. Tootsie took her in hand. "Let's go." She gently pushed the caterer out of the kitchen. "We'll clean you up in the bathroom. It's better we go."

"I'm sick," Nicole sobbed to her mother. "I'm sick of all of this."

"Well, you know what, Nicole? I'm sick of it too. I'm sick of your laziness. I'm sick of all my hard work and you still insisting on being a disappointment."

Nicole felt her body crumble.

Mrs. Hicks propped her up like an unwilling doll. "Now, you listen to me." She shook Nicole's shoulders. "You are a hostess here. You are my daughter and you are a Tri Delt. You will go upstairs and change. You will come down here and tend to our guests. Do you read me? With good fortune comes responsibility."

Nicole whispered, "I'm not a Tri Delt."

Mrs. Hicks let her go and Nicole's ass hit the floor.

Enveloped by her mother's shadow, Nicole looked up and into the face so similar to her own. She thought, *Maybe finally it's all going to be over.* No more clubs to be a part of. No more games to win and win.

"Did you hear me?" Nicole braved. "They kicked me out. I'm not a Delt."

"Well, then." Mrs. Hicks's expression lost its luster. "We're going to have to figure out the next best thing."

Mrs. Hicks held up her hand. Under the track lighting, her diamond ring shone.

Nicole hissed, "You're not marrying me off. I won't be a whore."

Her mother backhanded her, the ring leaving a gash on Nicole's pasty cheek. As she walked out of the kitchen, she gave her daughter instructions. "Clean yourself up, then join me with the others."

Nicole used her not-so-puffy short sleeve to stop the flow of blood. When she stood up, she knew two things: this was her party now and she wanted that ring.

On her way from the kitchen, Nicole pulled a butcher knife out of the block.

She gripped it at her side as she strode into the living room. *This is my party now. You will listen, listen, listen.* She shouted, "Listen!" but her mother did not flinch.

Mrs. Hicks kept her eyes on her cards, three card tables away from where her daughter entered screaming. The rest of her foursome tried to follow her lead. When Nicole raised the butcher knife, decorum was lost.

"Carolyn," said someone.

Cards were placed down at table after table. "Carolyn, for God's sake!"

Nicole was now running. She hiked her skirt and hurdled a chair. When her mother looked up, Nicole had no way of stopping herself. She was flying, flying, flying. She had wings and she had speed. She was out of control and the only thing that would stop her was the blade coming down.

When it did, Mrs. Hicks was caught pointing out queens full of jacks. Within a split second, Mrs. Hicks lost her daughter, her nerve, and two-thirds of her right index finger.

Nicole jerked the butcher knife out of the card table. She shivered as her mother dragged back her hand and Mr. Pointy stayed where served. The ring stood between Mrs. Hicks and her nub of her index finger. It toppled with a tiny thud.

The alumnae were out of control. They fled to the kitchen, upstairs, to their cars. Several women were so full of mimosas plus panic they squatted like ceramic frog plant holders and peed in the backyard. A few brave matriarchs remained in the poker room and darted between the buffet tables shoving banana bread and petits fours into their purses.

Mrs. Hicks stayed in her seat. She went pale as the blood drained from her face, and down her arm, across the tablecloth, from the hole in her hand. The blood pooled and lifted the queen of spades from the table. It slid to the edge, then fell, face first, splat on the beige, velvet-soft, steam-cleaned carpet.

Nicole spotted Tootsie leading the caterer out of the bathroom. She met her eyes as Tootsie registered the blood and the butcher knife and Mrs. Hicks slumping deeper into her chair.

"No!" she cried. "No, pumpkin, you didn't!"

Tootsie zigzagged between card tables, snatching cocktail napkins, shoving them down the front of her shirt. When she reached Mrs. Hicks, she applied pressure to the wound, pulling napkin after napkin out of her blouse to soak more blood.

Tootsie reached for the finger.

Nicole reached it first. With the butcher knife, she swept it off the table and it flew into a floor fan. The fan coughed and spit out Mrs. Hicks's now irreparable part. Blood and skin sprayed Nicole's ankle, her mother's cheek.

Tootsie cried "NO!"

Nicole grabbed the ring and started to run. *I can't go back. I can never go back.* She had no idea where she was going or how to get there or whether she would. She sprinted through the house without the proper shoes. Her pumps hurt her heels and she clenched the ring in her fist. She thought of her mother. *Now she's got nothing! Not moon rocks, not me!* She ran into the traffic congested outside her house. She ran as fast as she could until someone opened a door offering her a way to escape.

Back in the Hicks's house, the guests had evacuated.

Remaining were Tootsie and Mrs. Hicks and the caterer who had seen this incident from beginning to end. That young woman dialed 911.

In a house vacated by hatred and nonsense, Bitty Jack Carlson spoke as calmly as she could. "There's been an accident," she told the operator. "We need an ambulance. Hurry, you hear?"

Sarina

THE YEAR FOLLOWING Nicole's disappearance, Sarina kept her bedroom door locked and the shades drawn, and she never walked anywhere without a sister at her side. These were house rules and applied to every girl, not just the one Nicole had cut herself up for. The Tri Deltas were distraught. Terrified that Nicole might show up full of craziness. A bagful of butcher knives. Geared to collect souvenirs from sisters who had forgotten to tuck their hands safely beneath their covers.

Mrs. Summers told Sarina she had nothing to worry about. If Nicole was going to come back, she would have done so by now. If Nicole was going to hurt her, she'd had plenty of chances. In the wake of such an ugly situation, Sarina should do her best to find the good. Nicole had always been dead weight on her heels. She'd hung on. Slowed her down. Her junior year in college, Sarina had more important things to consider. Now was the time to move on unencumbered.

Sarina told her mother she wasn't scared.

Mrs. Summers answered frequently, "That's because that girl is gone."

Sarina knew Nicole was probably dead. Picked up hitchhiking, her thumb testing her doom like a turkey thermometer. Years from now, Nicole's body would surface. Kids would find it in the woods or parts of it stuffed in an abandoned refrigerator. By the time she was found, Tuscaloosa would have forgotten Nicole and come to view Mrs. Hicks's right-hand nub as an unfortunate birth defect and not the result of a bad seed gone berserk. Her dental records would be the only way to identify her. Unless Nicole still had that ring. That was an item T-town could identify.

During his five-minute editorial time, Mr. Hicks had shown enlarged pictures of the diamond in its intended place, his wife's first finger. He showed photos of Nicole. The most recent, her Tri Delta pledge shot. Sarina remembered how, every few seconds, Mr. Hicks shook his head as if he were trying to wake himself from what had become of his life. He wasn't too swift during the co-anchor banter. When he read the TelePrompTer segue into the football scores, his voice cracked and he didn't seem to care that Auburn trounced Bama at the end of November for the third stinking year in a row. Closing off, he apologized for his earlier lack of impartiality. The editorial had been a one-time plea for help in the locating of his lost, obviously disturbed, sweet, sweet child.

Sarina was pissed at Mr. Hicks's portrait of his daughter. Nicole wasn't the victim and she shouldn't be portrayed as one on TV. In Sarina's opinion, Nicole had done this to herself. She had screwed up her chances of being anyone worthwhile. Once upon a time, Sarina would have been more affected by the loss of her friend, but Sarina had let go of Nicole years before Nicole had surgically removed herself.

Besides, Sarina was too busy to be sad, scared, or bothered at all. Graduation was in sight. Less than two years away.

At every Delta meeting, it seemed, another senior announced her engagement. All the single sisters cheered and jumped to their feet. Champagne was uncorked and a serenade pilgrimage was made to the lawn of the groom-to-be's frat house.

Sarina wanted to be the subject of such songs. She wanted to move forward, beat her peers to Wife and Country Clubber. It would be good to have her future secured. Marriage was the logical step.

Of course, Sarina was aware of divorce stats and difficult men. She had grown up as a first-hand witness to a prime example. She knew. No one had to tell her. But her marriage would be different, a shining example. No man would dare to cross her. She just had to find a manageable prospect.

Sarina met Joe Diller at the Alabama Boat Show.

Diller Marine was the largest display in the center floor space of the Birmingham-Jefferson Civic Center. The family business had twelve bass boats surrounding a yacht that stood almost as high as the second-floor escalators. Joe stood on the deck of that yacht. He wore shorts and sunglasses despite an unseasonably cold Halloween.

Sarina was dressed as Cleopatra at the Tri Delta Trout Tub. She wore blood red lipstick and false eyelashes that hit her brows. Her dress had been doctored so she looked straight out of the movies. Cleavage everywhere. Faux emeralds pasted to leather straps making their way over and under ten polished toes. And there was more. Mrs. Summers had mixed glue, glitter, and Jergens to give Sarina's skin the golden glint sometimes found on expensive hood ornaments.

Her sorority sisters had come dressed as a mouse, Raggedy Ann, a bubble bath (who looked more like a cauliflower), and an Avon lady fresh out of hell. Even if Sarina hadn't spotted Joe, the night at the trout tub would have been a success.

Every year, Tri Delta sponsored amateur fishing to raise money for the Humane Society. They rented bamboo poles to kids or anyone who wanted to stand around a fiberglass pool, drop their hooks, and try to catch one of the hundreds of bass previously captured the hard way from Lake Tuscaloosa.

"Five minutes for a dollar," a Tri Delt would call.

"There's a big one in there. Almost eight pounds."

"Won't you?" Sarina would say, her voice soft like Marilyn's, not Elizabeth Taylor's. "It's for charity."

From the top of his yacht, behind his silver-tinted sunglasses, Joe pretended to survey the sales floor. He was a terrible faker. Sarina knew he was looking at her. She knew he was considering taking a break to say hello. To show Joe that she was a sporting girl, a woman he could lure to the lake at five in the morning, Sarina took the fish off the hooks by herself. She smiled as she stuck her hand into each gill, held it firmly, then dropped it into a Ziploc bag.

"Don't cry." She'd gather her dress and stoop to watery kiddie eye-level. "He'll stop squirming as soon as he suffocates."

Joe made his way down the yacht stairs to the bass boats. He took two steps at a time as if he had one just like it docked in his backyard. Sarina clocked him at twenty-eight, but indisputably he was in charge. Comfortable as the go-see. At ease with competition in every direction.

All the salesmen reported to Joe. If a customer wanted a better deal, he asked for a supervisor and was taken to Joe. If he wanted to see something back at the dealership, Joe gave him a business card and hints of special treatment. Joe signed all sale slips. He kept the catalogues stacked a foot high no matter how busy things got.

"Everybody likes to fish." Joe grinned at his customers, retirees or juniors with their Pampers brood in tow. "A little quiet time with nature. Just you and your thoughts. Come on." He'd wave his blond-knuckled hand. "Let me show you the rod bins. Seven-footers on this Cajun Beauty."

When Joe offered to buy her a Pepsi Freeze, Sarina knew she would bag him on their first date.

* * *

Joe took Sarina to dinner at the Cypress Inn. The restaurant was just across the Black Warrior River and Joe's new car handled the back roads beautifully. All the restaurant tables had a view of the water and the wait staff wore bow ties, even the waitresses. Sarina had been there just a few times. Each night, an occasion. High school Homecoming. The prom. While her suitors paid the checks, Sarina had noticed adults who were there only for Friday surf-and-turf. No special reason. Just dinner. Fifty bucks. Sarina had never been there in anything other than her fanciest dress. So she called her mother, who advised a nice pantsuit.

Sarina ordered swordfish, even though she hated swordfish. She drank white wine illegally. She ate all her vegetables. She was very attentive. She did not complain when Joe excused himself to make a business call and left her gazing at the river, a pecked-bald duck drifting determinately by.

After all, he was gorgeous. And rich. Not just some college boy.

Diller Marine was the most profitable dealership outside of Gulf Shores. Mrs. Summers had done some homework. She wanted to know who this boat salesman was. When she got the Dun & Bradstreet, she said, "Sweetheart, he's your man."

The Dillers weren't big socially, but the Summers could change that. They could push them into the Cheshire Country Club. Override Mrs. Hicks, that naysayer who used Mrs. Summers's divorce and, more than likely, that rush ring–stealing lie she'd threatened Sarina with, as ways to keep the Summers at the University Pool. With the Diller money behind them, the Summers had power. No due was too pricey. No Hicks strong enough.

Besides, since Nicole's disappearance, Mrs. Hicks had dissolved. She had become even thinner. Unattractively thinner.

She was quiet at sorority gatherings, her hands arranged carefully, poised in her lap. Tootsie Steptoe escorted her, pointed out steps, guided her through girls, uncomfortable in the presence of her cancerish condition.

Mrs. Summers said, "Now she knows what it's like to be robbed."

Sarina said, "She's lost it, all right."

With the Diller name signed in Sarina's bold penmanship, it would be impossible for Mrs. Hicks to override the application.

Joe told Sarina about his job. How one day, he would take over for his father. Turn Diller Marine into a chain of stores linking Alabama to Georgia to Mississippi.

"You mean Mississippi to Alabama to Georgia."

"Sure, sure." He smiled. "That's what I said."

Sarina pictured a future with Joe. Cutting red ribbons. Posing by his side in Sunday color-edition newspaper ads. She would water ski every summer. Oil herself up. Get the tan she knew she deserved.

"My father doesn't have my ambition. When I'm in charge, I'll take us places. Move to Atlanta. Get us out of this one-horse town."

"Us?" said Sarina.

"Sure. Why not?"

Sarina held her wine glass casually. She wanted him to see a woman who could always keep him satisfied. Who would stay this way forever. Who was better than the rest. She blew out the candle. She said, "Let's go."

Joe's apartment was small by Alabama standards. Shaped like a capital *L*, each door was indistinguishable: bathroom, his room, hall closet, one for linens. It was neat, but lacked identity.

"I know." Joe grinned. "It could use a woman's touch."

Sarina said she'd touch it and then Joe opened the fridge.

The little light lit up and the Maytag screamed bachelor. Parkay sticks, two brown eggs, left-over fast food, and an assortment of booze.

"Champagne?" Joe said. "Or," he opened the freezer to a lone bottle of vodka, "something stronger?"

Sarina said, "Whose wine cooler is that?"

Joe looked in the fridge as if he had unlocked the door to his neighbor's apartment. His voice curled into a question. "Mine?"

Sarina crossed her arms like her mother in certain circumstances. "What's her name?"

"She's nobody."

"Is Nobody who you spent half an hour with on the phone during dinner?"

Joe didn't move.

Sarina reached into the fridge and plucked out the wine cooler. It was Very Berry. A sissy girl's drink. She rolled it between her palms. "Why don't you call Miss Nobody right now and tell her that it's over. I'm not going to share you." She twisted off the top.

Joe leaned against the kitchen counter, his good posture heading toward the sink. "I can't do it over the phone. She's not as strong as you."

Sarina took a sip. The Very Berry was sickly sweet. She wanted to gag, but then she thought of the woman who had picked the four-pack off the grocery shelf. She was probably Joe's age. Fragile with the knowledge that her good years were gone. Sarina pulled the bottle away and the glass mouth made a little pop. She looked at Joe as if he should know better. She brought the bottle back for another swig. She thought, *By the time I finish drinking this, you sure as hell better pick up that phone.* What she said was, "So toughen her up."

Joe looked at her as if the other woman was his mother. God forbid he hurt her like that. God forbid he hurt a stupid little twit.

Sarina said, "It's your choice." But she knew there was no contest. How could there be? How could it possibly get better than this? Sarina knew she was a catch. She had the fries to go with her shake. She was all that and a bag of chips.

Joe took the portable into his bedroom. He shut the door for what, after ten minutes, seemed like would be a very long time.

Sarina took inventory of the bathroom. She put the plastic trash can on the commode and filled it with toiletries he would not be needing anymore. Pond's Cold Cream (even her mother was too young to use that), hair spray, a barrette lacquered with hair spray, roll-on deodorant shaped like a lavender penis, plus his only toothbrush. She knew it had been in that other woman's mouth. Joe should know it wasn't going back into his.

She opened the front door and hurled the wine cooler at the bushes that bordered the parking lot. It felt good to divide and conquer. When the bottle broke, the night air was filled with the sour, arousing tang of an ex-girlfriend gone stale.

Back at the Delta house she called her mother, who asked how it went.

"Pretty well," said Sarina. "I didn't call you too late?"

"It's never too late."

"I know." Sarina paused for a moment. She thought about this, the third year she would spend only school breaks at home with her mom. She asked, "Are you happy alone?"

"I'm not alone."

"I mean friends. You two used to be so social."

"I'm social."

"I remember the dinner parties," Sarina said. "Meena sneaking biscuits to my room."

"She did that?"

"I remember his laugh, even with my door closed."

"Willamina snuck you rolls?"

Sarina said, "What happened to all your friends, Mother?"

Mrs. Summers made no effort to muffle the sound of the cork she twisted out of what could only be her favorite brand of white wine. "I got the house." There was silence as she took a sip. "And you."

Sarina kicked her shoes off and lay across her bed. "How did you know he was Mr. Right?"

Mrs. Summers was silent as if she was trying to envision old ghosts. Maybe of the marriage she used to be a part of. Maybe of the days when three Summers were pasted in every photo album.

"Mother?"

"I'm still here."

"Tell me. How did you know?"

"I just knew."

"That's what they all say."

"Well, then," sighed Mrs. Summers, "they'd all be right."

Two weeks before finals, Sarina decided she and Joe would go all the way. It had been two months of teasing and, truth was, she had wanted to let him since he first put his mouth on her.

Joe was a good kisser. Give-lessons kind of good.

Sarina found herself as she had often heard it could be: caught up in the moment, captured by his every move. She didn't have to train him: shut her mouth to get his tongue out, draw her head back to slow him down. She didn't have to put her hand over his chin to keep his stubble from rubbing her raw. Joe always double-shaved when they got home from a date. He put his hands in her hair. He moved his lips along her face. He found a spot on her neck she never knew held interest. He touched her all over. Every instance, asking for more.

When she finally gave it to him, the condom came off. Got lost, in doctor speak, is the more accurate analysis.

They were on top of the covers, on top of his bed. Sarina, amazed that she wasn't the teacher. Joe taking over, making filthy little comments most women want to hear. After the *Are you ready?—Yeah—you?—Yeah*, Joe sat back on his heels and looked nervously into his lap. Sarina was unaware of what had happened until she saw the look on Joe's face and got up on her elbows to find his penis, extinguished, collected in his hand. Sarina winced and scooted sideways, out of range of the wet spot. But she was the wet spot. And that wetness made her feel like a stepped-on tube of toothpaste.

"I'm on the pill," she spat out. Which was true, but little comfort. When Sarina couldn't fill a B-cup before Varsity tryouts, Mrs. Summers had taken her to her gynecologist and insisted that her daughter get her share of regulation.

Joe said, "Why didn't you tell me?"

"Where the hell did it go?" Sarina reached between her legs. She felt the sheets around her legs. Nothing. Nada. That rubber was missing and they knew where it was. "Didn't you feel it coming off when we . . ."

"Hey, shhh." Joe leaned forward, onto all fours. He dropped his head and looked up at her through his sandy blond bangs sprung loose from the gel. "Hey, it's okay."

"It is most definitely *not* okay." Sarina swung her body off the bed. She stormed naked to the bathroom shouting, "Let's put a quarter up *your* ass and see who's okay!"

Sarina slammed the door and flicked on the lights. It was a shower-sized bathroom. The towels badly bleached. She sat on the toilet and tried to get it out. She stood up and put a foot on the sink and tried to get it out. She saw herself in the mirror, hair in knots, skin blotchy from his chest hair or soap or the inferior detergent he used on his sheets. She gave herself x-ray vision and saw that condom trapped inside her, cupping her cervix like another girl's diaphragm. She couldn't get it with her fingers. They were too short and too straight.

Sarina turned off the lights and called for Joe. When he knocked on the door, the sound almost broke her. She opened it and Joe reached for the light switch.

"Don't," she said.

"Shh, it's okay."

If she was as brave as she wanted, she would have asked for a coat hanger. Instead, she managed to ask for his help.

When she got back to the Delta house, Sarina thought her answering machine was on the blink. The red light was flashing. She couldn't count the number of times. She pressed Play and took her coat off, but she didn't sit down. She was sore from Joe's two fingers playing pliers. She was anxious and embarrassed. Tender from the night.

Message after message revealed her mother getting drunk.

Friday, 6:45 P.M.: "Hi, honey, I'm home. Waiting for your call. Wondering what you're wearing to the big game tonight."

Friday, 7:01P.M.: "Hi. It's your mother. I'm looking for you on television. Where are you? I don't see you."

Friday, 8:20 P.M.: "Sarina, it's your mother. Call me if you check your messages."

Friday, 9:00 P.M.: "It's your mother. Call me when you get home."

Friday, 10:00 P.M.: "It's your mother."

"Mother here."

"Just your mother."

"Call your mother."

Sarina thought, She knows. Somehow, she just knows.

Sarina paced in front of her twin bed. She had herself a sticky situation. If she didn't call, her mother might call the house mother whenever she came to. That could be early.

Before alarms. Before dawn. Her mother had told her, "It's never too late." But it was 3:00 A.M. Did she want to test that theory?

She called.

"It's me, Mother. Just letting you know I got in okay. Talk to you tomorrow. Go back to sleep."

"Wait," her mother croaked. "Wait a second. Hold on." Mrs. Summers cleared her throat. She coughed and coughed. "Hold on."

"Mother, don't worry about it. Go back to sleep. I'll call you tomorrow."

"Wait a second." More coughing. "You're still my daughter. I want to meet him. Bring him over. Lemme meet him."

"Mother, we're not in kindergarten."

"Well, you're hardly self-supportive. Do you want to get a job? Is that what you'd like?"

"Fine," said Sarina.

"Fine," said Mrs. Summers. "I'll see you Sunday at six. Tell him to invite his parents. We'll make three dates of it."

"Who's coming with you?"

"Oh, for goodness sakes. It's just an expression."

Sunday morning when Sarina reminded Joe of the dinner, he sat up in his bed and said, "You were serious?"

"You said you wanted to."

"I said my parents would love you."

"So?"

"So, it's only been two months."

"Ten weeks," Sarina corrected.

"Ten weeks, then," said Joe.

"Do your parents even know about me?"

"Of course," said Joe. "You're my girlfriend, aren't you?"

Sarina said, "You got that right."

* * *

The Dillers were not what Sarina expected. They were graying brunettes. They were old and laughed a lot. They sat close together on the living room sofa and nudged each other when one of them snorted. Tweedledum and Tweedledee. Every joke, a private one. Every story, a had-to-be-there. And, boy oh boy, did they love their Joe. They offered excuses when he was forty minutes late.

"I'm sure he's stuck in traffic."

"What traffic?" said Mrs. Summers.

"There's traffic," said Sarina.

"I'll bet he's closed a deal." Mrs. Diller turned to her husband. "You've been late before." She said to Mrs. Summers, "It happens sometimes. That last-minute customer. Last-minute, but serious."

Mrs. Summers got to her feet. "I'll just tell Will to put the roast back in the oven."

The kitchen door still swinging, Sarina was left alone with the company.

"So," said Mrs. Diller. "Joe tells us you're in a sorority."

"Tri Delta," Sarina nodded.

"Oooo," said Mrs. Diller.

Mr. Diller patted his wife's knee. His fingers were pink and chapped at the knuckles.

The doorbell rang and Joe arrived with red roses. They were not supermarket fare. They were long-stemmed and too large for the baby's breath to cover. "The deal was so close," he said to his father. He kissed Sarina on the mouth. He apologized to Mrs. Summers and offered her the flowers. He shook her hand. He laughed as he said, "Quite a grip you got there."

"So I've been told." Mrs. Summers made her way back to Willamina.

At the dinner table, Mrs. Summers seated Joe to her left

and Sarina to her right. She sat the Dillers to either side of them and left her ex-husband's seat without a place mat, chair tucked under.

Over the course of the evening, Willamina brought out one dish after the other. Salad and little rolls. Pot roast. Potatoes. Gravy boat and butter. Peas, greens, and corn.

Before dessert, Joe pulled a vibrating beeper from his sports coat pocket. He read it and frowned. "That same client. I've got to take this." He touched Mrs. Summer's wrist and Mrs. Summers held his gaze in a way Sarina had yet to master. He nodded to the swinging kitchen door where, behind it, a phone was surely stationed. "May I?"

"Far be it from me."

Joe left the dining room and his father was the first to speak. "I discouraged him from getting that thing. I'll never wear one myself. Never get a car phone, either." He reached his chapped pink fingers across the pot roast for his wife's hand. "After five, I'm a family man."

"Stop it," Mrs. Diller gushed and squeezed his fingers before releasing them.

Sarina picked at a second dinner roll. She joined in conversation. She tried not to let her gaze move from the three parental faces to the kitchen door that Joe was behind.

Mrs. Diller lowered her voice as she forked several peas. "My husband is going to kill me for bringing this up."

"Go ahead," said Mrs. Summers.

"No, don't," said Mr. Diller.

Mrs. Diller put her fork down and wiped her mouth. "Nevermind. He's right. It's tacky. I've drunk over my limit."

Mrs. Summers said, "Please, there're no secrets here. Ask us anything. Go on. We've got nothing to hide."

Before Mrs. Diller got the words out, Sarina knew what she was going to say. "What ever happened to that girl, Nicole Hicks?"

Clearly grateful his wife had opened her big mouth, Mr.

Diller added, "You must have seen everything. Tell us, is there anything the TV didn't say?"

Mrs. Summers said, "Honestly, there isn't anything else I didn't tell the police. You know the story. There was what happened. Then hysteria. But I never saw Nicole. Just a bunch of women running for their cars. Same thing I would have done if I had been a guest in that house."

The Dillers were visibly disappointed.

"But why'd she do it?"

"She's crazy." Mrs. Summers sawed a piece of meat with her knife. "But how can you blame her? Carolyn Hicks could make us all do crazy things."

"Like what?" asked Mrs. Diller.

"Whatever," said Mrs. Summers. "I'm just glad that girl's off the streets. She's dangerous, and *my* girl doesn't need to fear a Manson in her sleep."

Sarina smiled accordingly as her mother patted her hand. She wondered what kind of commission could keep her boyfriend in the kitchen so long.

Mr. Diller said, "How do you know she's not on the streets? I mean, where else could she be? She's a long way from anonymous."

Mrs. Summers said, "Now, really."

Joe was still on the phone.

"It's true," said Mrs. Diller. "She could be anywhere."

"Los Angeles," said Mr. Diller.

"But, honey, Oprah says runaways don't go that far from home."

Mrs. Summers mused, "You know . . . she could be watching us right now."

"Oooo," said Mrs. Diller.

"Did you check your back seat?"

"*Oooo!*"

"Don't you worry." Mr. Diller's pink fingers searched his wife's out across the table.

All this chatter and Joe was still on the phone.

"She's dead," Sarina said and pushed her chair from the table. "Dead as in door nail." She picked up the dinner roll plate.

"Let Will do that."

"No, Mother, it's okay."

In the kitchen, Joe sat on the green stool by the wall phone with the receiver pinched between his shoulder and ear. His back was to Sarina. He was facing the maid. Willamina sat at the blue wicker kitchen table, her arms crossed, her eyes on Joe. She took them away only for a moment to frown at Sarina. Joe saw the exchange and turned around, his cheeks flushed. He checked his watch and whispered into the mouthpiece, "I've got to go."

Sarina said, "Who were you talking to?"

"Told you. Client."

Willamina stepped forward. She took the empty dinner roll plate from Sarina. She stood behind her at the oven and pulled out warm rolls one by one.

"It's been over ten minutes."

"Well, what do you want me to do?"

Willamina shut the oven and tapped Sarina on the back before handing her the dinner roll plate. She crossed the room and made a lot of noise getting comfortable in the blue wicker chair.

Joe said, "You want me to lose the sale?"

"I don't know, Joe."

"Well, then, for God's sake gimme a break."

Sarina was annoyed by his impromptu little rhyme. She was even more annoyed when he offered to follow his parents home in his car. Mrs. Diller had drunk over her limit. Mr. Diller had poor night vision. It was a predicament. Joe would tail them and beep if they swerved into traffic.

"I'll meet you at the apartment," he whispered as he kissed Sarina good-bye.

"How am I supposed to get in?"

"Don't worry," said Joe. "I'll be there in twenty minutes."

Sarina and her mother stood on the front porch and waved. Both their shoulders set in knots as Mr. Diller sounded his horn and drove away to a loud, high-speed version of "*Look away, look away, look away, Dixie Land!*"

Mrs. Summers wrapped her arm around her daughter's waist. "Come inside for a second. It's time I told you the facts of life."

"You told me when I was ten."

Mrs. Summers sat down at the dining room table. "Those were the mechanics. What matters is the mind."

Sarina stood by her seat until Willamina finished shaking the crumbs off her place mat.

"Go on," said Willamina and patted her chair.

Mrs. Summers said, "Sarina, do you think he's the one?"

"I think so."

"Think hard."

Sarina closed her eyes as if that would help the process. For a few seconds there was peace. Quiet, save the shuffle of Willamina at the sink. Sarina was absorbed by the simple scene within her head. There was darkness and cloudy stars. Her mother's voice, the sharpest light.

"You know that wasn't a business call, don't you?"

Sarina said, "What?"

"He's got another girlfriend. Ask Will. She heard it all."

"She told you?"

"Didn't have to. I knew just by looking at him. I hate to tell you, he reminds me of your father."

"Meena!" Sarina screamed. "Meena, get in here!"

"Don't bother Will. Let her work. I'll tell you."

But Willamina was right behind her. Soap still on her apron, gloves dripping dirty dishwater all over the floor.

"Will, mind the carpet."

"What is it? What's wrong?"

Mrs. Summers said, "Take your gloves off. I just had this steamed."

"Well, what's she yelling about?"

"Take off your gloves."

Willamina shoved the gloves in her apron pocket. All the while, waiting on an answer. Looking at Sarina as if she'd clean lost her head.

"Well, what is it?"

Sarina couldn't look at her. She was too afraid to hear the answer. If history served, her mother was right.

"What is it, girl? You scared me outta my skin."

Mrs. Summers said, "Tell Sarina who Joe was talking to."

"Why she want to know that? He told her, 'client.' What makes y'all think it was anything else?"

"Will, please," said Mrs. Summers. She stifled a yawn. "You know and I know it wasn't any client. People talk in front of you like you're a goddamned lamp post. Just confirm our suspicions. Did he call her by name?"

Willamina folded her arms and sort of sat in midair. She sighed so severely. She said, "No name."

"But Mom, he told me it was over."

"Sweetheart," Mrs. Summers said, "these things are never over."

Willamina put her hands on her knees. She bent over and spoke to Sarina like so many times when Sarina was short. "Go get yourself a better man. A good man who'll treat you right. Cast a spell. You know, make a man love you like that boy in seventh grade."

"Stewart," said Sarina.

Mrs. Summers said, "That's quite enough."

"Yes, ma'am," Willamina said and, still slightly bent, went back into the kitchen.

Sarina felt the room spin around her like a funnel. Everything seemed to be growing and, at the same time, she shrunk.

She pictured herself too small to slide down the chair leg. When she finally spoke, her voice was a speck. "Fuck."

And then, "So I should call it off, tonight?"

"Watch your language," said her mother. "And I didn't say that."

"So what are you saying?"

"That marriage is a job. It's hard work. I'm sure you've been told this before."

"And?"

"And," said Mrs. Summers, "men cheat. They work late. They don't clean up after themselves. There's something wrong with every one of them. You just have to decide what you can put up with. I suggest you cross beatings and pedophilia off that list."

"Mother!"

"Sarina, Joe's a fine man. He comes from money and no matter how else he screws up, that money isn't going anywhere. He can open doors for you that, I'm sorry, I can't. Your children will be stunning. And after ten years, you'll get half, plus the house, plus child support. Alimony. The works. No judge is going to ignore photo evidence of adultery. You should be thankful you know his weakness now." She picked up her empty wine glass and pointed at her daughter with the stem in her hand. "Just don't let him near you without a condom. Have him tested before you get pregnant."

Sarina said, "Is that what you did?"

"We didn't have AIDS when I was a girl."

"No," said Sarina incredulously. "I mean, is that what you did when you married my father?"

"Oh, don't look so surprised. You come from my blood. You're hardly afraid to go get what you want."

"But is Joe what I want?"

"Lord knows," sighed Mrs. Summers as she got up from the table. "In today's world, he's as good as any."

* * *

When Sarina reached Joe's apartment, his car was not parked in his spot and the lights in his second-floor unit were out. It had been over an hour. Where the hell could he be? Sarina kept the radio low and car doors locked. She stewed in her seat. She got angrier and angrier.

When Joe showed up, Sarina was fuming. She stared at the steering wheel when he tapped on her window. She cursed herself silently for waiting at all. When he climbed onto the hood and made a blowfish face against the windshield, she fiddled with the cigarette lighter she had never touched in her life. She was mad and he should know it. She got out of the car and left him sprawled on the Prelude.

Joe followed her up the stairs to his apartment. All the while apologizing. Offering excuses to the beat of her heels.

Sarina did not say a word as Joe unlocked the front door. She shrugged her shoulders when he offered her something to drink. She was mute and damned impatient. As he unbuttoned the front of her pale Laura Ashley, Sarina kept her eyes straight and narrow.

"Go ahead," she finally spoke. "Try to seduce me."

Dropping to his knees, Joe took her panties in his mouth by the breathable cotton crotch. "I will," he managed with his teeth close to home. He tugged gently and, even though Sarina surrendered solely to the motions, like always, predictably, unavoidably, he did.

Well after midnight, Sarina woke up drenched in sweat. Joe was snoring loudly. She had been dreaming of stampedes.

She went to the bathroom and ran her wrists under cold water. She asked her reflection if she could pull off what her mother suggested. Could she handle Joe's cheating for a decade to come? Could she nail him to the wall? Play the gay divorcée?

When she saw the razor behind the toilet tank, she couldn't resist picking it up. As if left by the Infidelity Fairy, it had been laying there like a little reminder. It was pink and plastic and definitely not hers.

Sarina ran the blade under the faucet. There was no rust. Not a hair in sight. She thought, *This is something. Something downright unforgivable.* She gripped the plastic razor and considered her choices.

Bitty Jack

THE DRIVE TO Druid City Hospital was uncomfortable for Bitty Jack. Stewart had gotten the bad news on the Big Al Mascot Mobile portable phone. He crumbled and Bitty Jack took over the wheel. She did not bother to adjust the seat. She balanced her butt on the vinyl edge; her toes pushing the pedals, the steering wheel reachable by her fingertips only.

On talk shows, women always begged their men to bawl like big babies. To share their pain. To let it all out. Now Stewart was shaking, shivering in his seat. He was breathing fast and hard. He didn't bother to wipe his face. Bitty Jack wondered if those TV women had ever seen a grown man cry. It was a hundred miles from beautiful. It was not a special moment. Stewart's tears made his face raw and puffy. They slid into his mouth. They scared Bitty Jack out of asking questions.

Inside the hospital, routes were taped on the floors. Pink tape went to the maternity ward. Yellow tape went to cardiac care. Red, of course, sought the emergency room. Green, the cafeteria. Blue, substance abuse. Bitty Jack and Stewart followed the gray tape to the morgue.

In the basement, they looked down a long, chilly hallway.

Windowless steel doors guarded every room on either side. Twenty feet ahead, the Hicks were waiting. As Bitty Jack and Stewart got closer, Bert Hicks helped his wife up from an aluminum bench. She had gauze around her hands and fresh stitches on one arm. She seemed wobbly in her stance. She held onto her husband as he said what he must have been practicing for hours.

"I'm so sorry, Stewart. If it's any comfort, your parents have been taken care of."

"What do you mean taken care of?"

"He means," said Mrs. Hicks, her face tight like a fist, "they're at peace. Bert and I will take care of everything."

"Can I see them?"

Mrs. Hicks looked at her husband. She looked back at Stewart. She looked at her husband.

Mr. Hicks said, "It's not a good idea."

Mrs. Hicks said, "It's better you remember them the way that they were."

"Is it that bad?"

"Oh, Stewart," Mrs. Hicks opened her arms, an invitation for him to walk right in. "It was horrible." She pressed her face into the front of his button-down. "Horrible." She ran her hands through the back of his hair. Her nub lost in the layers recently grown out.

Mr. Hicks said, "Bitty." He petted his wife's back with long, soothing strokes. "Tootsie's introduced us, I'm sure, at the games. She told us all about your quick thinking at the poker tournament. We've never given you a proper thank you."

"Thank you," said Mrs. Hicks, her voice muffled by Stewart's stiff shirt.

Bitty Jack nodded and was left with Bert Hicks while his wife guided Stewart to another bench, six doors down, even farther into the bowels of the morgue.

"He needs to make some private decisions."

Bitty Jack said, "Can you tell me what happened?"

Mr. Hicks took her hand and looked as if he might start from the beginning, before the events of that morning, back to the days when the couples first met. He closed his eyes. He shook his head. He walked toward his wife, leaving Bitty Jack's hand adrift in the stench of wax polish and formaldehyde.

At this point, all Bitty knew was that the Steptoes were dead and she was being pushed out of the picture. The Hicks and her boyfriend were huddled down the hallway. Clearly no room for a young college girl. She wasn't the wife. She began to understand that the Hicks saw her as no use at all. So she'd seek out the doctors. She'd get some answers from someone.

The coroner was eager to talk. She was short and blond and looked as if she'd wandered in from a Tupperware party. "It was one of those alumnae tailgate parties. You know, twenty cars on their way out of state. Their Jeep hit a log truck. Heavy rain. Faulty brakes. There were tons of witnesses, but your friend's friends were in the car right behind them. Their injuries are obvious. A truck driver could tell you as much as I can."

"Did they die right away?"

"Most certainly. The paramedics said the man was dead on site. The firemen had to use the Jaws of Life to pull the log out. Every rib broken. Now, that's something to see."

"And Tootsie?"

The corner pointed to her own head for example. "Clean off," she said. "Shot it off like a pinball."

"Where—"

"Did it go? You didn't see the bandages? On your friend's friend. Her husband said she chased it into the woods. She wouldn't give it up. It was covered in glass, but she put it in their Pepsi cooler. She rode in the ambulance. Brought it in on her lap."

* * *

Bitty Jack called her mama from the waiting room. As she waited for her to pick up, Bitty Jack figured she was in shock. In her heart there was nothing. No sense of emergency. No hint of fear. So many times in her life, Bitty knew how things would go. There was a good feeling or a bad feeling. Something to accompany every trip she took.

When Mrs. Carlson heard, she said, "Sweet Jesus!"

"It's the worst thing I've ever seen."

Her mama said, "You saw?"

"No," said Bitty Jack. "You know what I mean."

"So what happens now?"

"That's the problem. I don't know. I'm just sitting here. They've got Stewart somewhere and I'm just sitting here, and I need you to tell me what I'm s'posed to do."

"Okay," said Mrs. Carlson. "Okay, let me think." She only thought for a second. "Baby girl, you've got to be strong. And strong means backing off. It sounds like those friends of his parents are taking care of everything. Let 'em. Let them choose the funeral home. Let them hold the reception. Let them smother that boy as much as they want and when he needs you, you let him come.

"I remember when your father's father died. You were little and we stood in the back of the church and he walked right past us like we were total strangers. I don't think he spoke to me for three whole weeks. I mean, baby girl, this is just the way it goes.

"I'm real sorry this happened. Real sorry. But give him his room because, I'm telling you, people are going to come outta the woodwork. People he never even mentioned are going to hear about this and show up at the funeral. You're going to feel lonely and left out, but stick it out, because in a few weeks, all those people are going to go back to their lives and all that'll be left will be you and him."

Mrs. Carlson added, "If you need to do something, clean his house."

"It's a big house."

"Baby girl," said her mama, "do one room at a time."

At the cemetery, Bitty Jack sat in the row behind Stewart. She had not seen him in two days. At the hospital, Mrs. Hicks had announced that Stewart would be staying with them for a while. Tootsie would have wanted it this way. He would take her son Rick's room. Rick was in the army now. On his way to becoming a general.

Stewart looked like he had lost a little weight. Maybe five pounds. Or maybe he was tired. From her brief phone calls with Stewart, Bitty Jack had learned that Mrs. Hicks had kept him busy. There was the service to plan, the caskets to choose—pine or oak, regular or moisture-sealed, silk-lined or synthetic—and clothes to pick out for the Steptoes's life together, forever and ever, in the sweet hereafter.

"She's so demanding."

"So leave, Stewart."

"I can't. Mr. Hicks has to work and she's acting really weird. He asked me to keep an eye on her. But I hate it. She's totally freaking me out."

"What's she doing?"

"I've heard her talking to my mom."

"Well, that's supposed to be natural."

"This ain't natural. Rick's room is right next to Nicole's. Mrs. Hicks goes in there and I can hear her having seances and shit. Moaning and shit. Calling out my dead mother's name."

"Stewart, leave."

"I can't. I promised. Besides she's always on me with something else to decide."

Stewart told Bitty Jack that Mrs. Hicks had vetoed his choice of the matching red blazers his parents wore to every football game. "She said it's not right. That it's tacky or something."

"What does it matter?" Bitty Jack had asked. "It's closed casket still, right?"

"Right, but she's got these beliefs."

"What beliefs?" Mrs. Carlson had asked when Bitty Jack told her.

"I didn't ask," said Bitty Jack. "I didn't want to upset him anymore than he is."

"Well," said her mama, "I can understand that."

Bitty Jack confessed that she wished they were coming.

"So do I," said her mama. "But, you know, your father doesn't do well with death."

Graveside, Bitty Jack had been better herself. Already, she felt selfish for missing her boyfriend. Until now, she had spent most nights in Stewart's apartment. Stewart was solid. A security next to her under the blanket. He slept soundly, every night weighing down his side of the bed, causing Bitty Jack to roll slowly toward his Fruit Of The Looms. In the warm spot where Stewart met the sheets, she pressed her body against his back and wrapped an arm around his shoulder. She patterned her breathing to sink and rise with his. She fell asleep more readily. It was good to be his girl.

Bitty Jack shifted in her fold-out wooden chair. Under the tent, there were three rows of six before two open graves.

They were deep holes, six feet under. They were exactly the same size even though, in life, Tootsie Steptoe stood at least a foot shorter. The pulleys to lower the coffins had been laid during the church service. The canvas straps were blue with a thick white stripe. They were wider than the handles of her daddy's duffel bag.

Bitty Jack's good pair of shoes were covered with condensation. The rain had returned and the grass was wet from the time before the tent was put up. It was crowded under the green waterproof tarp. Even the fair tents weren't this garish and far from this small. Whoever designed it was very insensitive. He obviously thought people kicked one at a time. There were no plane crashes or car pile-ups or semiautomatics.

Bitty Jack touched Stewart's shoulder to let him know she was behind him, two chairs to his left.

"Hey," said Stewart.

Bitty Jack said, "Hey."

Mrs. Hicks returned from talking to the funeral director. Throughout their conversation, he'd held her by the elbows, supporting her weight, careful not to touch the gauze on her hands, which had been reduced to one layer. She leaned into him as if she were drunk, her mouth working rapidly inches from his face. Her low banter was interrupted only by her own one-syllable cackles and sobs and "Huh-hmms?"

Mrs. Hicks picked up her purse from the seat saved beside Stewart. She did not acknowledge Bitty. She straightened her black suit that made her complexion appear slightly green. There were dark circles under her eyes and cream concealer caked on top. Her lipstick bled. Her hair seemed thinner. Bitty Jack winced as Mrs. Hicks ran her bandaged hands through her locks, each time dropping strands over her shoulder onto the grass by Bitty's good shoes.

Mrs. Hicks put her arm around Stewart's broad back. He flinched, but she persisted, scratching his shoulder, massaging his neck. Bitty Jack wondered if she was doing the right thing by giving Stewart his space and not forcing herself. Mrs. Hicks whispered and Bitty Jack leaned forward, straining to hear.

"Tell me she's not gone, Stewart. She always knew what to do. She had a second sense."

"You've told me."

"She always said that she'd find Nicole."

People were arriving by the carload. The funeral procession was so long it had delayed traffic significantly. Relatives quietly argued over who should get one of the few chairs remaining.

"Aunt Sallie can't sit in the rain."

"Well, you certainly can't expect Mee Maw to stand."

Mrs. Hicks hissed, "Would you *please?*"

Stewart again shifted anxiously in his seat.

"Here." A third cousin bent over Bitty Jack. "Scoot down three, so we can all sit together."

Stewart was out of her reach, so Bitty Jack relinquished her chair and walked to the other side of the plots where her boss, Tom, stood with a tremendous domed umbrella borrowed from the bakery's lost-and-found. Tom put his hand on Bitty Jack's shoulder. She knew he meant well, but she shook it off anyway. Tom had done enough. He'd driven her there and offered to cater the reception for free. Presently, two of the staff were setting up at the Hicks's house.

Bitty Jack scanned the faces and recognized very few. There were a couple of professors and kids from classes they shared. Alabama football players. Coach, too. Some of the cheerleaders stood in a pack. They cried a lot. More than the Deltas. There was a cluster of them, her old roommate included. Funny, Bitty knew her old roommate wasn't there to support her. In a school of thirty thousand, Greeks and Independents were socially segregated. Since she'd moved into the sorority house, she hadn't seen Bitty Jack. She was there to help Mrs. Hicks survive a Tri Delta loss. The sisters wore matching pendants. They held songbooks and wore veils. There were older people: friends of Stewart's parents, patients of Dr. Steptoe. Everyone tissuing their eyes like they had bottled their grief for this very moment.

The clouds over the cemetery were as dark as the shadows they cast. They rumbled. They made everyone cold. The rain kept coming and sometimes thunder. The patches of artificial grass laid around the fresh graves flattened and, more noticeably, could be seen as a different color than what was natural.

Under his breath, the preacher cursed the funeral director

for forfeiting a second tarp to a baby's burial two counties over. Mr. Hicks lent him an umbrella and, ready to begin the service, the preacher stepped into the downpour. He stood between the heads of the identical plots.

During his sermon, Bitty Jack noticed Mrs. Hicks was not paying attention. She seemed to look through the crowd, moving her head slightly at times as if to get a better view of something or someone that had a motion of its own.

Bitty Jack turned to see if she could spot what had divided her attention. She looked back at Mrs. Hicks, whose lips now formed two words so indeterminably it looked like she was chewing on the inside of her mouth. She said it over and over, never making a sound.

"My daughter, my daughter, my daughter, my daughter . . ."

In the far reaches of the cemetery, Bitty Jack saw no one. There was rain and there were headstones. There were statues shaped like angels. There were open holes and shovels stacked beside them. There were cars with their lights on and flowers beaten down.

When the preacher finished he nodded to the funeral director, who tapped the white carnation on his lapel to signal the pall bearers, who each wore white carnations on their lapels, to leave their loved ones and join him at the hearse closest to him.

There were no umbrellas this time. To keep the caskets dry, there would have had to have been six men to carry the coffins and six more to keep off the rain. Twelve men, plus a preacher, plus the funeral director and his two attendants would simply not fit around the two partner graves. Mr. Hicks and his partners emptied Dr. Steptoe's hearse first because he would lay next to the family seated on the first row, under the tarp. Then they got Tootsie, who lay next to him.

Rain beaded and rolled off the caskets.

Bitty Jack was not eager to see her boyfriend's parents lowered like furniture. She was sick of all the tears. This had gone on long enough. She hated this place. She hated the rain. She hated Mrs. Hicks, who had suddenly stood up. Following her lead, the extended family stood up, their soles caught in the mud, laces asunder.

Stewart never budged, his head in his hands. He didn't watch the caskets set down on the pulleys. He didn't sense the crackpot Bitty saw in Mrs. Hicks.

The funeral attendants pulled the motor levers, which started the caskets on their easy way down. The small engines churned. The pulleys were taut. All eyes, except Bitty Jack's, were on the Steptoes' descent.

Bitty Jack watched Mrs. Hicks sway close to Dr. Steptoe's coffin. Her lips were still moving, but they were unreadable. It was if she were slurring her words mouthed in tongue.

Mr. Hicks made his way around the sinking Steptoes to comfort his wife. He excused himself past the preacher, past the relatives, but in his effort to be courteous, he was too slow. Before he could lay a hand on her, Mrs. Hicks jumped.

She cleared Dr. Steptoe, but belly-flopped onto his wife's coffin that at this point was close to a foot below ground. She straddled the casket and snatched flowers off it like fistfuls of hair.

"Tootsie!" she screamed. "Where is she?"

"Carolyn," came her husband's voice. "Carolyn," through the rhythm of the rain.

The casket sunk even deeper, two, then three feet. The pulleys swayed under Mrs. Hicks's frantic efforts. Mrs. Hicks slid to one side, shifted her weight, regained her balance. She jerked up her skirt for better leverage. Her black panty hose tore. Her slim legs fattened against the sides of the casket.

Mr. Hicks tried to reach down for her, but she was too far gone.

She bounced on her friend. "Answer me!"

One of the pulleys broke and the foot of the coffin slipped and hit the hole hard. Mrs. Hicks hugged the coffin like a tree. "Is my daughter with you? Did she die worse than you?"

"Carolyn," said Mr. Hicks. "Carolyn—"

"WHERE IS MY DAUGHTER?"

Mrs. Hicks put her hands on the edge of the casket door. "*Tell me!*" She screamed and yanked with all her strength.

"It's been locked," said the funeral director.

"It's no use," said Mr. Hicks.

But Mrs. Hicks continued. Her fingers slipped off the waxed oak, her body flew backward into the mud, calves moving crazily against the upright casket.

"Is my daughter with you? Did she die worse than you?"

Mr. Hicks was on his stomach now. The funeral director joined him. He motioned to his attendants and all four men lay side by side. They reached into the grave, none of them quite reaching her.

Mrs. Hicks was stuck between the casket and the side of the grave. Her legs still in the air, the four men took swipes at her feet. One of the attendants caught hold of an ankle, but seemed hexed at the sight of Mrs. Hicks's orange thong.

The rest of the mourners were shell-shocked, but Bitty Jack came forward and told the attendant to "Pull!"

Within moments, the men gathered Mrs. Hicks in their arms, but Mrs. Hicks defied them. She pointed through the crowd. She thrust out both arms and screamed for her daughter. "Nicole!" She got loose. "Nicole! There she is!"

Mrs. Hicks tried to run but she stumbled, one shoe lost, on permanent loan to a size 6-narrow Steptoe. She hit the crowd like rows of Red Rover. Some people got out of her way. One gentleman tried to stun her with the handle of his umbrella. Everyone turned to see what she was trying for. But there was nothing. Just a storm settling and Mrs. Hicks falling for the final time that day.

She fainted, face first, into the mud.

Stewart made his first move. He came forward to help Mr. Hicks help his wife through the cemetery toward their car. Each took one arm by what was left of her biceps. They carried her this way: disheveled, legs like string.

Bitty Jack stayed back. She watched the mourners make way for the Hicks, but, suddenly, one woman stepped out of the crowd.

She wore a black turtleneck tunic and a long fitted skirt. Her body ballooned in the front and back. Her beads swung at the cliffs of her boobs. If Mrs. Hicks had looked up, the woman would have blocked her view entirely. She put a hand on each man's shoulder. She said something and Mr. Hicks nodded. Stewart nodded too.

The woman put her finger under Mrs. Hicks's chin. She raised it and spoke as if Mrs. Hicks's eyes were open. "Now don't you get upset about me stealing your party."

With a tiny chuckle, she moved aside and walked straight toward Tom, calling his name, waving as if she might be invisible.

"I live across the street," she said and shook Tom's hand. "We'll move the reception to my house. Call your people. The back door's open. It's the one with the magnolia. Willamina will let them in."

The first thing Bitty Jack noticed when she walked into the Summers's house was a silver-framed eight-by-ten of her thirteen-year-old foe. At the end of the front hallway, Bitty Jack stopped short at the glove table. Guests were filing past her, but Bitty Jack could not resist picking up Sarina's photo.

"My daughter," said Mrs. Summers and took the photo, rubbing away Bitty's fingerprints with the cuff of her blouse.

"Sarina," said Bitty Jack and then again to make it real, "Sarina Summers."

"You know her?"

"We went to camp together."

"Oh, yes," Mrs. Summers said. "Not the best experience for Sarina." She put the photo back, angling it toward the door. She took Bitty Jack's umbrella and placed it with the others in a tall brass container. "There was trouble there. I'm sure you remember. Some unfortunate business with a member of the staff."

"I remember," said Bitty Jack.

"So, who are you now?"

"I'm Stewart's girlfriend."

Mrs. Summers almost laughed. "Then this should really be interesting for you. Look around the house. There are photo albums everywhere. The ones with the blue leather spines are from middle school. There are pictures of Stewart before he gained the weight. Take a look. You'll barely recognize him."

"I'll keep my eyes open."

Mrs. Summers said, "You do that." She pointed Bitty in the direction of Tom's seafood buffet.

Stewart had gotten there before her. Mrs. Summers had planted him in a reading chair, an arm's reach from the peel-and-eat shrimp. Bitty Jack waved to him, but with every step she took, someone else stepped in front of her. There were so many people milling about. Everybody damp. Everybody eager for a napkin of their own. Bitty Jack tried to shimmy through the cliques, ribbing each other, keeping it light. Stewart was impossible to reach and, for the time, Bitty Jack was haunted by the possibility of Sarina.

God forbid she be in this house.

Bitty Jack made her way around the perimeter of the living room. Pictures were placed on tables and shelves, the bookcase, beneath lamps. It did not matter what the frames were made of—brass or cut glass or crystal or wood—every picture was of that girl. There she was at her sweet sixteen. There she was with her fluffy pom-poms.

"High school," explained a voice over Bitty Jack's shoulder. It was a voice, less shrill, that had deepened with the years. But Bitty Jack recognized it. It squeezed her throat and made her fight for every breath.

"That's me," Sarina said. "High school cheerleader. Rah, rah, rah!"

Bitty Jack turned and came to the shocking realization that her mother had been wrong all those years ago. Sarina was still beautiful. Worse than Bitty Jack could have ever imagined. She didn't seem unhappy, as Mrs. Carlson had predicted. Sarina was bright-eyed and cheerful despite the occasion.

Mrs. Summers came up behind Sarina and wrapped her arms around her waist and perched her chin on her daughter's shoulder. "This is who I was telling you about. Stewart's new girlfriend."

"So, how long have you been dating?"

"Over two years."

"Stewart's had a crush on Sarina since they were little." Mrs. Summers turned her head to pretend-whisper into Sarina's ear. "Remember how upset he was when you had to leave to go to camp?"

Sarina laughed and Bitty Jack remembered how she had bragged about some boy. *And then he undid . . . I made myself look . . . he didn't say anything when I . . .* But it wasn't some boy, it was Stewart. She knew that now.

Mrs. Summers broke Bitty Jack's trance. "You two went to camp together. Dear, what did you say your name was again?"

From Sarina's expression, Bitty could see that she had figured it out.

"Mother, this is Jack Carlson's kid."

"Whose?" said Mrs. Summers.

Sarina said, "You heard me."

Mrs. Summers reached out and took Bitty's wrist. She held

it tightly and Bitty Jack wondered if it was possible for bones to break under this kind of pressure. "I'm sorry," said Mrs. Summers, her apology surprising Sarina as much as Bitty Jack.

Bitty Jack concentrated on taking a deep breath. In her mind, she heard her mother, *Take a deeeeeep breath.* "I'm sure my father would appreciate that. I'm sure the owners would want to hear what you said."

"No, dear." Mrs. Summers squeezed her wrist even tighter. "You misunderstand. I'm sorry that you're here. I'm sorry that you're involved with the Steptoe boy and that I am going to have to ask you to leave. I will not have the daughter of a child molester in my house. No matter what the circumstance. No matter who she is." Mrs. Summers let go of Bitty Jack's wrist. She reached behind her to secure her daughter. "Please leave." Mrs. Summers stuck her neck out impatiently. "Tell Stewart you're not feeling well and go out the back door."

Bitty Jack felt dizzy. She put her hand on the banister. She closed her eyes and started counting to ten. At *one, two, three,* Mrs. Summers, again, had her by the wrist.

"Sarina," Mrs. Summers said, "tell Stewart that his friend has gone home. Tell him she threw up and was embarrassed and went home."

Mrs. Summers wrapped her arm around Bitty Jack and trapped her within the confines of her plump upper arm and double-D bosom. She nearly carried Bitty as she steered her through the crowded, noisy house.

"Poor lamb," she explained to every guest who seemed to care. "This is all so upsetting."

When they got to the kitchen, Mrs. Summers opened the back door and helped Bitty Jack into the garage with a swift kick in the butt. Bitty Jack lost her balance on the two cement stairs. She landed hard. Her funny bones keeled over and she turned her head to look at Mrs. Summers.

"No one hurts my daughter." Mrs. Summers braced herself in the doorway, the noise from the reception backing up her authority. "Not your father. Not the sorry sight of you."

Bitty Jack winced as Mrs. Summers slammed the kitchen door. She tried to get up, but she was stunned. She had to figure out a way to get back to the dorms. She had to figure out what to do next. She put her cheek on the cool, painted cement and watched the rain fall outside the raised automatic garage door. She felt a breeze wash over her. She looked under the two cars parked parallel.

Something moved.

Bitty Jack got to her feet. She grabbed a Hula-Hoop as her only defense. She crept around the cars, the sand within the hoop sounding off with every step. When she got to the other side, she put down her makeshift weapon. There in the corner, between the cars and a tool cabinet, was a shivering, curled-up, messed-up human being.

Bitty Jack could not be certain if it was a man or a woman. It was dressed in a gravedigger's jumpsuit and covered with mud. It sat in a wet, sloppy puddle. It was cold beyond a doubt. Not dangerous. Just confused.

"Are you okay?" said Bitty Jack. "Do you need any help?"

The stranger looked up and took off a worker's cap. A Rapunzel's worth of long flaxen hair fell around her face. It fell down the front of her. It fell past her elbows. It was a girl, all right, and Bitty Jack knew who. "You were there today. Your mother wasn't crazy."

"Haven't you heard?" Nicole seemed startled at the sound of her own voice. She licked the snot from over her lip. "I'm the only one who's crazy around here."

PART THREE

Off with Her Head

Sarina

For Sarina, it had been a very bad day. Cold without release. Rotten for many reasons. It started with the funeral, which she had missed because of Joe.

That morning, he whispered "Stay in bed a little longer." Kiss, kiss, kiss. His body warm. He held her down and made her love him. Turned the alarm off. Kept the blinds wrung tight. When she came back from the bathroom, she found him sitting up in bed. She was naked and on her period. He was stern, his lips curled down.

"I don't want you running to the side of some ex-boyfriend."

"I haven't seen him since high school."

"I don't care. I still don't like it."

Joe pulled back the covers and patted the blank spot. He smoothed the wrinkles on the butter yellow sheets. There was a dent in the partial down pillow he had bought just for her. It did look comfortable. Sarina crawled in and felt him press his body into her back.

"I am the tablespoon. You are the teaspoon."

Sarina purred as she always did when Joe flattered the two

of them and the way that they fit. She pushed her back against his chest. She closed her eyes at the sound of thunder, not far off, probably in Northport. Reaching back, she ran her hand along his peach-fuzzed hip. She was comfortable with his jealousy. Grateful for an excuse to stay out of the rain.

They got out of bed when Joe went for the shower. Time for work. Up and at 'em. They ate cereal and Joe walked Sarina to her car.

"Late night, again?" she asked.

" 'Fraid so," said Joe.

"Call me," she said. "I'll be at my mother's."

Of course, Joe did not call and that's the second thing that got on her nerves. If she were making a list, in order, it would be the third. The second would be thirteen cars parked on her lawn, twenty more curbed at the neighbors', the cars extending two blocks over. Sarina had to hike from her Prelude to the front door. She was surprised by the Steptoe party; her house full like when her mother was married.

That was the biggie, the first strike, the pisser: a Summers gathering. Her mother making rounds. Stewart as the guest of honor. That Chickasaw freak all up in her face. She should have gone to that funeral. Prepared herself. Worn the right clothes. If she had gone, she wouldn't have had to mingle like company. There would have been no surprises. She would have known what to say.

At one point Mrs. Summers asked about her boyfriend. "Where's your boyfriend?" she said. "Where *is* our dear Joe?"

Sarina knew her mother knew, but was tough-loving for effect.

"You've got to keep control of him."

"I'm trying."

"Don't try. Do."

Throughout the course of the reception, Sarina willed him to call. To show her mother that she'd whipped him. To show her mother that she wore the proverbial pants.

But the guests soon left and the caterers cleared. The furniture was moved back into place and her mother retired to her room to lie down. Sarina was left by herself in the living room. Not a chirp, not a murmur. Not a boyfriend who cared.

Through the window, she saw Willamina at her green Chevrolet. She had a trunk full of clothes, extra ironing done at home. She slung two dozen shirts over one arm and carried a stack of sheets on the palm of one hand. She moved steadily, her knee-highs rubbing at the elastic. Sarina waved and wished she could live like Willamina. Sort, press, fold. Spray, rub, wash. No complications. No wants. Not the smallest of desires.

Willamina plowed past her. Sarina followed, spouting details of the party Will had missed because she was helping caterers in the kitchen: some kid fingering the Swedish meatball platter; Stewart up close after so many years.

"What happened to him?"

"I don't know. I guess he went home."

"Home where?" said Willamina.

"*Home* home," Sarina said.

Willamina patted the tight gray curls that fit her head like a cap. "That's a lot to happen to such a young man."

"Hey, Meena, are you cooking dinner tonight?"

"Not my night. You forget. Your mother's had me on a schedule for over a year. She likes the house to herself. Come tomorrow. I'll do something with that left-over shrimp."

Sarina said she would, but she knew that she wouldn't. It was the weekend which brought new movies. Alabama vs. Georgia in a women's gymnastics meet. It was a time to be seen. Tomorrow, date night.

Sarina left her mother to sleep, and she beat every red light back to Tri Delta. Inside, dinner was being served, but Sarina snuck up the stairs and locked her bedroom door behind her. She kept the lamps on low settings. She ate two cherry-frosted untoasted Pop-Tarts. She drank a Coke from the mini-fridge, but wanted a beer. She watched a string of sitcoms and did not answer when sisters knocked or called her name. When Joe phoned, she refused to pick up. She just stared at the answering machine, the button blinking as he spoke.

Sarina did not know how long she could teach lessons. Today's was: *You Can't Find Me, See How It Feels.* But Joe never called back. He didn't hound her like her mother. One message, all night long. One message, that's all he wrote.

Nevertheless, she kept trying to mold him into shape. *Don't lie to me. Don't cheat on me. Call me when you say you will. Tell me I'm the only one.*

The problem was he told her that, but she knew it wasn't true. There were items in his bathroom. Late arrivals. Sudden gifts. For a while she took advantage. He was conscience-stricken, so she asked for more. The Cypress Inn. Large popcorn, forget the small. Maybe a sweater or a new compact disc. How about local theater, Joe? How about two tickets, first-class, to the moon? When totals were tallied, she did not offer to contribute. She just looked at him like an innocent girl, easily impressed by a wallet flipped open.

Mrs. Summers agreed that she was handling him correctly. She said, "Treat him like a dog. When he strays, slap his nose with a wet rolled-up newspaper."

In human terms that meant act like a rag. Don't sleep with him, don't flatter him, make him wait, be late. Make sure he understands there are girls for a good time and girls you marry. There should be no question that Sarina was the marrying kind.

The following spring, Mrs. Summers was not as gung-ho about her daughter's pursuits. The funeral reception had been such a success, Tuscaloosa society had welcomed her back. When Sarina called her mother, she was often cut short by a five-card-draw game beckoning from the blue wicker table. On Saturday mornings, she went to aqua aerobics. There were potlucks and Birmingham trips and teas and movie Mondays. Mrs. Summers was involved. Dressed in gusto. Self-improved. At the Steptoe reception, she had discovered other wives with children grown and hours to fill.

"So what am I, chopped liver?" Sarina huffed and she puffed. "Am I a hole in the head? Am I your sorry sloppy seconds? I'm just your daughter. You know, your own flesh-and-blood. Is it too much to make time for me? Is it too much of a strain on your busy social schedule?"

Mrs. Summers said, "Of course not," and made good on her words. Every Sunday they beat the church crowds to lunch. In every restaurant, Mrs. Summers spread marmalade on toast. She listened to her daughter's predicaments as if Joe were misbehaving for the very first time. She gave her dog theory, her bug theory, pep talks that started, "When I was your age . . ."

"But how did you stand it? Was my father this bad?"

"Your father was tolerable and you were born right away. I was too busy to be bothered. I was too tired to care."

"But how did you stand it?"

"Sarina," said her mother, "you are a beautiful girl."

"And your point is?"

"You expect a lot. And you should. You *should* expect to be treated like a princess. But there are times when you have to consider the payoff. When you marry Joe you can live like a queen."

One Sunday Sarina showed her mother the razor.

Since she'd found it in Joe's bathroom, she had kept it in her purse, in the side zippered pocket, in a plastic sandwich bag. Rickety, pink nothing. Always knocking against her hip. Always blocking the way to her one Chanel lipstick. It made her sick, that skanky razor. Every time she touched it, it made her want to puke. To know that Joe was gallivanting. Keeping a spot warm in his medicine cabinet.

"So what?" said Mrs. Summers.

"So how do I get rid of her?"

Mrs. Summers tossed the package back to Sarina. "Sweetheart, pink razors are exactly like mice. Where there's one, pussy follows. There's no changing Joe now."

Sarina decided to try a less traditional approach. She found Willamina pushing the Dumpster up the driveway.

"Go on," said Willamina at Sarina's Lady Bic in a bag. "Bin's empty. Drop it in."

"It's not that," said Sarina.

"What, you want more?"

As Willamina parked the Dumpster outside the garage, Sarina fiddled with the razor. She waited for Willamina to figure out what she wanted. She always had an opinion about what she thought was best.

"What?" said Willamina. "You want it for supper?"

"Meena, be serious."

"Well, what then?"

"I need your help. I wanna get Joe."

"Get Joe," Willamina repeated. She kicked down the brake and crossed her arms atop the Dumpster. She leaned forward. "How you think we gonna do that?"

"You're from New Orleans."

"So?"

"You know how to do things."

"What things?" Willamina grinned and confused Sarina with the way that she smiled.

"Things like," Sarina stammered, "you know, voodoo."

"Voodoo." Willamina laughed. "Voooodoooo!" She wagged her arms like a ghost. "What you think, child? I'm gonna take that little thing and make a soup, stick pins in it? You think I got the power?" She scratched dried bird crap of the lid off the Dumpster. She flicked at it. She blew the spot clean. "You the one with the power. Dump his ass."

"I don't want to dump him. I want to stop him from screwing around."

"Well, I can't help you there."

" 'Cause you don't know voodoo?"

" 'Cause, obviously, I don't know you. I can't believe you want to live like your mother. Same old housewife, same old shit."

"You don't know what you're talking about."

Willamina smirked. "I'm sure I don't."

"You don't know how hard it is."

Softer now. "I'm sure I don't."

"What am I supposed to do?" Sarina opened her arms as when she was six, stepping out of Mr. Bubbles, anxious for Willamina to towel her off before the cold set in. "Huh?" She wrapped her arms around Willamina's neck. She snuggled into the soft places even though Willamina's arms remained at her side.

"You're too old for this."

"Why?" Sarina said and wiped her eyes on the strap of Willamina's apron. The mascara left a smudge. Again, she said, "Why?"

"Because you are." Willamina sighed, pushing Sarina back with her breath. "You are."

Sarina kept her hands clasped as Willamina tried to pry them apart.

"Let go," Willamina said and pushed at her shoulders. "You think you gonna hold on forever? I'm not your mama. Your mama's inside. She's layin' down on her bed. Go cling onto her."

"But, Meena, why? What'd I do? You've always been like a mother to me."

"Get off me, girl."

Sarina stepped back. She noticed bags beneath Willamina's eyes.

"Like a mother," said Willamina. "Like a mother, what's that mean? That I cook for you? That I clean your dirty clothes? What, 'cause I'm nice? 'Cause I used to give a damn?"

"But what about biscuits? What about my Mammy doll?"

"It's a job, girl." Willamina opened the door to the kitchen. She didn't look back, but Sarina heard her just the same. "For sixteen years, it's just been a job."

By the end of her junior year, Sarina had fallen short in her Tri Delta responsibilities. In her attempts to discipline Joe, then woo him back, then keep him to herself, Sarina had missed several house meetings. She'd shown up late to the Kids Carnival for Cervical Cancer. She was distracted and failing to set an example. Secretly she had been told that she was on probation.

She called home, crying to her mother. "You've gotta help me. I've got to do something or I'm gonna get kicked out."

Mrs. Summers assured her that she would not lose her membership. If the Tri Delts tried anything, she had an ace up her sleeve.

"What?" Sarina sniffed.

"Never mind," said her mother.

"But if it has to do with me . . . "

Mrs. Summers cut her off. She suggested that Sarina organize a mother-daughter luncheon for the active Tri Delts. "We can have it at the Cotton Patch. Burn our letters into the tables."

The Cotton Patch was a restaurant, forty minutes away in Eutaw, Alabama, where the dog track used to be. There was a gas station nearby, but besides some stray greyhounds, that was about it. The Cotton Patch was a real log cabin with only one room for dining but the restaurateurs turned it into one of Tuscaloosa's finest establishments.

Everything at the Cotton Patch was fried and smothered in white gravy. Pickled watermelon rinds set out as the appetizer. A stack of Sunbeam bread. Plastic bibs. To drink: Coke or cold beer. The waitress uniform resembled Aunt Jemima's and, like Aunt Jemima, the all-black wait staff was encouraged to say little more than *Yes, ma'am* and *No, sah* and dole out specials like sugar on the table.

It was tradition to leave your name on the premises. People came with Swiss Army knives. Some used their dinner forks. The gas station sold disposable lighters. Little girls pulled barrettes from their hair. The walls and the windowsills, the tables and benches, the floor and the ceiling were wood and more wood. An untarnished spot was like heaven to touch. To squeeze in two initials guaranteed your immortality.

Sarina had reserved ten tables for the Deltas. Most sisters attending were newly inducted. They were chatty and giddy and showing off for their moms. Mrs. Summers had bought a skirt and blouse, especially for the occasion. The skirt was long and pleated. The blouse came with a vest sewn to the shoulders. All the officers were required to attend, except for the treasurer, whose mother had eaten roach repellent and hung herself in the yard. The lunch fit perfectly into Greek Week. Everyone was undeniably impressed. It showed visitors a little culture. Down-home cooking. The smell of skin.

Sarina thought it couldn't get any better until the fried pies were served and Joe and another woman took a table in the corner.

"I can't believe it."

"I know," said Mrs. Summers. "They still use real butter!"

Sarina pinched her mother. "By the kitchen. I can't believe it."

Joe was holding the woman's hand across the table. They

were playing finger games. Leaning forward. Tête-à-tête. Joe brushed a lash off her cheek and told one of his dead-baby jokes, which sent her reeling. He always made that face when he told a dead-baby joke. The woman snorted and everyone turned.

"Sah-ree!" she cheeped. "It's my laugh. I'm so embarrassed."

Joe tugged her hands away from her face. She was blushing and he liked this. Sarina knew. He'd told her the same thing. He cradled both her hands now. He thanked the waitress for the rinds.

Sarina roasted her nail file over a Playboy lighter she had picked up at the gas station. She held it firmly, the white profiled bunny ears sticking out within her fist. The nail file turned black. The odor masked the scent of her fried peach pie topped with cherry Breyers. She imagined singeing a lover's cross on Joe's forehead. JD + SS should send a clear signal. A message like that should keep the bitches at bay.

Some of the Tri Delts had caught on by this point. They had seen Sarina's boyfriend. They had heard her refer to him as marriage material. Sarina could guess what girls were whispering to their mothers. She could imagine the rumors let loose after lunch.

Mrs. Summers leaned close enough to cut Sarina's meat. She took the nail file by the handle and tucked it under her plate. "This is it," she whispered. "This is how you'll get your ring."

When Sarina stood up, she was filled with her mother's venom. She had been instructed to walk past him, barely notice, then stop and chat. Make him squirm. Greet them both with salutations torn out of *Charlotte's Web.* Charmed, charmed. She should treat him like her husband. *It's so nice to finally meet you.* Shake her hand until it breaks. *Take a good look, Joe,* she should say inside her mind. *This is class. It's Jackie O. You've been bad, so make it better. Sit up, you lousy mongrel. Beg.*

Play dead. Trade your shame in for two carats. I want a platinum band for this damn stunt.

When she tried this, Sarina was met with reserve. Joe's nerves were unshakable. His face a field of unreadable marks. Before him, she felt like an ornery gal. Nothing to get upset about. Where was his chicken-fried chicken?

"Who's this?" Sarina broke.

"Mary Druthers," said Joe.

"What's this?" Sarina said.

"Pickled rinds," said Joe.

"Oh, for Christ's sake, don't bullshit me!"

"What do you want me to say?"

"Tell her that she's meaningless. It's over. Good-bye."

Joe kept his mouth shut. The Tri Deltas were silent. Mrs. Summers had chosen this time to leave the table to powder her nose. Mary Druthers looked at Sarina like she was a retard lost from her short yellow bus. She took Joe's hand as easily as she had done throughout the hors d'oeuvres.

"Fine," said Sarina. "That's fine. That's just fine." She tried to hold Joe's gaze, but she couldn't. She was frantic. "You're meaningless," she said hoarsely. "It's over. Goodbye."

From the gas station, Sarina called the only person who might still care. She knew the number by heart. She had made this call when things weren't right in the past. Desperate times called for desperate men. Stewart said she could come right over.

Pulling into his driveway, Sarina thought back to when they were kids. She had never been to his house as a girl. He had always come and gotten her. Always shown up right on time. It was later when she'd visited Tootsie's prescreen Delta parties. Then the yard was full of promise, the house packed with kick-up-your-heels. Turning off the ignition, Sarina wondered if this was what she had missed: a quiet place where the roses stayed open, the metal flag on the mailbox as bright as the day.

Stewart had lost weight since the last time she'd seen him. It was only twenty pounds, but Sarina could see the potential for more. Grieving had agreed with him. The dark circles under his eyes made him seem older, wiser, reliable at all costs.

He led her to the living room where, on the overstuffed floral sofa, he appeared out of place. This was no bachelor pad. Surrounded by antique furniture, framed paintings, and throw pillows, Sarina appreciated the years of work made-to-order.

She said, "So, you're doing okay."

"Let's not talk about how I'm doing."

"Sorry," she said.

"Don't be sorry. Just talk. Tell me what happened with your big, dumbass boyfriend. Let me feel bad for someone else for a change."

So Sarina let the stories fly. She started from the beginning: the boat show, the family dinner. She called herself a fool and an idiot and Stewart said, "No." She said she should have known better. In hindsight, she tried to set the scenes a little differently. But at every misreport, Stewart interrupted. "Are you sure that's what he said . . . You mean it didn't seem weird when he . . . Jesus, Ree, you've got to be kidding!"

By the time Sarina got around to the Cotton Patch, it was dark outside and dark in Stewart's house. The grandfather clock chimed eight in the hallway. Dust was more visible beneath the moonlit skylights.

Sarina said, "Aren't you lonely living here?"

Stewart said, "No."

"Aren't you scared sometimes?"

"Scared of what?" And then, "You?"

Sarina liked the second alternative. She hadn't been fierce in a very long time. She scooted closer to Stewart, one cushion beside him. "Of me?"

He nodded slightly.

"Of me?" She pushed her body into the warmth of his side. She settled into his groove. She felt the rhythm of his breath drawn deeper with the years.

Stewart kept inhaling, exhaling, inhaling. At the moment it seemed it was all he could master. Sarina pulled his arm from the back of the couch. She snuggled under and stroked it like a heavy old wrap.

She climbed on top of him. Her knees on his thighs, his knees beneath her shins. She could not straddle him. Her cheerleading days behind her, she was even less limber. On top of his legs, she felt tall and in charge. She could see out the back windows. She could see the possibilities. Moving in on Stewart would require little work. He'd inherited a lifestyle. Lots of money. Two-and-a-half baths. Tootsie's taste was her taste. No struggling years required.

And despite what he'd become, there was chemistry when she kissed him.

Maybe it was repeating what they had first tried together. Maybe it was puppy love barking closely at her heels. But, to be certain, there was something. Something wicked. Something sweet. Sarina closed her eyes and forgot her plans and schemes.

Stewart grabbed her hands as she fiddled with his zipper. "Don't."

"Don't why?"

"I'm with someone."

"Just once." Sarina pushed her shins against his sweaty shirt. Her ass was on his thighs. Her toes around his belt. She gripped the sofa back, locking the two of them in place. She said again, "Just once."

And Stewart kept his mouth shut. He did not argue. He did not dare.

When the phone woke them up, Sarina knew it was his girlfriend. *Where are you?* she must be saying. *Didn't we say such and such a time?* Stewart had reached up and taken the phone from the side table. He now sat naked, cross-legged on the carpet, a sofa seat cushion balanced modestly on his lap. He wound the phone cord around one finger. He apologized profusely. "I just fell asleep."

Sarina stood up and stretched right in front of him. Meow, she mouthed and reached her fists to skylight night. Stewart was listening to that Chickasaw freak, but he watched Sarina, parading slowly, strutting her stuff.

See what a woman is supposed to look like. No pock marks, no freckles, no deceiving underwear. I'm covered in curves and I glow after sex. Can you see me glow, baby? I am extraordinary. I could be yours.

Sarina strolled around the sofa, making sure his eyes went with her. Out of sight, she pulled an orange juice carton from the side shelf of the fridge. She drank some, but let most of it miss her lips and hit her body.

I glisten, she thought. *I glimmer. I'm gold.*

Taking long strides as if she'd kept her heels on, Sarina returned to her first and future love. She smiled at Stewart, naked on his knees, fishing for his boxers somewhere beneath the sofa.

With both hands, Sarina slapped Stewart on the ass. Stewart scuttled to his feet and awkwardly stepped into his shorts. He froze as Sarina pressed her sticky stomach teasingly against him. She held him close, arranging her breasts so that he could see her nipples. She looked into his face, so serious, so intent. She let herself relax. Hang back. Look alive. This time she would be ready. Savor everything he said. When he told her that he loved her, she would not interrupt.

"Ree," he started.

Sarina waited for the gush.

"Tonight was a mistake."

"A mistake?" said Sarina.

"A stupid mistake."

Stewart pushed her away and she lost her footing, toppling onto the couch like a preteen in stilettos. She sat there in shock as Stewart scrambled with his clothes. Zipping up his pants, he walked hurriedly from the living room. He shouted as if she might be in the backyard. "Let yourself out. I'm sorry. I gotta go."

Sarina was dumbfounded, but still willing to kill. "You know that she'll smell me all over your clothes!"

"No she won't," Stewart returned, as if to make his point final. "She won't." He shook his head. "She's not like you."

With Stewart gone, Sarina didn't feel so pretty. The orange juice had dried. Her pubic hair clotted as if it she'd romanced the Elmer's Glue cow. Her makeup was a mess. Her lipstick rubbed off. She was cold. She was clammy. Belly empty. She stank.

What was wrong with her? Where was the control she used to carry like cover-up? Her life had always been Win, Win, Win. Now it had dissolved to No, Not Again. Sarina was paranoid. Itchy. On guard. The windows betrayed her. Her mind pulled rabbits. It was as if there was some sort of conspiracy brewing. As if a spy was outside, writing feverishly on a birdseed bag. She could feel the eyes of judgment take aim through night goggles. Stalk her. Mock her. Memorize her every move.

Well, this had to end.

When there was no one left to trust, she could always trust herself.

She deserved Stewart and she would go get him. According to playground rules it was fair and it was square. She saw him first. She tagged him eight years ago. He was covered in her cooties. He was hers. He was hers.

Yet, she had to be careful in her approach. She couldn't just show up and tell Bitty Jack she'd screwed him. She couldn't sit in his house until he returned. No, in this case, it was definitely bad to be the bad guy. No matter what the circumstances, Stewart would never propose to the bad guy.

So she would take him on the rebound. Make Miss Bitty Jack undesirable. Once Stewart left Bitty, Sarina would mend his broken heart. She would be there through the tough times. She would remind him of how good she could be to him when she wanted.

What would it take to make Stewart break up with her? What was too distasteful for Stewart to forgive? When Sarina concentrated, the answer came easily. It was as if the trap was right under her nose. It was infallible. Divine. Told-you-so-ish. God-approved. Sarina would hit that freak where it hurt.

Take Back the Night had been promoted for weeks. There were flyers posted on telephone poles, ads run for free in *The Crimson White.* The march would start in the Bryant-Denny Stadium parking lot and weave through campus to end on the Quad. It was an event dominated by double x-zomed GDIs. Unlike the Greek girls, God Damned Independents did not consider date rape to be part of a beer buzz. The National Organization for Women ran the show. The dormitory indies turned out in droves. Tuscaloosa's twelve lesbians were sure to attend. Golden Key could be counted on. Even feminists would show their faces. To combat stereotypes, sororities marched. They had T-shirts made, colorized by house. There was a sign-up sheet on the Tri Delta bulletin board. Sarina's name was the last on the list.

The Tri Delta president was pleased to see Sarina involved. "It's such a dirty subject. I'm surprised at you, Ree."

Sarina said women's safety was important. "What happened to the days when we could walk alone at night? When we could jog and have a drink and, like, totally feel okay about it?"

"Aren't you the little speech-giver."

"Hey," said Sarina, "I do what I can."

"I'm beginning to see that. If this goes well, you're off probation."

In the Bryant-Denny parking lot, Sarina passed out candles to the Tri Delta marchers. She had been waiting for this night, biding her time, practicing exactly how the evening would go. She had refrained from calling Stewart and, with the certainty of converting Stewart's taste from white trash to diamond girl, she had weaned herself from checking the answering machine. Did Joe call? Joe never called.

The parking lot was getting louder. Women practicing their chants, passing fire wick-to-wick. There was every shape and size. Big bangs and buzz cuts. Unkempt armpits and electrolyzed eyebrows. There were no men allowed, except for one who was there for the photo opportunities. At the front of the crowd Big Al stood solemnly, his arms behind him, his head bowed in respect.

Stewart was in there, and where Stewart was, Bitty Jack Carlson was surely close by.

Somebody fired a starting pistol and everybody screamed. The march moved forward, stopping traffic with a loud, slow momentum. When the crowd reached the Quad, the leaders and Big Al climbed the Amelia Gayle Gorgas Library stairs where a microphone was already in place. Sarina steered the

Tri Delts toward the front for better news coverage. Their picture would look great in the sorority newsletter.

One woman after the next came out of the crowd. They spoke of rapes and muggings and run-ins and sex wars. One freshman was locked in the Brass Monkey bathroom. One woman accosted in two different dorms. There were scars shown and abortions admitted. Tears came like comets and then Sarina took the stage.

The Tri Delta president looked shocked, but hushed her girls. The NOW leader asked Sarina's name and introduced her, passing the mike.

Sarina stayed silent, sucking in humid air. She scanned the crowd for the Chickasaw freak. She was easy to find. Ugly girl, three o'clock. The candle Bitty Jack held cast a glare across her glasses. She looked like a bug, her line of sight undeterminable. She might be staring straight at Sarina. She might be looking at Stewart one foot behind.

"I was a victim," Sarina said strong and clear, "but not the kind you've heard about tonight. What happened to me happened a long time ago, when I was twelve years old and completely defenseless. It was horrible." She shut her eyes as if reliving the moment. "To be a child and taken advantage of by an adult, a grown man."

"What happened?" came a voice.

"You can tell us," encouraged NOW.

"I can't," Sarina whispered making the microphone squeal. "I can't," she repeated a little louder than necessary. "I've been able to forget for so many years. But I can't do that anymore. I don't get to do that anymore. Every day," she aimed her finger directly at Bitty Jack, "I have to see his goddamn daughter and know her father's never paid!"

The crowd gasped and Bitty Jack dropped her candle. She ran, her figure shrinking until all eyes lost her and turned back to center stage.

Sarina false-fainted and two NOW girls caught her. They called for Big Al. "Help us get her off the stage."

Stewart came forward and took Sarina in his gray felt arms. She wrapped her hands around his neck and pressed her face into his giant ear. The elephant skin was so soft and comforting. It was like she was being carried in a purse or a pouch.

Stewart lay her down in front of the library doors, twenty feet behind the mike stand, the cement columns making her efforts seem heroic. In the distance, Sarina heard the roar of the crowd for another confession. Stewart leaned over her, his Hulkish costume blocking everything out. Sarina tried to see Stewart through Big Al's black mouth screen. She apologized for exposing his girlfriend for what she was.

"You're lying," she could hear him. "You're lying!"

"No, it's true!"

"God, Ree, don't you think I'd remember? You pulled the same crap when we were sixteen!"

"No, this is different. It really happened. I swear."

"Bullshit!" said Stewart.

"The other night wasn't bullshit." She grabbed his trunk with both hands. "Have you told her about that? Have you told her you fucked me?"

"I fucked you all right."

"She'll leave you."

"Let go!" Stewart jerked his head back. He put his front feet to his ears. He yanked and he yanked till he yanked his trunk free.

"I'll take you back," said Sarina.

But Stewart was gone. Jogging down the library steps. Elbowing his way in the direction that Bitty ran.

Back at Tri Delta, the sisters were split.

Some were behind Sarina one hundred percent. They had

taken back their night. They had taken Sarina back to the house. In a way, each one wished that she could trade places. To be the one known for something. A survivor. A fittest.

Others were pissed off, humiliated, waiting up. They had seen Sarina's confession on the ten o'clock news. Bert Hicks had gone live and there she was, camera ready. She had shamed the Tri Deltas. She had aired her dirty laundry like soiled panties at a prison rodeo. Delta girls did not kiss and tell. They were never molested. They were not spectacles-in-waiting. People's parents were calling. Alumni asking, *How did this trash get past?*

And then, there were sisters who hadn't even noticed. They were reliving Spring Break up in their rooms, trading peach schnapps for rum, comparing their hickies.

Everyone else was in the front hall, waiting. Sarina was escorted through the house by the Tri Delta president. "Has my mom called?" she asked over questions and insults. "Am I back on probation?"

The president didn't answer. She put her hands on Sarina's back and steered her through the pack of girls, some in Take Back the Night T-shirts, others in rollers and PJs, slippers and robes. Everyone clamoring to talk to Sarina. Everyone wanting a piece of her pie.

It disturbed Sarina that things had not gone as planned. Stewart sucked. A school year of her life had been taken by Joe. She'd been out of the social circuit. Forgotten by college ring–bearing, upper-class men. So she had to throw herself back into the arena where sex sold and there were no returns. She had to start over. Become someone no man could refuse.

There was one thing left.

Sarina imagined herself on the Alabama football field. The AstroTurf had been shampooed and ninety thousand people had shown up to see her. On her scalp, she felt the weight of good rhinestones and 14 carat-plated gold. She was next year's Homecoming Queen.

Winning that title would prove her life theory right: that all was controllable with the proper gut wrench. As queen, Sarina would be back on top. Everyone's favorite. The prime pedestal pusher. A few good men would be in that stadium. After the Homecoming game, she would pick one and start over.

Nicole

In her bathrobe, Mrs. Summers paced furiously between her daughter and the sliding-glass doors. She held a rolled-up newspaper with Sarina pictured at Take Back the Night. Mrs. Summers seemed iffy. At a loss in her living room. She put her hands on her hips. She put her fists in the air. She opened her mouth and her mouth warped to Why.

"*Why?*" she asked Sarina, who sat still on the sofa. "*Why?*" she asked the backyard as if the answer was out there, camped beneath two bed sheets and a bristle-less broom.

The only one out there was Nicole Bernice Hicks. She was rooted like a weed on the confines of Deerlick. She sat in one of her many viewing spots. She adjusted her binoculars. She watched closely. She saw it all.

For eighteen months and six days, Nicole had been watching Sarina. She followed her on dates. She followed her wherever she could. Nicole had been present for the sad seduction of Stewart, Sarina's speech at the library, so many other things. There was always a window shade raised just high enough. Blinds never shut tightly. A porch light illuminating a hint or a dare.

When Sarina was home, Nicole watched from the woods. She sat on the moss, her back against the tallest pine. After so much time, the roots had grown around her, made room, saved her place. Nicole was sure she would never be caught. No one ever climbed that tree or had a picnic in the shade at the edge of the woods.

If they did, the rumor mill would have churned out fresh malarkey. The tree had Ree's name on it. The last time she counted, Nicole had carved it ninety times.

Through her binoculars, Nicole could see Sarina tucked within her mother's arms. She was crying, crying, crying. She was faking, Nicole could tell. Never in her life had she seen Sarina lose it. Her lip was as stiff as upper lips could get. To get herself started, Sarina must have bit her tongue, imagined herself with no fingers, no nose. Whatever the tactic, Nicole was impressed. Sarina's face was flushed with color. Her mouth trembled. Her breath came quickly. Every sentence, hijacked by coughs. Blue eyes, bloodshot. Puffy lips, pale. She was so beautiful this way. So luscious, wet with tears.

Nicole wanted to rush the sliding-glass doors, break through the plate, and tackle Sarina. She'd tell her that she'd always been there. She'd never left. *Hi, Ree! It's me!* Rolling across the carpet, Nicole would press down when on top. Glass would be everywhere. Shards net between them. Slivers on the floor. There'd be blood, blood, blood. Nicole could share her pent-up pain. The cut glass would keep cutting, embedding past their lines of flesh.

Nicole knew better. She would not endanger, least not ruin, what she had.

After all this time, Tuscaloosa had forgotten her. The reward posters had come down. Too old for milk cartons, Nicole's photo had been filed. Police had put away their flashlights and moved on to simpler cases. With the proper disguise, Nicole could blend into a crowd. She fell in with the trees. Quiet as a bee's knees. Hers was now like any other face: eyes, nose, and chin. Hers was now a simple story often taken as just that.

Once upon a time there was a girl who hurt her mother, who loved another, who ran away.

Nicole had become the ultimate ghost girl. She was a shadow, a memory, a fettered voice in the night. She spoke to Sarina without making a sound, without ever being spotted, but she knew she got through. Sometimes, Sarina turned right and not left, put her hair in a barrette, wore that cardigan set. All these signals told Nicole that Ree heard her. That she knew Nicole was watching. That she knew Nicole still cared.

Nicole had Sarina exactly where she wanted. She had Sarina *when* she wanted. She watched and followed. Followed and watched. Nicole was content to observe Sarina from this distance. Even if she didn't always like what she saw.

At the moment, she didn't like seeing Sarina so tightly knit to Mrs. Summers. When the two of them got together, Nicole always felt unsettled. The two of them together made Nicole extremely nervous.

Nicole got onto her stomach and crawled through the hole she'd dug under the fence. She lay still in the bushes that bordered the woods.

As Mrs. Summers led Sarina from the living room through the house, Nicole dashed though the empty backyard. Mrs. Summers had dismantled the swings long ago. There weren't any trees. Just a barbecue grill. Nicole squatted by the watering hose, curled in circles, hung with a nail on the brick siding. Through the window above, she heard the two women speaking.

Mrs. Summers said, "What's done is done. We'll have to use this Carlson business in the best way we can."

"How?" said Sarina. "Delta still might kick me out."

"Nobody's kicking anybody. I'll take care of it tonight."

"How?" said Sarina.

"Just leave it to me. If my daughter wants to be a Delta, that's what she'll be. If you want to be Homecoming Queen, you'll be that too."

When Sarina drove away, Nicole moved to the Summers' garage and sat in the nook between the wall and tool closet. Nicole knew what was in there: Tupperware bowls full of nails grouped by size, screws and *Playboys*, hammers and bolts. The tool closet was left behind by Sarina's wayward father. Mrs. Summers never went near it.

In that spot, Nicole savored her handmade reality. Nobody bothered her. Surprised her. Denied her. She could be comfortable in this corner. Absent from the world.

She fell asleep and, in her dreams, met a very nice girl made of all kinds of candy. She was Sarina, only better. Her hair, untangled licorice. Her lips filled fuller by cherry syrup injections. Chocolate-sprinkled freckles. Glazed and sugar-coated. Bonbon boobies and congealed joints. She could not run. She just stood pretty. A gingerbread piece for a quiet, good girl. Nicole would surprise this confected Sarina. She would kiss her frosted skin. She would bite into her shoulder and know that muscle tastes like taffy.

Nicole woke when the sun set, when Cheshire cars came home for supper. Her father's car was the only one missing. As usual, he had a date with the six o'clock news. Her father had always been pulled away by reporting. Flood, feast, or famine, he was anchored to his anchor chair. His eyes chockful of community concern. His sports coat tucked neatly under his ass. Mr. Hicks was a man who was conveniently absent. Gone from his home when the dirty stuff went down.

What happened that night was that Mrs. Summers crossed the road. She marched swiftly to Nicole's parents' front yard.

Nicole knew if Mrs. Summers put her finger on the doorbell, her mother would let her stand there until she died of natural causes. Mrs. Summers must have known this too. She walked directly to their dining room window and rapped briskly on the pane.

"Carolyn, it's time we talked!"

She called, "Carolyn, yoo-hoo!"

Rap, rap, rap. "Yoo-hoo!"

Rap, rap, rap. "I know you're in there!"

Through the binoculars, Nicole saw her mother pull back the drapes. She did not look well. Worse than at the funeral. Her hair was clipped at the back of her head. Brown roots, an inch in length. Sunken eyes, dark as sautéed marbles. Not pretty. No, not too pretty. In the vein of If-I-Was-Dead-Then-She'd-Really-Be-Sorry, Nicole was glad to see her mother affected.

Mrs. Hicks said something that Nicole could not make out. Her mother moved her mouth too quickly. She barely spread her lips apart. Balling her hands into tiny fists, she pounded on the glass, but Mrs. Summers did not flinch.

Mrs. Summers simply strolled to the gray-stoned front walkway. She sat down and got comfortable, spreading out her long denim skirt, pushing up her sleeves as if she might pull jacks from her cardigan pocket.

Nicole noticed neighbors peeping out behind their blinds. Opening their doors a crack. Watching and waiting for the clash of two titans.

Mrs. Summers waved hello to Mrs. Three-Doors-Down. She nodded to a woman with a trash bag half empty.

Nicole knew her mother could not tolerate such a scene. So she wasn't surprised when Mrs. Hicks stepped outside. What did surprise her was that she sat down to talk. She sat opposite Mrs. Summers. Both women's legs on the walkway, both butts in the grass. Six-ticket fun-house mirror versions of the other. Fat and skinny. Fraught and frail. They spoke over each other. One whispered. One hissed. The middle-aged she-devils eloquently at war.

Then Mrs. Summers said something that shut Mrs. Hicks up. She said it again and Mrs. Hicks' neck jerked. In the corner of the garage, Nicole wondered what she'd said. In all her life, Nicole had failed to find the words that could quiet her mother.

Mrs. Summers reached into her pocket, wriggled her fingers, the knuckles making waves beneath the densely woven cotton. It seemed she was trying to torture Mrs. Hicks, hunt for something in that pocket among lipstick, keys, and gum. Mrs. Hicks did not appear to draw a breath in those few seconds, her eyes on that pocket, stroking her nub as had become her gross habit.

Nicole shifted nervously, anxious for the big surprise.

Mrs. Summers produced something small and shiny. It was the size of a nickel, but a higher-ranked color. Nicole craned her neck forward as if that would magnify the binoculars' effect. She had to make sure it was what she thought it was.

As if to help Nicole as well as Mrs. Hicks get a closer look, Mrs. Summers held the object away from her body. Her elbow bent, her thumb and first finger pinched the object half a foot from Mrs. Hicks's face. Nicole was scared at what her mother might do. But Mrs. Hicks just sat there, wide-eyed and weary. Her shoulders slumped. Her posture that of a woman defeated.

As if to provoke her, Mrs. Summers flipped it like a kick-off coin. Falling, falling, falling, the object flickered in the glow of the lamp post light.

Mrs. Summers caught it clean. She stood up and started back to her house.

Nicole hugged herself to smother the shock. She was right about that item. It was her mother's diamond ring. The same ring she had swiped when she cut out and ran. The same ring that now left her mother as idle white as the moon.

"Where did you get that?" came Mrs. Hicks's voice across the street.

Mrs. Summers kept walking.

"Wait. Where did you—" Mrs. Hicks was running now. In truth, she was stumbling in a fast, awkward manner. Her arms dangled at her sides. Flat feet upon the pavement, her head wobbled without posture like a puppet with one string.

Mrs. Summers did not look at her. She looked straight ahead. She moved toward her own front door, seemingly confident that her neighbor-slash-nemesis would never catch up.

But she did.

Mrs. Hicks grabbed Mrs. Summers by the back of her sweater and hung on as if she could be dragged until Tuesday. Although the sweater was now pulled snug at the armpits, Mrs. Summers kept walking as if hindered by a weight less than the dead.

"Where did you get that? It can't possibly be mine!"

Mrs. Summers stopped short, two feet from the garage. She whipped around. "You bet it's yours."

Mrs. Hicks said, "Let me see it again."

"Forget it. You saw. Besides," Mrs. Summers gave Mrs. Hicks a slight shove, "you've said all along that I'm nothing but a thief."

"You've got her?"

"Wouldn't that just be the cat in the hat."

"*You've got her?*"

"Now, Carolyn, that's not at all what I'm saying. But I'm surprised you didn't think of that before. You've held that Tri Delta prank over my head for twenty-some years. You and Tootsie Steptoe. Setting me up for whatever reason you had."

"You stole Tootsie's ring."

"You know I didn't." Mrs. Summers reached into her

cardigan pocket. "And for your information, I didn't steal this one either."

Nicole tried to curl herself into a ball. She closed her eyes and hid her face in her lap. If she couldn't see them, the reverse must apply. She covered her ears. She pursed her lips to shush her breathing. *Don't move,* she told herself. *Don't move or they'll find you.* She stayed this way for a few minutes more. Then her peace was cracked open by the slam of a door.

Nicole watched her mother storm across the street to answer Mrs. Summers with a door of her own. As if to top her, Nicole's mother turned the knob, opened, and swung hers shut a second louder time.

Nicole thought, *What the mother-fucking hell is going on?* Everything was going so well, so damned right. She had her binoculars, her freedom, her tree, and her Ree. Her life was as she liked it. She had an invisible shield. But now that shield had a great big hole in it. Cut away with a diamond as if she were trapped in a phone booth.

Nicole stormed into the kitchen and rammed Mrs. Summers into the fridge. She caught her fall on the vegetable crisper, but dropped her wine bottle onto the tile floor.

"What are you trying to do to me, huh?" Nicole grabbed a knife from the knife block and yelled, "Tell me! Tell me or I'll—"

"You'll what?" said Mrs. Summers, her skirt soaking up the white Zinfandel, one hand reaching for the egg shelf for leverage. "You'll cut me? Oh, please. You make one move and I'll tie your hair to your mother's mailbox. I'll blow my horn till the cows come home!"

Nicole put the knife on the counter.

"That's not where it goes."

Nicole put the knife in the knife block.

"Much better."

Nicole handed a paper towel roll to Mrs. Summers and

stared into the faces of bunnies and ducklings as they sopped up the white wine under Mrs. Summers's pressure.

"You're sending me back to my mother, is that it?"

Mrs. Summers stuffed the paper towels into the trash can. She took off her skirt and lay the wet part in the sink. Her blouse hung over the control top of her panty hose. The cardigan hit hip level and, in the pocket, Nicole could see the precious rock's bulge.

"I gave that to you so you'd keep quiet about me."

Mrs. Summers sat down at the blue wicker table. The seat crunched beneath her. She shifted on the cushion and the seat crunched some more. "Nicole, when you came here I didn't ask any questions."

Nicole remembered running, halfway crazy, halfway scared. Tri Delt alums, in the street and in her yard, in her house, in their cars, panic-stricken, somewhat drunk. Everyone screaming, chatter-boxing round the bend. In the distance, Mrs. Summers with her front door held open. She offered an alternative. An escape hatch without springs.

She took such good care of her. Ran a bath and washed her hair. She wrapped her in Sarina's pink robe. She gave her a slight sedative and Nicole slept for days.

"Sarina wants something and my mother can help. Is that it?" Nicole asked. "That's why I lose my life?"

"You're not going to die, Nicole. Your mother misses you. You'll see."

"What did you tell her?"

"That I knew where you were."

"She'll call the police."

"They won't believe her. Need I remind you of her very public nervous breakdown?"

"My father will believe her."

"She's not going to tell him. She's trying to convince him she's still fit to live at home. I told her she'd see you when

Sarina won that crown. You'll be surprised. She really misses you. She'll be happy to have you back."

Nicole imagined her mother holding her like she had held her best friend's coffin. Maybe she would be grateful just to have her alive. Maybe she'd let her be whoever she wanted. But how long would that last? She'd be forced back to school. She'd be required to wear lipstick. Make the grade and hook a man.

Nicole would lose the ability to watch Sarina like she had been. Once she came out, restraining orders would be enforced. Sarina's guard would go back up. The town would sit on porches with sawed-off shotguns, waiting and watching and wishing for trouble.

In bed that night, in Mrs. Summers's attic, Nicole thought about her future and what she could possibly do to salvage it.

The time with Mrs. Summers had been the best of her life. Until recently, Mrs. Summers had let her sleep in Ree's bed. The sheets were so clean. They smelled clean. They felt clean. She slept sounder than she ever had. She barely moved in the night. But with all the social gatherings since Stewart's parents died, Nicole found herself in the attic for hours.

The attic was comfortable. Mrs. Summers had installed all the modern conveniences. There was a TV and a boom box, with headphones for both. Not to mention the mini-fridge. Mattress, books, cross-stitch, and cards. It was the playroom Mrs. Hicks had never allowed her. Mrs. Summers was a guardian who let her do as she pleased.

That is, as long as Nicole stayed out of the papers. Stayed away from Sarina. Stayed missing. Stayed gone. The deal was Nicole could look but not touch. Mrs. Summers would board her in exchange for her absence.

"We must help Sarina be all she can be. If you really love

her, Nicole, you won't interfere. Stay out of her way. Be a good girl. Be sweet."

Nicole had agreed, but over time, she had seen that Sarina was miserable.

There had been so many boys, her brother, Rick, the backseat fumblers. Stewart Steptoe. That goddamn Diller. It was high time Sarina learned that sex was not the end-all and be-all. It was not the harness Sarina hoped it could be.

If Sarina cared for guaranteed, zombie-style, killer loyalty, she should have searched harder for Nicole when she ran. Nicole had always been what Sarina wanted. She had bent over backwards. She'd sacrificed. She cared. Yet, everything Nicole did, Sarina took the wrong way. Every way Nicole adored her was to Sarina a nuisance.

So if Nicole's life was to be ruined next Homecoming weekend, why wait? Why go back to her mother, when she could go down in flames? Nicole would take care of Sarina real good. She would put her out of her misery. Make her see how she felt. In fact, Nicole would be the last person Sarina laid eyes on. Sarina's vision would close in on her, the rest of the world becoming part of her haze.

There was a way to link herself and Sarina in history. Their names, like schoolgirls, would go hand in hand. They would skip lightheartedly into Ever After. Repeat the same move on TV and home video. Like Norville hugged Pauley. Like Conway cracked up Corman. Like Hinkley's bullet made Reagan call Mommy. Summers and Hicks would, at last, be inseparable. Together forever. Yes, this time. The end.

Bitty Jack

When spring semester ended one week later, Bitty Jack's troubles followed her home.

Stewart insisted on coming to camp. He had worked as a Black Foot the past two summers. He was committed to helping with maintenance, as always. Even though Big Jack told him he could find a last-minute replacement, Stewart said, "Sir, I'm calling from the car."

Bitty Jack was not happy to hear this. In the hours following Take Back the Night, Stewart had confessed he had made a mistake.

"It was a stupid mistake."

But it was what every girl fears. Not impotence or when-I-was-twelve-I-shot-twenty-squirrels. Not fear of commitment. Not two years in the Merchant Marines. Stewart had been with someone else. He had cheated. He'd screwed up. It was more than Bitty Jack could try to understand. She didn't want to understand. It was worse than his tears.

For months, Bitty Jack had attributed Stewart's lack of libido to the death of his parents. He didn't touch her like he used to. He didn't let Bitty Jack touch him for long. When she sat on the couch, he sat in a chair. When she offered him popcorn, he stared at the movie screen. He was pulling away from her. He was distant and moody. Without him, she was lonesome, lonelier still in his bed, while Stewart paced about his inherited house.

After a while, Bitty Jack knew that the problem must be her. Her, Stewart had lost any passion or thirst for. Her, he wasn't interested in. Her, he didn't love. Bitty Jack found herself suspicious when he was late for their dates, forgot to call, criticized her outfits, was thoughtless, not himself. She was afraid that there was someone else he wanted. Someone whom he'd lost. Some girl, the cliché girl, who had gotten away.

"Sarina Summers," he'd confessed.

Who else could it have been?

"But it was only one night. It didn't mean anything, I swear."

Bitty Jack didn't believe him. The two had known each other their whole damned lives. Sarina was the first woman Stewart had slept with. She was the only woman, besides Bitty Jack and, now knowing her identity, that suddenly wasn't good. Why wouldn't he still want her? Look at her. She had everything. She was pretty. For chrissakes, they had the same initials.

At Take Back the Night, Bitty Jack had been hurt, but not surprised. It was as if Sarina Summers was Destiny's pit bull, taken out for yet another walk, happy at the chance to bite Bitty Jack's ass.

As the campers unpacked, Stewart knocked on Bitty's cabin door. He was wearing the overalls her father had bought him his first summer at Camp Chickasaw. Day one on the job, Stewart had worn shorts to chalk the softball field. The chiggers had all but eaten him alive. The welts lasted for weeks.

Stewart was miserable. So Mr. Carlson had taken him to the Summons General Store. They shopped for work clothes in the men's department, which consisted of two round racks beside the aisle stocked with Q-Tips, chips, and Dinty Moore Stew. At the moment, Bitty Jack thought Stewart was trying to pluck at her heart strings. To bring back fond memories with soft denim and "I'm sorry."

Bitty Jack did not want to listen to Stewart's apologies. His sob story retold. His dumb, dumb excuses. She turned her back to Stewart, who, as a maintenance man, was not allowed over the threshold without counselor consent. She talked with the new crop of twelve-year-old girls until her good old-fashioned silent treatment rang loud and clear. Stewart stepped backwards and away from the porch.

Big Jack had told Bitty to give Stewart another chance. Men did make mistakes. Trusts could be broken. Most things, repaired.

But Bitty hadn't told her father who Stewart had slept with. For that matter, she hadn't told him that sex was involved. If she talked about sex, Big Jack would lose his little girl. If she said Sarina's name, she might bring back all that pain.

But pain came to Chickasaw without Bitty Jack's permission.

It showed up at supper with sixteen lackeys, news reporters on the scene. As she poured her campers bug juice, Bitty Jack saw the camera lights swarmed outside the mess hall windows. She heard correspondents shout questions before they elbowed open the doors.

"Where's Jack Carlson?"

"Is it true what they've said?"

Luckily, Bitty's father was not there to answer. Maintenance ate earlier. The press wasn't prepared.

Neither were the campers. Bitty's girls wanted to know.

"What do they want with your daddy?"

"Did your dad do something wrong?"

Bitty Jack didn't know what she should tell them. Fresh faces lined down the table, eyes expecting an explanation. "Whatever they tell you, don't believe it. It's not true." But why should her campers trust her? They'd only known her for a day.

The owners grabbed giant cookie sheets from the supper serving line. They dumped the yards of brownies and used the sheets as buffers to block the cameras. They threatened the reporters and bullied them out.

As the reporters backtracked, mikes in the air, Bitty Jack ran past them, toward her house, up the hill. She had to warn her parents. Tell them what was going on.

The Carlsons, unfortunately, were already aware. They had their TV turned on. The nighttime news was running clips from the twelve o'clock coverage.

Mrs. Carlson said, "Bitty, lock the door behind you."

Sarina Summers had fed her regurgitated lie to the press.

Everyone believed her, Mrs. Hicks included. While Stewart was on the road and the Carlsons painting final coats on front porches, Mrs. Hicks had joined her husband on Channel 5 Afternoon Update. She'd said, yes, Sarina's Take Back the Night speech was out of character for Tri Delta, but as the Standards Chair, she knew that some standards had to change. After all, this was the New South. Young women couldn't be expected to hold their tongues and take it on the chin. Sarina Summers would certainly not lose her membership. She was a brave girl who should be commended, not shunned, for her courageous behavior.

Bert Hicks said, "Let's go to Summons for on-the-spot coverage."

The Channel 5 blue screen showed the Carlsons' back door. There was the wooden plaque with THE CARETAKERS chiseled by Big Jack's prize chisel. There was the banister Bitty'd held onto as a girl. An investigative reporter made a fist before the camera. The Carlsons heard the knocks before they saw them on TV.

"Jack, what do we do?" Mrs. Carlson whispered as if the house was bugged.

The phone rang before he answered. Big Jack picked up. "You've taken care of it?" he asked the owners. "They're on my front porch! No. We talked about this years ago, you know it's not true. It's crazy! It's a damn lie. I don't know what that girl's trying to pull."

Mrs. Carlson gently pried the kitchen phone from her husband. She rubbed his sunburned neck and guided him toward a box of Crunch 'n' Munch resting open on the counter. She said very calmly into the receiver, "Do I have to call the authorities? Or would it be better I speak to the press? Tell me, would you, what should I do?"

Bitty Jack was the only one left watching TV. Several minutes of dead door time did not make good television. Bert Hicks had gone to weather. Judy Buckley was predicting summer showers, highs near sixty.

Bitty and her parents sat at the kitchen table. They passed the box of Crunch'n' Munch. Mrs. Carlson hung up the phone. "We're gonna talk with the owners before reveille tomorrow. This is bound to die down. Worse things could happen."

Unfortunately, Mrs. Carlson was absolutely right.

In the dark hours of the morning, parents drove past the parking lot, onto Chickasaw grounds, and woke up their children. Bitty Jack lost three girls before the sun came up. When she asked the parents why, they warned the other counselors to get Jack Carlson's daughter out of the cabin.

"It runs in the family," one mother said. "I'm from Tuscaloosa. I've seen where she works."

"She makes dicks outta dough," her husband supported.

"Yes, dear, that's right, help upset the children."

The girls *were* upset. They wouldn't let Bitty near them.

"You saw me change for dinner!"

"I'm in my nightgown, get away!"

A few other counselors tried to quiet the campers. Hungover from Trinka's, two stayed on their beds, pillows over their eyes, pretending to sleep through the REM racket.

Bitty Jack felt like a monster in sweatpants. She fingered her drawstring. She knew she had to go. She left the girls crying, stewing, some chatting excitedly. Maybe they'd get to be interviewed on TV. Maybe their parents would now buy them anything they wanted. Bitty Jack wished this would all go away. She walked to her house to see how much damage Sarina had done.

On the campgrounds, cars were parked by the assembly bleachers. There was a Mercedes by the swings. A silver Saturn by the tire crawl. Campers were locked alone in each backseat. Some lucky enough to have a sibling to talk to. Others stole maps and markers from glove compartments to make signs to communicate with other kids in other cars. CAMP SUX read one. Another answered BJ WANTS BJS! Headlights were left on to light up the area. Parents compared stories and Bitty Jack overheard.

Mrs. Hicks had gathered so much support in advocacy of Sarina that the Alabama Greeks had boycotted Camp Chickasaw. Greek alumni had been alerted. There were parents upon parents who sent their kids there every year. It was shameful that the owners had covered up such a scandal. No one wanted their children to summer in a cesspool. No one wanted to pay for a camp cleaned by a criminal. They didn't want *theirs* mixing with people like *them. Them* was the likes of Big Jack Carlson. A pedophile. A pervert. A man who should be hung and then shot in the face.

Bitty Jack found herself running fast on her bare feet. The

grass was wet and she stumbled over roots and rough patches she had avoided all her life. Her glasses clouded in the Alabama fog, but shoulder-high bright lights lit up her yard. This wasn't over. The news cameras had returned.

Reporters sat on the steps to the back door. They were probably playing pinochle on the front porch she never used. They waited as if the Carlsons might change their minds. Come out and talk. Give publicity a go.

Bitty Jack unlocked and snuck through the garage door. She pocketed the spare key from the Chock Full O'Nuts can to the right of the doormat. The Chock Full O'Nuts can was the same one she'd used at bonfires for the past fifteen years. Bitty Jack was still slim enough to fit inside her father's teepee of logs, tie a string to the coffee can filled with sulfuric acid, then yank it to spill onto the powder chemical combo. Boom. There was fire. The coffee can, still alive. It was dented and smelled funny, but reliable nonetheless. It was almost as black as her heart felt right now.

Bitty Jack imagined a fire of her own. One set for better reasons than because tradition told her so. Her fire would mean something. It would burn more than logs. The flames would stretch high fueled by cameras, mikes, and Dictaphones; the smoke consume indifference, reporters' callous remarks.

Bitty Jack thought of what else she could burn: the sounds of campers crying, of their parents giving them a false reason to do so; the day that Stewart's parents died, the day she stopped trusting him, her anger and pain; her hatred for Sarina that now smothered every hope.

In fact, Bitty thought, she wouldn't mind if that girl fell in. She could see Sarina in front of her fire, laughing, oblivious that she had started it all. Bitty Jack could see her hands on Sarina's soft shoulders, one last straw away from pushing her in. Maybe the fire would bring everyone to their senses. Burning, Sarina would come to know the hell she so carelessly sent everyone into.

In the kitchen, Bitty found her parents holding hands across the table. The Crunch 'n' Munch was in the garbage. They made do with a block of store-brand mild cheddar. Stewart was slicing it, placing what he'd cut onto generic saltines.

"What's he doing here?" Bitty asked.

"He wanted to help."

"Daddy, how can he help?"

"He's good with the cheese."

Mrs. Carlson said, "Baby, things are gonna get worse. You've got to get out of here. Stewart said he'd take you. Let Stewart take you home."

"This is my home."

"Baby girl," said her mama, "not for long."

Bitty Jack listened to her mother predict their future. More parents would come. Campers leave. Money change hands. The only way the owners could salvage their business would be to get rid of the Carlsons. Plain and simple. Wash their hands.

"We want you to go. It's best that you go."

Stewart said, "Bitty, you can stay at my house. I've got plenty of room, till the dorms open up."

"So you want me to live with you, but then get the hell out. So you can bring that bitch home again? So you can—"

"Bitty," said her father, "that's enough, you hear me?"

"But you don't know the whole story!"

"I know what you told me."

"I'm telling you I should stay here. We've got to fight this. This is happening for no reason!"

"We can't fight this," said her mother. "I'm sorry, baby, we just can't."

"Mama, what are you gonna to do?"

"We're gonna be okay. We've got family. We work hard."

Big Jack said, "There's always a job."

"But this job was so perfect. It's been our whole life!"

"Life goes on," said Big Jack.

Mrs. Carlson said, "Go."

On the drive home, Stewart said, "I hope I got everything."

Stewart had packed Bitty Jack's duffel bag. He had gone to her cabin while the remaining campers ate breakfast. The owners had prohibited the Carlsons from campgrounds. They were to stay in their home until further instruction. Bitty Jack hated the thought of Stewart packing her panties. Folding her bras. Zipping her tampons into the secret side pouch.

She couldn't remember when she'd last been this angry. At least she'd had time to take a few mementos from the house. Her spare keys, the plaque, other things she might need. She managed not to speak to Stewart for the five-hour ride.

It was established that Bitty Jack would stay in the guest room. It was furthest away from Stewart's. It faced the backyard, while Stewart's room faced front.

Bitty Jack did not like the guest room. The theme color was peach. Peach bedspread. Peach curtains. Peach carpet. Peach towels in the adjoining full bath. She wondered if the sheets had been changed since his parents died. There was a thin layer of dust covering the window sills and towel rack. But there was a TV. Never in her life had Bitty Jack had a TV she could watch from bed.

What she saw was the house from where Stewart had just taken her.

Reporters banged ruthlessly on the Carlsons' back door. They claimed the public had rights. Didn't the Carlsons want to tell their side of the story? Didn't they want to set the record straight?

At last, Mrs. Carlson appeared behind the rain-warped screen door. "We know the truth." She crossed her arms over her pastel flannel shirt. She looked into the cameras as if she knew her daughter was watching. "Trust when I tell you that we'll be all right."

In the days that followed, those were the only words the reporters got out of them. If Mrs. Carlson drove the Ford to Summons General Store, she kept her head high and spoke politely to the cashier. Although the camp had closed, Mr. Carlson kept up with his duties. He'd been given two weeks to pack his things and move out. On camera, Bitty Jack watched him mow straight lines across the soccer field. Twenty reporters, like mites at his heels.

Bitty Jack was trying to figure out a life for herself. Tom had hired her back for the summer. Stewart had given her use of his parents' taupe Taurus, keys to his house, a shelf in the fridge.

"It'll be like we're roommates," he told her one morning. "Until maybe you forgive me. I'm so sorry—"

"Stewart, stop. Just because you're sorry doesn't mean you get the girl."

Bitty Jack spent most of her time away from that house. She worked double shifts. She catered parties. Made deliveries. She kept herself busy. She did anything for a dollar. The more that she saved, the sooner she could leave. She hated those moments when she passed Stewart in the living room. All she could think was *Did it happen in here? On the sofa? Or that chair? How was she? Was she worth it? Do you want me to leave, so you can move her in here?*

Bitty Jack Carlson was a woman divided.

She wanted to stay hard and make Stewart suffer the way that she had. The way that she *was.* But she worked such long hours and it took energy to stay mad. At night, her defenses were often let down.

And Stewart was being so goddamn nice.

He left precooked dinners on her refrigerator shelf with heating instructions written out on Post-It notes. He washed her towels. He changed her sheets. He put peach roses by her bedside. He tried to stay away from her because that's what she had asked.

Sometimes when Bitty Jack saw him sitting on the sofa, she wanted to sit beside him. To wrap her arms around his neck. To cry for the first time over what had happened to her family.

But the reason her family was experiencing a crisis was the reason that she and Stewart had broken up to begin with. It was the same reason she was tortured and had nightmares as a kid. Why her father was persecuted and she watched as a kid. It was why she lost Johnny Iguana, a chance to travel, another life. Maybe she would have been happy without college, without Stewart, without a bakery job and rent to pay. Maybe there wouldn't have been a Chickasaw boycott if Bitty Jack hadn't been banned from the freak show. Because of Sarina, she'd never find out. Because of Sarina, so many choices were botched.

Bitty Jack lay in bed and tried to forget about Sarina by watching TV. She knew her life was better than Diane Sawyer's report on birth defects. At least she wasn't a crack baby. At least she wasn't a Siamese twin. Now, those kids had problems. She flipped the channel and tried to laugh at Lucille Ball's crazy antics. Where was Ethel? Had she been wallpapered to death? But Bitty had seen this episode before. She knew Ethel was in the closet. Ethel was always in a closet.

Bitty Jack usually fell asleep by midnight. Her bedroom door locked, so Stewart couldn't surprise her. One window cracked open for the August night air.

Bitty Jack was not a light sleeper. But one time, she woke up to that window being raised.

Maybe it wasn't the sound of one window frame slowly

sliding over the other. Maybe it wasn't the dream where she's falling. More than likely what woke her was the sense that she'd been watched, that someone had studied her from the backyard for hours, that someone wanted a much closer look.

"It's Johnny," came his voice. "It's me. Can I come in?"

Bitty Jack grabbed her glasses off the nightstand. She put them on quickly and brought her old boyfriend into view.

"Johnny?" Her whisper rushed up her throat. "Johnny, it's really you?"

"It's me," Johnny said and put his right leg through the window. The rest of his body followed and Bitty Jack marveled at how he'd become, most definitely, a man. He was still in black Levi's, same style button-down with a Hanes T-shirt underneath. His hair was longer and curled, not like in summer. She wanted to let her fingers get lost. He was slim and six feet tall. Still with that slight slump from ducking under doors.

Bitty raced to him, oblivious that she'd gone to bed in only a tank top and panties. She was so happy to see him, all she could do was open her arms.

Johnny took her like she'd hoped that he would; as she'd imagined since Stewart had slept with that bitch. Johnny could show him how you treated a girl who you loved. He held her cheek to cheek, picking her up in a powerful hug. Bitty's feet were off the floor and she wished that they would never, never touch down.

"How'd you find me?" she said.

"It's all over the news. I called your parents. They said you were here."

"Oh, Johnny, I've missed you," Bitty said in the air.

"So come with me," Johnny said as he put her back on the floor. "Let me take you away."

"Back to the freak show?"

"It's a good life."

"I know."

"Come with me," said Johnny. "It can be like it was."

Bitty slid her hands into the sleeves of his shirt. She felt the old familiar. His skin was like a road map leading back to her young heart.

But Bitty Jack had learned that things were never as they'd been. In her soul, especially. She was too old to go back to the girl who held the hose, who rode the Matterhorn like a school bus, who handled snakes and played with ducks. Now she knew blue Squishies were not the gods' nectar. They were shaved ice with sugar, food coloring, and false flavor.

Bitty Jack was tempted to run away from Tuscaloosa, from Sarina Summers and the wake of her destruction. But Bitty Jack knew she'd be haunted for a lifetime. As long as Sarina was celebrated. As long as mean women were encouraged for what they did.

Johnny Iguana accepted her answer. He didn't put up a fight or beg her to leave. He didn't kiss her good-bye, because it would just be too hard. She said no and then Johnny was gone, his big body shrinking as he walked from the window.

Bitty Jack wished he would come back and get her, kiss her at least, let her know that she could find him, when she was ready, at the fair.

Back in bed, Bitty heard a shuffling outside. She sat up, ready to spring at his sight.

But it wasn't his face that popped up behind the window. It was Nicole Hicks and she didn't ask permission to climb into Bitty's black room.

Bitty tried to scream for Stewart, but her voice wouldn't work. She made tiny gasping sounds as she tried to remember how her arms and legs moved. She had seen Nicole before and, that time, she'd run.

Her mama had told her, "Believe what people say. If a person tells you she's crazy, believe her, she is. She knows herself much better than you do."

As Nicole moved closer and stood by the bed, Bitty Jack was motionless, rigid with fear. Her eyes were stuck open. She didn't know what to do.

"Stay with him," Nicole said like a benevolent ghost. "Stewart. Stay with him and we can go get that girl."

"Who?" Bitty managed.

Nicole said, "You know who."

Nicole

IT WAS NOT hard to get Bitty Jack to help her. Bitty Jack seemed interested in every word Nicole said. She sat in bed wide-eyed as Nicole fed her lies about revenge and how she was the only one who could feel Bitty's pain. Almost two years ago, Nicole told her, she had escaped from this world, run by the likes of Sarina Summers and Cheshire mothers. Together, Nicole told her, they could teach Sarina a lesson. Bitty simply must cooperate. She could do that. Couldn't she? She would do that. Wouldn't she?

"Just tell me what you want, Nicole. Whatever you want, I'll help you, you hear?"

Nicole told her they would wait until October. Sarina had already launched her campaign to be Homecoming Queen. The campus had never seen a crusade to compare. Nicole was sure that she'd win. She was positive. She had to. At the Homecoming halftime, when the float was brought out, the stadium would be packed and everyone would see.

"See what?" Bitty asked. "What'll we do?"

"*You're* going to help me get Stewart's Big Al costume. Once I'm inside, I can get on the field. Once I'm on the float, I can do what I want."

"What's that?"

Nicole started to make her way out the window. "Just be at the stadium where he dresses at noon."

"Then what?"

"Just be there. When I find you, I'll tell you."

Nicole thought it best to get out of there quickly. Before Bitty Jack asked questions like: *Where've you been? Are you crazy? Is your mom home? What's her number?*

But Bitty Jack said little. She just watched Nicole go. She did not call for Stewart, sleeping somewhere in the house. She did not phone the police. Nicole never heard a siren. Thus, Nicole knew Bitty Jack could be trusted to do more than help her; she'd help her legend live on.

When Nicole had finished with Sarina, Bitty Jack would feel compelled to confess. She would tell the police of this night through the window, how she'd helped Nicole plan revenge, but not to this extent. She would be so, so sorry, but Officer, really, she'd never known it'd go so far. If Nicole were around, she'd swear to it. She would.

Back in the attic, Nicole sharpened the ax. It was the same ax she'd used to chip Sarina's name in that tree. The same ax she'd found months ago, heaven sent.

When she'd uncovered it in that camp trunk, Nicole wondered why it wasn't kept in Mr. Summers' tool closet. Laid next to a birthday candle, burned to sixteen, the ax was wrapped in two towels and bound with duct tape. The handle was just under two feet in length. The blade was rusted. Or were those the tiniest, old-brown drops of blood?

Maybe the spots were Sarina's young blood. Maybe there'd been an accident and Mrs. Summers had hidden the ax in the trunk for safekeeping. Nicole liked the thought of mixing her O-negative with Sarina's A-positive. No matter the method.

No matter the pain. Within her hands, Nicole squeezed the metal head firmly. She watched the dark liquid slide out of her skin and coat the brown spots like paint.

Every night since she'd found it, she had polished the ax with rocks from the woods. The grating sound was soothing. The tip ever so bright. With every stroke, the blade got thinner. Nicole's own destiny, razor sharp in her mind.

Nicole had tried everything to be with Sarina. She'd made the high school cheerleading squad. She'd flunked out and sabotaged the index-card war. She'd tried Tri Delta. She'd lived in Ree's house. She'd shadowed her and studied her and been her companion. Her island. Her rock. But at the coronation, the crown would go down onto Sarina's scrubbed scalp and, with it, the relationship for which Nicole worked so hard.

Unless Nicole made one last effort.

The lie she'd told Bitty Jack had been a good one. That they were the wronged trying to set their lives right. The truth was Nicole needed Bitty Jack for one reason: to help her hide Stewart after they'd gotten his costume. He was too heavy for Nicole to move alone. They could each take a leg. Work together as a team.

At halftime, Nicole would pull the ax from Big Al's sleeve. She would hack Sarina in the throat, along her arms, across her face. Hopefully someone would shoot her to stop her. They'd have to kill her to stop her. They'd have to cut off her arms.

In heaven, Sarina would realize that Nicole's love was what she wanted. She'd be willing and waiting. She'd wave at the gate. Nicole would come running and never have to let her go. She could hold on forever. Kiss her lips and brush her hair.

Sarina

By October, Sarina had done what no other Homecoming candidate had done in Bama history. While the Greek party had slated the queen slot for a perky Phi Mu, Sarina had spent September drawing an independent sympathy vote to go against the Machine.

She spoke in classes, at women's groups. Anywhere people wanted to hear about the beautiful girl who had been damaged as a child in that Chickasaw toilet stall. It was amazing how the lie became more true each time she told it, with each detail she chose to add. Jack's muddy boots. A broken blood blister on the tip of his thumb.

Some GDIs appreciated her struggle. Some simply savored Sarina turning on her own, standing up to the front-running Phi Mu who drank so much she puked at gymnastics meets. Sarina was a woman who could handle her liquor. She could handle most anything. Anything that came her way.

The Machine recognized this and, one week before elections, put their support behind the outspoken Tri Delt who'd split the vote. The Phi Mu was crushed, but Sarina didn't care. She'd fought and she deserved it. She couldn't wait to take that crown.

When Sarina rode the royal float into Bryant-Denny Stadium, ninety thousand faces would see her time had come at last. The day would mean more than a new dress for another special occasion. Her life would change forever. New doors open. Old challenges pass.

Bitty Jack

HOMECOMING DAY, Bitty Jack watched the parade on the TV in Stewart's guest room. From those early mornings at the bakery, Bitty Jack knew that the participants had been lining up before dawn. Pledges and drum majors and all sorts of people would buy dozens of pastries for 5:30 feedings. Bitty Jack always imagined them there, backed up through downtown, warming their hands with hot chocolate she'd made.

Bert Hicks and his co-anchor were covering the parade from atop the roof of the Bama Theater. Although the marquis was lit up behind their shoulders, the commentators looked cold: Bert Hicks in orange hunting gloves and a sports coat, asking the weekend weatherman to come forward and show himself. "'Mild and sunny,' that's a laugh!"

"Oh, Bert, buck up," his co-anchor elbowed him. Half his age, she had been pulled in from the traffic helicopter as soon as Bert's usual partner tossed her thin mints on a Brownie troop during the preshow. She'd told the producer, *Morning sickness gets 'em every time.* Barbara Bush pearls secured, she was raring to go. "Ready or not, here come the Shriners!"

Yes, there were the Shriners who were always in front.

Turning circles for the crowd on their mini go-carts, their fez tassels twirled like pinwheel beanies on little boys. The Shriners was the oldest men's club. For every parade, they deserted their lodge to lead hundreds of marchers, control their pace, and leave time to show off their motor skills through the minor twists and turns of the Tuscaloosa route.

The parade went down Greensboro Avenue or "First Street" as the yocals called it. All the big churches sat side by side: First Baptist, First Methodist, and First Presbyterian. Every weekend there was a wedding, rice strewn haphazardly along the edges of tar.

The parade took a right onto University Boulevard, which led into campus, most notably the Strip. As Bert Hicks and his co-anchor, who had started to wink as if they'd been partners for years, faded out for commercials, news cameras scanned the Strip restaurants and bars, freshly decorated during Paint the Town Red.

PTR was as traditional as Sing Night. Homecoming week, sororities painted business windows with red-and-white "Roll Tide"s and "Go Bama Go"s and "Welcome Home"s and portraits of Big Al, wild with excitement. The Booth, the Brass Monkey, and the Ivory Tusk oozed with Bama spirit, but Gallette's was the most popular bar with the Greeks. Even the sidewalk out front was painted. There was a line to get in. It looked like a blood bath.

The Shriners were making so much noise gunning their engines and blowing their horns, the Central High School marching band was thrown off rhythm. County High's band wasn't too far behind. Tubas collided. Cymbals were dropped. "Baby Elephant Walk" sounded like "Drunk Baby Elephant on Big Elephant Tranquilizers."

But the Million Dollar Band could always be counted on. With 330 members, nothing could distract them. They were a loud musical robot led by the beautiful Crimsonettes.

Bert Hicks said, "Ah, the beautiful Crimsonettes."

"You know, I was a Crimsonette, Bert."

"Really? How marvelous."

In simpler terms, Crimsonettes were baton twirlers. With names like Chastity and Brandy and Coco Clementine, they filled out their uniforms before they even got dressed. White plastic boots zipped up to their knees. Shiny silver fringe swung from cleavages to meet the waistlines of their satin leotards. They wore rhinestone earrings and great big smiles. Sometimes they set their batons on fire. But not during parades. In the past, too many spectators were singed.

The Color Guard followed, each member carrying six-foot "Alabama" banners, the poles secured in small cups on their belts.

Bert Hicks said, "Note the recently added Rifle Line."

"Ooo," wink, wink, "I'd love to get my hands one of those. I bet I could flip it twenty feet still today!"

Bert Hicks seemed to shudder at the thought of his co-anchor with a big white shotgun and her assertiveness training.

Bitty Jack sat up in bed to get a closer look. Were those guns loaded? Were the girls who carried them more fierce than their long white dresses implied?

Bert Hicks said, "Looks like they'll give the Crimsonettes a run for their money."

His co-anchor pointed out that, in certain circumstances, batons could be considered the most brutal of lethal weapons.

Bert Hicks said, "Let's hear that Alabama Fight Song."

As if taking his cue, the Million Dollar Band burst into: "Yea Alabama! Drown 'em Tide!"

"Yea Alabama," his co-anchor winked with the left eye this time. "Vanderbilt hasn't beaten Bama in over twenty years."

Bert Hicks said, "Well, let's be honest here. You don't schedule a Homecoming game with a team you're gonna lose to."

"Poor old Vanderbilt. You wonder why they keep showing up."

Bert Hicks loosened up a little. "With such a high level of

academic excellence, you'd think they'd be smart enough not to come here and get their brains beat in."

"Oh, Bert." His co-anchor swatted his shoulder. "You are too mean."

The Greek floats came next. Cross-dressing seemed the popular theme. Every house thought that they were the first to put girls in football jerseys and guys in cheerleading uniforms padded with Kleenex. When the Alpha Chi Omegas started to sing, Bert's co-anchor joined in, bobbing in her seat every time she clapped her hands.

"Your sisters?" asked Bert.

"My sisters!" she signaled.

The Alpha Chi's signaled back. The ATO men tried to steal the camera's attention by doing stripteases and hanging upside down off the side of their float.

"They're crazy," Bert's co-anchor said with a giggle.

The black fraternities were something else. They walked like soldiers, but dressed in crisp tuxedo shirts, tuxedo pants, and patent leather shoes. Accessories were simple: suspenders, cummerbunds, and magician-like canes. They stopped at every block and performed excerpts from their Homecoming step-shows. Their feet kept a beat apart from the band's.

The law school float followed.

Bert Hicks said, "Now that's what we all get out of bed to see."

The law school float was a fifteen-foot flatbed covered in drunk third-year law students screaming crude remarks. They wore frock coats and plastic bowler hats. Groucho glasses, mustaches attached. There was no other sign of decoration. Not one crepe paper pomp stuck to a shoe.

Dorm floats came after. Then honor societies: Mortarboard, Jasons, then Thirty-One. The grand marshal was near the rear. Some alum Bitty Jack had never heard of. In past years, she'd recognized Jim Nabors from *Gomer Pyle.* She'd eaten at Joe Namath's restaurant. She'd known Sela Ward.

But the Homecoming court was what the crowd had been waiting for.

Bitty Jack raised the volume as if it were a zoom control. The Channel 5 camera focused in on a trail of convertibles. Homecoming runner-up. Runner-up. Phi Mu. Then came Sarina. The winner. Machine Queen. She sat in the backseat, her butt on the boot. She wore a pink wool suit and black patent heels. On her head was the crown from the pep rally last night. The former queen had passed it on, on the steps of Gorgas Library, in front of the bonfire, on the center of the Quad. On the convertible, Sarina looked happy. Happier than Bitty Jack. The happiest one there. She waved to everyone as if everyone were waving back.

Bert Hicks said, "Isn't she a sight for sore eyes?"

Bitty Jack wondered if she would be for long. Nicole had never told her what she had in store for Sarina. What her great plan was. What would be done. Maybe Nicole would dump the classic bucket of pig's blood à la Stephen King. Maybe de-pants her. Could she have rigged Sarina's dress? Maybe Nicole would just steal her crown. Maybe beat her up. Coldcock her. Snatch her bald-headed. Maybe she would scar Sarina's pretty face for life. Whatever it was, was okay by Bitty Jack. As long as Nicole got onto that float. As long as Nicole got to Sarina.

Behind the court the cheerleaders followed. The girls hung on to the sides of the campus fire-truck. The boys held megaphones and shouted from the seats. The station was thirty feet from Bryant-Denny Stadium, where the parade dispersed. The cheerleaders cheered all the way there.

With them was Big Al, the much anticipated caboose. He straddled the firemen's ladder, which jutted out from the back of the truck. His big feet dangled. From his over-the-shoulder bag, he tossed Dum Dum Pops and Now & Laters. To grab the candy, Stewart sported his white polyester gloves. They were stretched across his hands, his fingers stubby at the tips.

Bitty Jack worried that, during the football game, the coach or cheerleaders might recognize those hands. Nicole's were half the size of Stewart's. The gloves would be loose. What if they realized that Stewart wasn't in there? What if Nicole didn't move like Stewart's Big Al? Stewart bounced and prounced and dove. He wore that costume like those gloves fit his hands. He was comfortable inside. The weight of the elephant head as light as a cap.

When the parade ended, Bitty Jack went to the stadium to find Stewart.

At 11:00 A.M., the campus was crawling with all the people who were going to fit in that stadium, which, when full, constituted the fourth largest city in Alabama. Most everyone was dressed in red-and-white combinations. Men wore boutonnieres. Women's dresses and sweaters sagged from the weight of grapefruit-sized mums, with pipe-cleaner-made "*A*"s glued to the petals, pinned above their hearts. The saying was "You got to have a shelf to hold the books." Without a C-cup or better, Homecoming chrysanthemums hung from clothing like tired, hungry children.

Kick Off on the Quad had started right after the parade. Bitty Jack parked the Taurus behind Gorgas Library. Before she walked around it, she heard music from a radio station broadcasting the pregame show from a stage on the steps.

Tents and booths covered the lawn. There was one for every school: Engineering, A&S, Business, you name it. Alumni had a tent. Bama Boosters had a tent. Alabama Power had one with a ten-by-twelve dance floor. The Waysider dished out their secret recipe biscuits. The smell of Jimmy Dean sausage filled the air like napalm.

Bitty Jack moved on. No one paid her any mind. She was just another student with a canvas backpack. A young woman on her way to the game of the year.

Bryant-Denny Stadium was so big it looked like the flying saucer that so many residents had spotted for generations had finally quit teasing and landed smack dab in the middle of town.

RVs surrounded it. Portable TVs lit up the windows. Mini-grills warmed all sorts of cured meats.

Fraternity pledges in khaki pants and navy blue sports jackets staggered past the ticket takers. It was their job to arrive early, save Actives seats, and keep their intoxication at a respectable level. Except for inside the president's box, alcohol was illegal within the stadium. The frat boys' pants always bulged in weird places. In their briefs, they hid flasks filled with Jim Beam or Crown, Canadian Mist or Southern Comfort.

Known to stadium security as Big Al's girlfriend, Bitty Jack passed through the player's entrance with no trouble at all.

The locker room was empty as Bitty Jack had predicted. An hour and a half before kick-off, the players, still in suits, walked the field from end zone to end zone. It was a Homecoming tradition. A psych-up for them. A psych-out for the opposing team.

As Bitty Jack approached Stewart's dressing room, she pulled her copy of his key from her pocket. She knew that he would be there soon. He never missed a chance to wash up between extended performances. She put the key in the lock, but found the door already opened.

Inside Nicole was waiting, the small of her back against the utility sink.

"I picked the lock."

Bitty Jack said, "You did more than that."

Helmets, kneepads, and footballs covered the floor. The

four lockers stood open. Their ancient contents laid out and rooted through. Nicole held the overhead lightbulb in her hand.

Bitty Jack said, "What were you looking for? We've got to put this away."

Nicole and she hurried, shoving stuff into lockers, anxious with the certainty that Stewart was near. Bitty Jack remembered to secure the door from inside. A few minutes later, Stewart's key slid in the lock.

Bitty Jack and Nicole moved quickly for cover. Each fit her body between the wall and a locker, the utility sink between them, barely visible to the other.

Bitty Jack whispered, "What'll we do?"

Nicole hissed, "Be quiet! Just do what I do."

Big Al's head under his arm, Stewart lumbered in and yanked the overhead string to turn on the light. Jerk. No light. Jerk, jerk. Not a spark. Stewart looked up to find the bulb was plum gone. He looked left, he looked right, turned around to face the door. Bitty Jack got worried, but Stewart shrugged. The janitor probably took it. He'd knock on the door soon enough with a replacement.

Stewart put Big Al's head onto the wooden crate. The combination lock hung undone. There was nothing to protect. Everything in the crate was on Stewart's body. But not for long.

Stewart started to undress. He stood between Bitty Jack and Nicole. When he bent down to take off his elephant feet, Bitty Jack looked across his back and saw Nicole's eyes, bloodshot and wide, carefully, consciously watching him too. Bitty Jack was surprised at how possessive she felt. She didn't like Nicole seeing what only she was once privy to see.

He stripped down to his boxers, laid his costume in pieces across the crate to air out. He slid off his shorts and Bitty stopped breathing. She had seen him do this at least a hundred times, before games, in her dorm room, under the bleachers, by Chickasaw Lake. Every time he did it, Bitty got a little thrill. To see him naked, crouching over, coming toward her, hands outstretched.

Bitty Jack had not seen Stewart this way for a very long time. She liked what she saw. She thought about calling the whole damn plan off.

Stewart rolled a bar of Irish Spring under the running water. He soaped his pits and his privates, his face, ears, and hair. As he reached for a sponge, Bitty Jack saw Nicole move. She edged down the wall and, in her hand, Bitty saw something large, round, and white.

Nicole stepped out of the darkness. Stewart heard her and turned.

Before he could wipe the soap from his eyes, Bitty Jack saw Nicole hike a football helmet high in the air. The spit-tarnished face guard was caught in her grip. She swung it full force across Stewart's wet face.

He fell and Nicole jumped on his back. Stewart had no time to react. He looked shocked in his circumstances: no clothes and the white-and-crimson helmet coming down out of nowhere.

Nicole hammered his head. She pummeled him. She was determined.

When Bitty Jack saw blood, she said, "Nicole, that's enough!"

"He's not unconscious."

"He is. Look how slow he's breathing. It's like he's asleep."

Bitty Jack pulled Stewart's arm. She tugged at his leg. She huffed and she puffed. "See, no reaction." The blood on his face curdled her backbone.

Nicole ran from the room.

Bitty Jack wiped Stewart's blood away to find a very small cut. Careful not to get blood on her clothes, she bandaged his head with the same roll of athletic tape she used to secure a clean, balled jock strap in Stewart's open mouth.

Bitty heard Nicole loose in the locker room. She pictured what she heard: Nicole tearing down the Bama Boosters' banner, dragging it between the long lines of benches. Together, the girls rolled Stewart tight in the banner. They put their feet under his back and rolled him, vertically, up the side and into the costume crate.

Nicole fastened the combination lock. Bitty Jack locked the door to his dressing room.

"Why'd you have to hit him so hard?"

"He'll be fine," called Nicole, who was already at the players' benches, almost vaulting into Big Al's gray legs.

"Those are huge on you."

"Does it matter? Come on, help me before the players show up."

Bitty Jack adjusted the costume suspenders. The elastic was bent where Stewart had worn the buckles for years. To Bitty Jack, it was obvious that this Big Al was an imposter. Nicole made the mascot's giant eyes vacant. The elephant skin hug loose on Big Al's appendages. The belly vest helped. The feet were like big slippers, one size fits all. But Bitty Jack was right when it came to the gloves. They were noticeably smaller, like cotton swabs sticking out of two toilet roll tubes. Big Al's head was clearly too much for her. Nicole wobbled as she walked. She held her arms out for support.

Bitty Jack said, "You've got to entertain the crowd for hours."

From inside the suit, Nicole's voice was muffled. "Don't worry about it."

"You've got to spot the cheerleaders."

"I can do it."

"Are you sure?"

Nicole put her elephant arms on her elephant hips.

Annoyed, she cocked her elephant head, which sent her stumbling sideways until she regained her balance on the Coca-Cola machine.

Bitty Jack hoped she could trust Nicole to follow through. It was important that Nicole make it onto that float. It was important that Sarina get what she deserved.

"I'll lead you outside," Bitty Jack said and touched Nicole's shoulder.

"Don't," said Nicole. "I need to get ready. Leave me alone, so I can get ready."

Bitty Jack took two tissues from her backpack and wiped the blood off the tiles she'd tracked out with her shoes. Stewart would be okay. He'd wake up soon enough. When Nicole was unmasked, he'd be searched out. For sure. Bitty Jack flushed the tissues and left Nicole, in her ex-boyfriend's alter ego, by herself in the locker room.

Walking through the players' tunnel, Bitty Jack heard the echos of her rubber-soled shoes against the cement. The daylight streamed in. Her nerves invaded her veins. She tried to step softer, but there was no point. The fans were filling the stadium. The tunnel was dormant, save for the rustle of crepe paper in the wind.

The royal court float was parked, at the mouth, for presentation. It was so tall, Bitty Jack didn't know how Nicole could possibly mount it. The twenty-foot flatbed was hooked like a trailer to a regular truck. The wooden platform was built three feet off the flatbed and left hollow so that holes could be cut to secure the big props. This year, props included eleven stakes with papier-mâché black-and-gold Vanderbilt helmeted heads. Plus poles for the Homecoming court to hold onto as they stood at the corners. Planted firmly, in the center, were the legs of the throne where Sarina would sit only after being announced. Everything was covered in chicken wire and crepe paper. The float was large, but very delicate. NO SMOKING signs were posted along the tunnel. One cigarette ash blown too close, and the float would be ruined. Up in flames, in an instant, would be two weeks of work.

Bitty Jack noticed a rectangular hole cut in the back of the float platform. She looked inside and saw the maze of poles and pulleys and the legs of the throne. Bitty Jack thought she was skinny enough to take a closer look. She was curious what it would feel like in the stomach of that vehicle. What ninety thousand cheers would sound like on the fifty-yard line.

Bitty Jack placed her hand into the platform and felt the coolness of its shade. She stuck her head in. Then half her body followed. Her backpack got stuck, so she had to empty the contents to pull it in behind her. It was dark and dank in the flat bed, but a place she'd never been. Bitty Jack was curious. She explored and set up camp inside the queen's royal ride.

Half an hour later, fifteen minutes to kick-off, Bitty Jack made her way to the president's box. Stewart had given her his parents' season tickets, which the Steptoes had pre-purchased, $25,000 per season for the next seven years. Bitty Jack had not seen a game this semester. Not since the Chickasaw boycott. Not since the boycotters would be occupying that box.

By the time Bitty reached it, the Vanderbilt team was taking the field. They did a lap, then took their benches. All heads turned toward the Sony JumboTron screen.

The guard outside the president's box took Bitty's ticket and glanced in her backpack for guns, knives, or Mace. She passed approval,but the guard didn't open the door right away. He was mesmerized, as was the crowd, by Paul "Bear" Bryant's voice coming out of the Sony JumboTron.

The dead coach's gravely words were the only noise within the stadium. Bear Bryant was like God and when he returned, in whatever shape or form, witnesses were respectful. They shut their mouths and paid attention.

The Sony JumboTron could be heard three miles outside the stadium. It wasn't unusual for drivers to park their cars or for McDonald's cashiers to bow their heads in respect.

Since Bear Bryant's death, this had happened every year: techies edited his speeches, pep talks, and interviews and created a retrospective of his twelve nationally ranked number-one teams, narrated by himself, the best coach that ever lived.

There were tears in people's eyes, including the guard's at the president's box. But the spell was broken when an *Elephas maximus* appeared on the giant screen and blew a noise out of its trunk that shook everyone in their seats.

The crowd went crazy and the Alabama players were announced one by one.

Bitty Jack made her way through the president's box toward a seat at the front of the room. All the hotshot alumni avoided or ignored her. They couldn't do much more than that. Bitty Jack had a ticket. She had a right to be there.

Sarina's win had earned a prime viewing spot for her mother. Mrs. Summers was seated to the right of the Hicks. She kept nudging Mrs. Hicks. Whispering in her ear as if vying for the spot of her new best friend.

Mrs. Hicks was not responsive. She stared at the field as she had stared across the cemetery. She looked like a skeleton Mrs. Summers could snap in two.

The model of impartiality on his way to the snack bar, Mr. Hicks asked Bitty Jack how Stewart was getting along.

"He's fine," said Bitty Jack. "But I couldn't find him before the game."

"There he is." Mr. Hicks gestured toward the football field. Big Al was seated on the twenty-yard line, pretending to row a boat as the band played the theme to *Hawaii Five-O.* "That's a move I haven't seen."

"Is it?"

Mr. Hicks nodded and Bitty Jack excused herself to take a seat in the front corner.

The head referee blew his whistle and what followed was nothing Bitty Jack had not seen before. The stadium was sold out. The fans rowdy, their cheers rising up, pouring into the president's box windows, opened to feel the cool autumn air.

No one sat beside Bitty Jack, but she was constantly distracted by the gossip growing louder, and mean-spirited rumors deadening her dad.

Mrs. Summers took a moment to tap her on the shoulder. She said, "See what happens when you fuck with my family?"

Bitty Jack refused to look at Mrs. Summers. She rummaged through her backpack for binoculars and Chap Stick.

Throughout the first half, Nicole held her own. She found ways to take breaks from the heat and inevitable physical exhaustion. She performed the *Hawaii Five-O* move to songs that had nothing at all to do with the sea. She sat by the cooler and passed out Gatorade. Laying on her back, she made snow angels on the AstroTurf. She peed doggy-style on the Vandy Commodore.

But something was unnatural about the way Nicole moved. Her right arm never bent. It was as straight as a stick.

Mrs. Hicks noticed this too.

"Do you see it?" she said above a normal speaking tone. "There's something not natural! Look at Big Al. He's not right. Can't you tell?"

The alumni were doing a good job of dismissing her. Mrs. Hicks was being treated like a bad child who, if no one encouraged her, might finally behave.

Bitty Jack swung her binoculars in Mrs. Hicks's direction. She caught a close-up of Mrs. Summers's jaw wagging, her foundation two shades darker than the skin on her neck. She was still badgering Mrs. Hicks, who had taken a pair of binoculars for herself. Constantly turning the focus finder, Mrs. Hicks aimed her field glasses toward the action on the green. Her posture was intent. She shrugged off Mrs. Summers. She moved her binoculars every time Big Al moved.

She couldn't possibly know. Bitty Jack began to worry.

The second quarter ended. Bama, 12. Eggheads, zilch.

The players left the field and the Million Dollar Band members marched out of the bleachers. Their capes blew behind them. The Rifle Line ladies propped white guns on their shoulders. Mr. Hicks moved from his seat to an announcer's microphone. As a local celebrity and personal friend of the president, Bert Hicks often introduced the halftime festivities.

"LADIES AND GENTLEMEN." His voice took a rich tone. "THE PROUD MEN AND WOMEN OF THE UNIVERSITY OF ALABAMA MILLION DOLLAR BAND!"

The crowd went wild.

With their bodies, the musicians spelled Bama Bound in cursive. The sax players twisted to jazz up the routine. Drummers beat the rear. Flutists tooted at the front. The Color Guard waved giant flags of red and white. The Crimsonettes did splits. The feather on the drum major's hat blew easy in the breezy. All was as it should be until Big Al jogged past the mellophones and attempted to take the drum major's position.

"AL!" Bert Hicks jokingly warned.

"*Al!*" the crowd parroted.

Big Al bumped the drum major, but the drum major played on. Everyone laughed and Bert Hicks's chuckle, too close to the mike, sent a screeching sound over everyone's heads. Yet, good old Big Al gave it the old college try.

Bitty Jack focused her binoculars on what Nicole was using as a drum major's baton. It was an inch wide and made of wood. Half out of her sleeve, one end tucked within Big Al's cuff.

As the band played "My Home's in Alabama," they formed a line to encircle the field. Mr. Hicks followed the cheerleaders' lead. "ROOOOOOOOOOOOOOOOOOOOLL . . . "

"*Tide! Roll!*"

"ROOOOOOOOOOOOOOOOOOOOLL . . . "

"*Tide! Roll!*"

The male cheerleaders threw their partners high in the sky. Funny enough, Alabama male cheerleaders were not considered homosexuals. They were athletic and could kick any antagonizer's ass.

"There she is!" cried Mrs. Summers.

Bitty swung her binoculars toward the home-team players' tunnel. Sarina was being helped onto the royal court float. She wore a bright blue gown that, even in the shade, gave off a thousand sparkles. Her hair was poofy, from White Rain, thicker than what could possibly be natural. The sun parted the clouds as if it knew this was her moment. Her skin was so porcelain, Bitty wondered if she'd burn.

With the aid of a stepladder, Sarina placed one high-heeled shoe onto the platform. She stepped gingerly across the crepe paper, careful not to catch a heel in the chicken-wire carpet. In the center of the float, she steadied herself by holding onto a slim metal pole. As tradition dictated, she would not take her throne until Bert Hicks broadcast her name.

"LADIES AND GENTLEMEN, PUT YOUR HANDS TOGETHER. THE UNIVERSITY OF ALABAMA IS PROUD TO PRESENT THIS YEAR'S HOMECOMING QUEEN AND HER COURT!"

The crowd rose to their feet as they had during the national anthem. The truck motored slowly, carting the float toward the center of the field. The Sony JumboTron featured Sarina's tall face, her eyes like flying saucers, her teeth like church doors.

Mrs. Summers turned to everyone behind her, squealing with delight. "Can you stand it? Can you stand it?"

But Big Al stole the scene.

Nicole stood on the fifty-yard line. With that excuse for a baton and her other hand raised with it, she led a spirit shout-off between the three home sections. "We've got spirit, yes we do, we've got spirit, how 'bout you?!" She turned to her right and the student section cheered. "We've got spirit, yes we do, we've got spirit, how 'bout you?!" She spun to her left and alumni went nuts. The Bama fans made more noise than them all. We've got spirit, yes we do, we've got spirit, how 'bout you?! Nicole made a circle and led a Crimson Wave.

As the float got nearer, she gave signals to the driver like she was guiding a 747 in for a landing. *A little to his left, now steer a little to the right. That's it. Nice and easy. Straight ahead. Keep her steady as she goes.*

Bert Hicks said, "AL . . . "

The crowd joined in, "*Al!*"

Sarina waved to Big Al, sure that Stewart was inside him. Bitty Jack cringed as Sarina blew him a dark, full-lipped kiss. She made a grand gesture. Holding her French-manicured hand in front of her mouth for three seconds. Holding that pucker for three seconds more. She kept her hand hovering in Big Al's direction until he responded by catching that kiss and holding it ever-so close to his heart.

To catch that kiss, the big wooden baton had to slip back into Nicole's elephant skin. This made Nicole's arm rigid again. She looked gawky in motion, running toward the float as the truck driver set his gear shift to Park.

She looked gawky despite that unbending arm. Every time a foot slapped the field, the Big Al costume seemed to spring off her limbs. The gray skin sagged at the knees and elbows. Nicole's pace was tipsy from the weight of the head.

The crowd ate it up.

Mrs. Hicks cried, "It's wrong!"

"There's nothing wrong," snapped Mrs. Summers. "Keep your comments to yourself. You're ruining the moment!"

"The hands." Mrs. Hicks thrust the binoculars between Mrs. Summers's bosoms. "For God's sakes look at the hands!"

"AL . . . " Mr. Hicks bellowed into the microphone.

"*Al!*" cried the crowd, drowning Mrs. Hicks out.

The stadium shook with laughter as Nicole did her damnedest to mount the royal float. She locked her fingers into the chicken wire on top of the platform. She swung her hips left and right in an attempt to get one of her elephant legs up. The Homecoming court jiggled, but held onto their poles. Unsure of what her ex-boyfriend was after, Sarina let go of her pole and took two steps backwards. The insides of her knees pressed against the seat of the throne and the wooden legs wobbled enough for Bitty Jack to get nervous.

"Stay put," Bitty whispered.

Bert Hicks said, "BIG AL! . . . "

"*Al!*" the crowd chanted. "*Al! Al!*"

Nicole was finally on the float.

Mrs. Hicks cried, "Not Al!"

Five feet from Sarina.

"*Not Al! That's Not Al!*"

Nicole started to charge, ripping off the mascot's head, her long blond hair streaming out for all to see, the bad-ass baton sliding out of her sleeve.

The ax was in the air and Sarina's mouth opened. The cameras were still rolling and everyone's eyes were seized by the Sony JumboTron screen.

Mrs. Summers said, "What the hell-fire devil is this?"

Mrs. Hicks kept screaming, but only Bitty Jack believed.

"It's my daughter! It's my daughter! I SHOULD KNOW MY OWN HANDS!"

Before anyone could answer, Nicole tackled Sarina. The two hit the throne and all four of its legs gave out.

It was as if Big Al had a grenade in his pants. Within seconds, the float went up in flames. The heat against his back window got the driver out of the truck. The male cheerleaders ran to rescue the court, their arms outstretched to coax the two who were too scared to jump and save their skin.

Although the fire department was thirty feet outside the stadium, the firefighters had been watching the halftime show from a stadium gate. They wore only their T-shirts and heavy rubber pants. They had to run to get the truck, to get their uniforms, to get in gear.

But their efforts would be pointless. The float was too wide for heroic attempts. Already the center of the float was a crackling inferno. Big Al's costume burned like a marshmallow. Sarina's ball gown fueled the fire.

The crowd was eerily silent. Eyes not on the field but on the Sony JumboTron. No one moved or came up with bright ideas. There wasn't a single extinguisher in sight. The Rifle Line ladies had no one to shoot. The sprinklers were turned on, but only sprayed at ankle level. The flames enveloped the bodies. Forever and ever, Sarina would be caught in the deathgrip of what once constituted Nicole's sun-kissed arms.

Over the loudspeaker, Mr. Hicks was struck speechless.

Mrs. Summers, shell-shocked.

It all happened so fast.

Mrs. Hicks broke first and rushed to her husband, yanking his arm, her daughter's name garbled in her throat. The crowd looked up at the president's box. Mrs. Hicks's cries blasted through her husband's microphone. Every syllable cut air. Each bawl was like a bullet.

She was out of control, flailing her limbs, running toward those behind her in the president's box.

But then someone took charge.

Mrs. Summers hooked Mrs. Hicks's neck with one fleshy, fat arm. She locked her other arm around her chest. She said, "You're not going down there."

Mrs. Hicks bucked.

But Mrs. Summers kept her in hand. She closed her eyes as if to keep alive the grand picture of Sarina that had been so publically praised just a few instants ago. She kept hold of her emotions and of Mrs. Hicks and of time. It was if she was giving the fire a few more minutes to leave less of a mess of her now charbroiled child.

"Let her go," Mrs. Summers whispered. "Let her go, let her go."

As alumni gathered around the two strickened mothers, Bitty Jack crept out of the president's box. Surprisingly, the spectators were not running scared. Most everyone remained in their seat as the fire trucks tore the turf, firemen slipping in their race across the field.

Gingerly, Bitty Jack made her way through alumni. She walked toward the presidential elevator, abandoned by the operator, which would take her to the parking lot. As she descended all those stairs, she heard the crowd sizing up what they would be speaking of for years.

The elevator doors opened and Bitty Jack walked forward, the stadium like a mausoleum, a little fuller, right behind her. The crowd could be heard over the walls. News helicopters hovered above the stench that was left. Mr. Hicks's voice could be heard on the Sony JumboTron.

"Ladies and gentlemen, please stay in your seats. You'll be the most help if you don't crowd the exits. Please remain calm. It's all over. There's nothing to see."

When the firemen sifted through the remains, they would discover Nicole, as her mother suspected. In her embrace would be Sarina and what had happened would be clear. It was a murder/suicide. Death by obsession. No further questions asked.

If the firemen searched past the burned, girlish bodies, they might ferret out a blackened coffee can. The brand could be identified if they took it to the lab. Chock Full O'Nuts. "The Heavenly Coffee." More than likely, the technician's favorite.

Even if the string that tied the coffee can to the front legs of the throne still existed, even if the saw marks remained on those legs, even if they found traces of sulfur and acid and charcoal, the blame would still go to Nicole.

Bitty Jack, one day, might feel bad for what she'd done. But worse things could happen. In fact, worse things had. Besides, Bitty Jack was comfortable with her future. She had savings and bus money. She had courage. She would dare.